DESIGNED TO DIE

Books by Chloe Green

GOING OUT IN STYLE

DESIGNED TO DIE

Published by Kensington Publishing Corporation

DESIGNED TO DIE

Chloe Green

KENSINGTON BOOKS
http://www.kensingtonbooks.com

To Wayne

KENSINGTON BOOKS are published by

Kensington Publishing Corp.
850 Third Avenue
New York, NY 10022

Library of Congress Card Catalogue Number: 00-109721
ISBN 1-57566-665-0

First Printing: June, 2001
10 9 8 7 6 5 4 3 2 1

Printed in the United States of America

Chapter One

SEATTLE

*M*y foot slipped, and I watched in a B-movie, cue the music, slo-mo kind of horror as the stirrup, that had secured me to the rope while I hung over the edge of Seattle's Experience Music Project building, fell away. It went straight between the monorail tracks and landed on the ground—forty feet below.

One foot swung free now. I clenched the handheld ascenders with sweaty hands. My heart raced. My hearing vanished. I pushed the left-hand ascender up and pulled myself after it with a trembling arm. I slid my right hand up higher.

The rope slipped.

I flung myself at the aluminum roof and caught it with both hands. I clung to the building, still for a second.

The way up was smooth as glass.

The way down was a long, hard drop.

My hearing returned. With a vengeance.

The woman below me, a model in Joan Jett-esque rock-wear and neon wig, swore in her native Scandinavian tongue. Across from me, the makeup artist in DKNY gray, *dark glasses, and a T-shirt that read "9 Out of 10 Men Prefer Camels to Women," screamed. It was a New Yorker's scream that warned all the neighbors to shut their windows and turn up their TVs.*

My life wasn't flashing before my eyes, but the past few weeks were.

I was the next victim. For the sake of those people who I'd come to care for, I hoped I was the last. It happens in fours, I thought. Not threes.

Why me?

Who wanted me out of the way? Who was left?

It would just read like the jinxed photo shoot had claimed anothr life.

Bizarre, hard to believe, but as they say, truth is stranger than fiction.

There was no reason to kill. All I knew were suits. That wasn't worth dying for.

This wasn't what I'd had in mind when Lindsay, my erstwhile agency rep, had pitched this job to me. "It will be a killer shoot, Dallas," she'd said.

Truer words had never been spoken.

"Dallas, darling, don't you miss the great outdoors?" Lindsay had asked me over the phone.

It was ninety-four degrees, and I was stuck on the parking lot commonly called Loop 635, with three thousand dollars' worth of Nordstrom's merch in my trunk and only hours before time was up on returning it. "There is nothing I miss," I said. I'd had to turn the AC off in my classic Mustang for fear of overheating, so the great outdoors was flowing through my rolled-down windows. Sweat made a suction cup between my ear and the Nokia.

"Not in this wretched heat," she'd said. "Somewhere beautiful, with mountains . . ."

Colorado?

"... and rivers ..."

Minnesota?

"... the ocean with jagged cliffs ..."

Maine?

I was highly suspicious, because the last time I'd been sucked into Lindsay's tall tale I'd ended up babysitting fourteen kids, with attendant parents, siblings, and nannies, on a catalogue shoot in, of all places, Uncertain, Texas.

For a week. They license mosquitoes there. You can rent them as transportation.

"Sounds nice," I said. "Are you going somewhere?"

"Of course not, silly," she said. "You are—that is, if you want to."

Then the seduction had begun. Male talent, Washington State with mountains, rivers, and ocean, five-star accommodations, gourmet meals, and a whopping fat day rate. I had to slam on my brakes when she told me.

"Are you sure where that decimal point is?" I'd demanded.

"Yes darling," Lindsay said, her English accent a little stronger. "The client saw your mermaids in that issue of *Metamorphosis*. The shoot will be rather like James Bond meets mythos, or something. Bob Mackie-style dresses on beautiful women, with dashing gents and expensive toys in the background. Fantasy shots."

I ooched my car forward. In Dallas, tailgating is an art. You have to protect your place in traffic, or some yahoo will sneak in before you. So you have to drive two inches away from the bumper in front of you. It wears out your clutch and your nerves pretty fast.

"Who's paying for it?" I asked.

"It's a vendor's promo piece. The design team will be on the set as the creative and art directors—"

I couldn't help it: I groaned. A quiet little groan, but still. *Yikes.* Lindsay chose not to hear me.

"He liked my mermaids?"

"He is actually a they," she said. "Imagine if Calvin actually had a Klein, or Ralph really had a Lauren. It's a design team, Tobin Charles."

I slammed on my brakes again. "Those—his—their clothes were just mentioned in that article in *W,* the next Tom Ford or something—"

" 'Elegant, timeless, stylish, sharp and sensible.' Yes, exactly! I knew you'd recognize the name."

"They liked my mermaids?"

Lindsay laid it on thick. This design team, Tobin and Charles, had specifically asked for me. Lindsay had shipped my book—the cumulative portfolio of shots I'd designed—for them to see. They adored my color sense and my understanding of shape and symmetry, and were convinced that I could make these mythology-meets-James fantasy shots come alive. "What's more, they are looking for a stylist who is active, physical, knows the outdoors, and isn't afraid of a little adrenaline rush," Lindsay had said.

I sucked in my abs for a twenty count when she said "active." "Why does that matter?"

"You will be in all sorts of precarious positions. That's the beauty of the thing. 'Ostentation,' Tobin said. 'Grandiose. Glamorous. Ironic.' "

An ironic fashion shoot? "So one of them *is* named Tobin?"

"Right, he's Tobin Marconi or something, and she's Kim Charles. Together, they're Tobin Charles. The producer is Dee, I believe. They sounded completely delightful on the phone."

"It's all their clothes?" Meaning, were they providing all the merch, or would I be expected to max out my AmEx on the girl's wardrobe and hope I could return the stuff.

"Exactly," she said. "The promo is for the men's attire, but the fantasy dresses will be theirs too; they're just not selling them."

"So, what, this is the second collection?" I put on my blinker and began cutting through to the access road.

"Right. Seasonless, really."

"Who's the market?"

"High end. The same people who sell Zegna and Brioni, but not as fashion-forward as, say, Prada. Though the same price points."

"Then, The Store, Bergdorf's, Barney's?"

"Very visible," Lindsay said.

She didn't have to tell me what a bonus it would be to get film that was not catalogue or advertising, for my book. It would help me expand my professional horizons. "Just answer a few questions for me," she said, zooming in for the kill. "Then I can make your reservations today."

Finally I had reached the relative safety of Montfort Road, and I zipped up to the Galleria. "Hang on; what do you mean by Bob Mackie clothes?"

"Well, something Barbie would wear."

This could be a lot of fun. Not to mention helping me get back on my feet financially. I'd recently switched over to free-lancing, after years at The Store. Building a clientele took time and money. I was running short on the latter. "How many days?"

"He wants to book you for twelve, but that includes pre-production, the days of prepping the merch, and six days shooting. But leave some flex in your schedule, since this is location."

I smiled. "When?"

"Monday week. They'll send you the information, so you can use your contacts here. You'll arrive, have the pre-pro meeting, and start the next day in Seattle before you move on."

"It's not in Seattle?" I said, slowing down to go into the parking garage.

"Some will be shot in Seattle, some in the woods, or rivers, or something."

"You're so delightfully vague."

"Now I need you to answer a few questions."

"Shoot," I said, pulling into an empty lot across from the underground parking garage. If I went in, I'd lose her altogether.

"Do you ski?"

"Snow or water?" I asked.

"Either."

"Both."

"Hmm. Do you mountain bike?"

"I have," I said.

"Rock climb?"

"I have." Once, in a gym.

"Ride horses?"

"Of course."

"Sky dive?"

"Uh, ya got me on that one."

"You haven't?"

"Not from a lack of wanting to, but no, I haven't."

"Could you do so by, say, next week?"

"I guess, though that schedule is pretty tight."

"By the way," she asked, her mind boomeranging in another direction, "how did you do all this stuff? You live in a city. A concrete one at that."

"Not when I was growing up. And my parents didn't believe in gender designation," I said. "So my brothers were given dolls and my sisters and I were sent to adventure camps. Then we'd visit my father, and everyone had dancing lessons, fencing lessons, horseback-riding lessons. Mom and Dad worked for the same end through different means." What could I say? My mother was an aging hippie, my father her codependent polar opposite. "Am I really going to have to do all those things as a stylist?" I couldn't imagine the amount of money, not to mention the insurance burden Tobin Charles would be carrying, if the talent had to do this stuff. "I thought he—they—wanted me for my mermaids."

"Well, you were the first choice for that reason, but they needed to know you could do the other stuff. Don't forget, eight hundred a day plus expenses."

"Just call me Dallas "Danger" O'Connor," I said with a laugh. A giddy laugh.

"Excellent! I knew you wouldn't let me down. Are you going to jump out of an airplane before you go up to Seattle, or are you going to just tell me you did?"

"Consider it done," I said.

The next week was harried, but it went off without a hitch. It was looking like the first problem-free location shoot I'd ever been on. D. Andersen, the producer, was excellent. The talent was outstanding, and confirmed. The weather was predicted to be sunny and dry. They advanced me money to pick up a few props in Dallas—watches, cufflinks, rental jewelry. The Polaroids and swatches were clear. The tearsheets showed me what feel they wanted. E-mails, faxes, and overnight deliveries flew back and forth between my M-Street-district home and their headquarters in downtown Seattle.

Every day was a joy; they were paying me to do what I love.

The taxi picked me up, my flight wasn't crowded, and I got upgraded to first class.

The first indication that the portents might have been wrong occurred when my plane was rerouted and then had an unplanned landing due to weather before leaving for Seattle in the dead of night. I landed in a downpour, exactly fourteen hours late.

Chapter Two

So I arrived. It was raining. I'd missed the pre-production meeting, I hadn't been able to get ahold of anyone, and I was still a virgin to sky diving—the one thing on my to-do list that I didn't get to do. There was no driver waiting for me, no one to carry my overweight bags, and no rental car. Obviously I wasn't talent.

I got a cart, loaded my tons of luggage onto it, and wondered when call time was this morning. The sun was already lightening the sky. My cell phone beeped to tell me I had a message. In it Lindsay said that the hotel where I was booked had changed from being quaint and European to being heavily atmospheric and nautical. "Tobin Charles wants to get you in the mood," she'd said.

I finally found a cabbie. "Where to?" she asked in an almost Canadian accent.

"Seattle," I said, and she threw my stuff in her trunk and smiled brightly while she asked me how my flight had been. I tried not to growl.

Leaving SeaTac was like traveling through any suburb. I could have been outside Kansas City or Austin or Boston. "I thought you had mountains around here," I said to her, looking out the windows. It was lush, green, hilly, but nothing like the Rockies, where it seemed you could reach out and touch the mountains.

But the light was awesome.

"Weathermaker will be in today," the cab driver said, catching my eye in the rearview mirror.

"Weathermaker?" I repeated.

"What the Indians called Mount Rainier. When the mountain is in, that means it is covered in clouds. Wind comes off the Pacific and hits Rainier; that's why we get rain on this side of the Cascades and have desert on the other side."

"There's desert in Washington?" What I knew of this state could be summed up in a few brand names: Starbucks, Nordstrom, Microsoft, Eddie Bauer, Boeing, and REI. I knew that it rained, some people committed suicide, others were in bands, and the rest of them were stinking rich.

"Whole, huge desert. Miles of it. Lots of Spanish too."

"In Washington?"

"*Si,*" she said with a smile. "Apple orchards."

Of course, migrant workers.

"Look up there," she said. "You're about to see Seattle."

The city was laid out before us, sparkling and glittering in the early sun—the rain had stopped. High-rises, the Space Needle, and a zillion other buildings that were under construction poked up from the water's edge. And everywhere, huge, green bushes flowered.

"So where's your hotel? At the market?" she asked.

"Originally, it was close to Pike's Peak Market, but not anymore."

She caught my eye in the mirror. "Pike's Peak is in Colorado. Pike Place is the market. Don't confuse the two; it irritates the natives."

Suitably chastened, I looked out the window. Seattle. Washington. It was wonderful here; in Dallas we'd already had 90-percent humidity with 90-degree days. It would be nice to wear a jacket at night for a couple of weeks.

"So where to?" she asked.

"Umm, a pier on Lake Union."

"You staying on a boat?"

"You know, I have no idea. We were meeting at BluWater, which is supposedly right there at the dock, but I'm a little late."

"Great restaurant," she said. "You'll have to go there this evening." I rode silently for a while, watching the traffic pick up and wondering if it was as bad as Dallas's. Seattle was a city of construction, with as many cranes and "men working" signs as there were buildings.

"A Starbucks!" I said, stopping her as we drove downtown. "In Seattle! Stop!"

"A Starbucks in Seattle—that's a worthy stop," she said, not bothering to hide her sarcasm. "Blondie, I'll stop here if you want, but trust me, Seattle's Best Coffee is the best. You're here, why don't you try that? You can get Starbucks at home, right?"

"Well, you have a point." I didn't want to tell her I'd had SBC at the gate in Dallas before I left.

She went around the corner, we parked in one-hour parking, and she bought me an iced coffee from SBC. "My treat. Welcome to my city," she said. She was a big girl, in khaki shorts, a tank top, sweatshirt and a meticulous pedicure in pastel pink.

I ran back inside for a straw. "You're right, this is amazing," I said after the first sip.

"You drink coffee through a straw?" she asked.

"Protects my teeth," I said, flashing her a smile that was dazzling white thanks to the miracles of modern dentistry. And straws.

"That's a great idea. I'm gonna start doing that." As she

spoke, she shrugged off her sweatshirt, revealing a tattoo on her muscled shoulder. "Esmerelda."

Girlfriend? Mother? Or was that her name?

We got back in the car and drove through shopping central, complete with a downtown mall. Monorail tracks ran two stories over my head all the way to the Space Needle.

"What the heck is that?" I asked, staring out the window at the sprawl of color and texture at the foot of the Needle. "How did they build it?"

"Three hundred million dollars in action," she said as we waited for the light. "It's the rock 'n' roll museum. It's just as cool inside."

"You've been inside?" It didn't look like any building I'd ever seen. "There's not a straight line anywhere, is there?"

She cruised past it. "Nah, but I've heard. S'posed to look like two electric guitars smashed into each other," she said. "When they built it, the workers were strapped to the building like mountain climbers. It was wild."

Each side was a different color—Hendrix purple, lipstick red, beach-ball blue—and it looked like frets crossed the top of it. "Very cool. Weird, but cool," I said as we went down the hill to the lake. She pulled into the parking lot and we unloaded my gear in front of the now-closed restaurant. I paid her, tipped her, and she gave me a card.

"Don't miss dinner at BluWater," she said. "Call me if you need a taxi. I also rent my RV. You gonna be okay?"

I was standing beside the Pacific Ocean in the Northwest. Either the air or the coffee suddenly cleared my head, and I felt excitement bubble inside me again. "I'll be perfect," I said. "Thank you."

From the gate that led to the marina, I saw an ageless man mince his way out to an idling van. The blue streaks in his hair matched his eyes, and his jeans were by Lang, his mailbag by Prada.

"You're with the Charles fashion shoot?" I called.

He stopped dead in his tracks. "How did you guess?"

"You aren't wearing Birkenstocks?"

"Oh, girl, Satan invented those ugly things. I'm Fredrico, of the Fredrico Salon in New York, but I was born Freddie Eauneau—it's French—in Baton Rouge. You are?"

"Dallas O'Connor."

"Let me guess: are you Texan?"

I laughed.

"Actually, your face gave you away. Texas girls have the prettiest faces. And they weather well—just look at Jerry Hall or April Alexander. Oh, bad example since she went psycho. But she is a beauty."

"She is."

"Do you know Jan?"

"Everyone knows Jan," I said, smiling. "She's a doll."

"So you are a little late. We wondered what gotcha last night."

"I tried to call," I said.

"Oh, girl, don't worry about it. The airline was calling us just to let us know you weren't dead."

My smile felt a little wan. "I didn't know that had ever been a possibility," I said. "Where should I put my stuff?"

"Oh my goodness, this is all your shit, isn't it," he said, looking at my assortment of bags. "Being a makeup artist is so much easier. Here, let me help you," he said as he grabbed my wheeled styling kit. "We're on a boat. I have the worst seasickness for a boy born on the bayou, but I tell you, it's a cute little boat. Follow me." I picked up my shoe case, my overnighter, and my backpack and trailed behind him, pulling along my suitcase as we started down the pier lined with cabin cruisers and sailboats.

At the end I could see the outline of a two-tiered boat. It was quiet and peaceful out here. Someone was brewing espresso; from somewhere else I smelled baking muffins. My stomach growled. A few dogs barked, and the wind, remarkably free of salt or sting, blew. "It's a tugboat," I said, finally recognizing the shape.

"It is just that, and it has better-planned storage space in one room than my whole apartment in New York." We walked down a private dock sprigged with potted flowers and benches and stepped aboard. "It was about here that I was sure I was going to just puke like a little fish, but it's remarkably steady," he said.

It didn't even have that wobbly feeling like a boat. We entered a dining room with wraparound windows facing the Space Needle and the multi-colored music museum. Off the port side across the water rose a gentle hill with clusters of houses. "It's wonderful," I said. "Is the whole crew staying here?"

"Yes and no. Well, everyone except the producer, who has some inner-ear thing and can't walk on a boat. And no, because only one model has arrived so far. But," he said, putting his hand on my arm and leaning close, "Richard is coming."

I smiled; I couldn't wait to see him.

"Ah, the chatelaine," he said as a sprite of a girl in head-to-toe Polo appeared with fresh-squeezed orange juice and a smile. "This is Hope," he said to me.

"Rough night?" she said.

I nodded.

"Your roommate is still in your quarters," she said. "But I think you are all leaving in a half hour or so."

"Roommate?" No one ever shares on a shoot.

"We're all squeezed on here," Freddie said. "Some of us had to double up. Since you weren't here last night—"

"Is that a problem?" Hope asked, concern on her fair, heart-shaped face.

"Uh, no, no," I said. "It's fine."

"Dallas can use my shower to freshen up," Freddie said.

He *was* a Southern boy—that was a polite way of saying I looked like I needed a week at the Greenhouse Spa. "Thank you so much," I said, and I let him guide me up the narrow, nearly vertical ladder, out on deck, around the side, through a cabin with a queen-size bed and porthole windows, and into a tiny shower. I had to keep ducking my head—sailors were supposed to be short?

"The head is through there," Freddie said with a giggle. "I just love saying that."

"What's the head?" I said as I peered into the shower.

He pulled the other curtain back, revealing an airplane-size commode. "Oh," I said.

"See you in a few."

Chapter Three

I was still running late. My cabbie followed the directions I'd been left and I arrived at the small yacht, our floating RV, alone. This fantasy shot was the only one without a woman—just a man on a tugboat, pulling an ocean cruiser in from sea. Seattle was behind us, Canada to the right, and the Olympic peninsula curved off to my left. Not that I could see it, but it was there. The air was cold—not cool—cold. The hazelnut double espresso with whipped cream, handmade by Hope, was warm in my hand.

It was so quiet, I could hear the water lap against the ship. Early-morning sun had faded to gray skies, and I wondered where everyone else was.

It had been a long time since I'd seen the ocean, and this was the first time I'd seen it so far north. I picked up some binoculars beside the door and looked up at the birds, around at the shoreline behind us, and then at the ocean liner we were going to be shooting. "So that's where they are," I said out loud as a parade of people who didn't look exactly like Seattle passed by on the ship's upper deck. I looked at a few of the boats in the water—a couple sharing a morning kiss while he steered, an older man and young boy zooming toward the open ocean. I was in Seattle! "Where did they film that Meg Ryan movie?" I asked myself as I continued to scan the passing boats.

A Donzi—it was written on the boat—purred up just off the side of the yacht . . . port or bow? Or was it starboard? I needed to learn this stuff. They cut the engine and the two people turned to each other. I zoomed in with my binoculars. Both men were hunched against the cold. One was tall and striking, the other was shorter and a little . . . slick-looking. They were talking animatedly. One slapped the other on his back, it looked like encouragement from here. I tried to see their faces, but it was hard to focus with them bobbing in the water. Brothers? Best friends? Lovers?

The men shook hands, and I grinned. They were making a bet with each other! One looked around, staring especially hard at the cruise ship, then slipped the other an envelope. The other man opened it. I did a close-up of the envelope. He counted out money. A lot of money. A two-inch stack of hundreds. He looked around again. "Furtive," I muttered. That was exactly how he was behaving. The first man turned away and started the engine again, coming closer to the boat. This was a little creepy. I didn't know who these people were, but I'd rather they not see me.

I replaced the binoculars and escaped to my impromptu dressing room at the back of the yacht, taking my coffee with me.

After setting up my pressing gear, my props, opening the shoe boxes and lacing the shoes up, I opened the first suit bag and whistled in appreciation.

"I'm gratified," a voice said from the door. I turned to see a dark-haired man in a suit over an (I was sure) Armani cashmere T. His hair, black and gelled, was brushed forward, and he wore tiny framed glasses and silver cuff bracelets. But he radiated masculinity, like a Roman soldier decked out in tassels and jewelry. He patted his forehead dry with a handkerchief, and when he put it away I saw an envelope inside his jacket.

"I'm Tobin Marconi," he said. "You must be Dallas O'Connor. Glad you made it safely."

His coat was different now, but he was the man who had just received a boatload of money and was carrying it in his pocket as we spoke.

"Thank you," I said. He asked a few questions about the flight, I apologized about its lateness, and we discussed the weather and a little of what I'd missed last night.

"We'll have the pre-pro meeting tonight," he said. "My partner Kim hasn't gotten in yet either, and we can't really get started without her."

He didn't sound pleased about that, but then again, time was money. "This is beautiful," I said, turning back to the suit and examining the three functional buttons on the sleeves, the precision of the pinstripe as it ran from the shoulder, met the Armani pocket and the ticket pocket, and continued uninterrupted to the hip. It was a perfect Neopolitan cut with higher armholes, and a more tapered, softer shoulder. Aware of Tobin's gaze on me, I turned the edge over, examining the stitching. "Silk thread?" I asked after a moment.

"Yes," he said, his fingers flexing.

"Slow machines, right?"

"Most people think they are hand sewn," he said, caressing the edge of the suit. "What makes you guess machine?"

"A sewing machine has a rhythm," I said. "See here?" I pointed to a stitch that was not more than one millimeter above the others. "It does this every fifteen stitches. A human hand wouldn't be that precise."

He glowed.

I turned the jacket inside out, and checked the internal canvas, the floating chest piece so the coat could mold more

easily to the human body. The undercollar was lined and inter-
lined, the armholes set in by hand and taped in with cotton.
The inside jacket had two pockets, one cut longer for a bill-
fold. "This suit is the real thing," I said. Sometimes demos
made for photos didn't have pockets and things like that, because they were just samples.

"It's a small operation," he said, running his finger over
the seam. "I can't afford to make twenty-five suits that can't
be sold."

I would have never guessed it to be a small operation, based
on what he was spending in advertising. "Are you the designer
and the tailor?" I asked. Tobin Marconi was in love with his
suits.

"The tailor," he said. "I'm the hands-on person," he said,
touching the fabric, checking the knots on the buttons. "I
love to feel the fabric, to shape it through heat and pressure.
To cut it, to drape." He laughed self-consciously. "I've lost a
lot of assistants because I just can't delegate."

I'd been an assistant to that kind of person; it was miser-
able, especially if you were honestly trying to learn something. "You must have a real gift," I said. "This suit's beautiful.
Just the pressing alone—"

"It can be quite a job," he said. "It's pressed probably
twenty times during construction. That's something an assistant can help with."

I laughed. "How old were you when you started?"

"I was a boy," he said. "I'm Italian; it's in my family."

The best tailors grew up cutting their teeth on scissors, I'd
learned.

"Kim, the designer, moved around, worked for a lot more
people than I did. I spent most of my time in New York and
Milan."

"Y'all do make magic," I said, caressing the suit, too. It
just begged to be touched. This job was going to be so awesome. "It's beautiful," I repeated.

"That's where we met the first time," he said to me.

"Who met?" I asked, half paying attention as I checked out the reinforcement on the waistband.

"You and me."

I turned and looked at this man; I'd never seen him before today. "Really?" I said. Best not to contradict someone who signed your check. "Whaddaya know."

"I was working with Beene."

He had me confused with someone else. "I, uh—"

"You don't remember at all, do you?" He was curt. His gaze moved over my face, to my throat and back to my eyes.

My trips to New York had been brief and infrequent. "I'm sorry," I said. "It's always crazy when I'm there. But I would have remembered your suits. This is incredible."

"I wasn't designing then," he said. For a second his eyes shone with anger, then it was gone. Or I'd imagined it. "The suits are divided into groups, for each of the models," he said abruptly, moving forward and touching the suits.

I nodded as I opened up the suit bags.

"The ectomorph is Richard, a forty long with a thirty waist."

Skinny for a suit model, but he was *Richard*.

"Tom Fly is forty long with a thirty-two waist. George is forty-two long with a thirty-two waist, and Wes is also forty-two long, but with a thirty-one-inch waist."

That was perfect; each model had a backup. "They came in for fittings?"

"Of course," he said. "I wouldn't trust anyone else with this task. Shirts, ties, all the merch I'm supplying, are in the next room. I presume you have watches and accessories?"

"Yes," I said. I hoped I had enough to go with this many suits. "Do you have today's shot list?"

"Just this," he said. "Wes, our Tobin Charles man, in one of his suits. Today's an easy day," he said with a smile.

"Oh, great," I said. "Then I'll get to work. Nice to meet you."

We shook hands and he left. I turned to prep the suits. Wes's choices were great, and I started pressing the shirts that would go with them. Then I wondered who had given Tobin money on a boat, and why? And cash too; that was unusual.

Freddie burst into the room, and I glanced up. "Your face is clashing with your hair," I said. "Why don't you take some Dramamine?"

"I did. I threw it up," he said, slumping into a chair. "The waves are just getting bigger. I'm going to die!"

"We're in a bay, there are no real waves. You're not gonna die."

"I want to die."

"No, you don't," I said as I reached into my styling bag. I grabbed two thick ponytail holders and some back-flanged buttons. I snipped the holders and laced them through the flanges, then retied the elastic. "Put these on your wrists," I said. "Mark three fingers down from the crease in your wrist to find your pulse point. C'mon, do it. I can't have you barfing on eight-thousand-dollar suits."

Weakly, Freddie felt for his pulse points.

"Now put these on so the button is pressing into the pulse point."

"Is this some sort of voodoo?"

"That's your part of the country, *cher,* not mine," I said, and I handed him the bracelets.

He slipped them on. "They're tight."

"Just lean back and relax for a minute," I said, returning to the finer points of prepping the clothes. My cell phone rang and I looked at the caller ID. It was Kreg, one of my best friends from home. "Dr. Alder, paging Dr. Alder," I answered.

"You are impossible to surprise since you got ID on your cell."

"The only surprises I want are ones I can translate into cold, hard, cash," I smarted off.

"It seems a certain Latin gentleman wanted to give you a diamond, but you resisted."

My mother's only advice on getting engaged was to get the biggest diamond you could—so you could hock it for more. "I'd rather have the cash."

"He would have taken care of you. Money wouldn't be an issue."

"Ah, Alejandro," I said wistfully. "But it's just not fair for a divorced person to marry someone who hasn't been married before. It's a different form of cradle robbing. One person is a skeptic; one person a romantic—it's just a mess."

"So should I screen only those who are shopping for wife numbers two through four for you?"

"Don't bother."

"You've got such issues with being a trophy wife."

"There is a statute of limitations on being a trophy," I said. "I think it ends when you hit thirty."

He laughed. "And how are you entertaining yourself today?"

"Right this second I'm turning my iron on 'cotton.' "

"I stopped by your duplex and got your mail. I met that student you leased the other half out to—"

"He's a divinity student at SMU," I said warningly.

"Heaven certainly came to *my* mind," Kreg said.

"His girlfriend is on a mission, feeding the homeless in some backward nation," I said. "Hint, hint."

"Message received. I won't be the corrupter you obviously fear I am. I just realized we are going to miss brunch this week."

Kreg and I had been friends for—ouch—decades. When I finally moved to Dallas, we set up a permanent brunch date, with a permanent location and time. The only excusable absences were to be at least one time zone away or attending a funeral.

"Pacific time," I said. "Though thankfully, no funerals."

"Perhaps we should just brunch up there. Lowell's has a spectacular view."

I rolled my eyes; Freddie was snoring. "I know what this is about," I said. "And it's not me."

"How do you like Seattle? As a caffeine junkie, you must be in paradise."

It was almost nine-thirty. "Doctor Alder," I said, "I would love to chat, but I have a mountain of prep work to do."

"Don't you have assistants for the lowly tasks?"

"My assistant is having a baby," I said. "Couldn't find another one."

"It's only menswear, right? Suits?"

"Yeah," I said. "*Only* suits, with French cuffs, silk ties."

"You know, I can iron!"

I snorted.

"That was not polite."

"Your idea of ironing is to drop a shirt off at Bibbentucker's and go have martinis," I said.

"I have a suggestion, I'll come up there and be your assistant. You can order me around and I will prove to you, beyond doubt, that I can iron."

"And mountain bike when I am not using you?"

"Well, there was this great article in *Bike* magazine," he said.

"You're insane," I said. "I can't pay you. And I can't put you up. Just come and bike, if that's what you want to do."

"When my dearest Dallas is slaving over a hot iron? I wouldn't enjoy myself."

"Oh, please, you just want to get your hands on some male models."

He snickered. "Live a little. We could have fun—just for a few days. I'll see if I can hitch a ride with Mark," he said, naming Dallas's newest billionaire bachelor. They played basketball together at Premier. "I think he's heading to San Jose on Friday."

"That's a little south of here," I said, watching the minutes tick off my watch. I really needed to get an earbud for my phone. Then I could iron and talk.

"Don't worry, I think I can find Seattle. I'll call you when I'm at the airport."

"Love you." I clicked my phone shut. "Certifiably insane," I said aloud.

Freddie jerked awake. He was once again flesh colored. "I feel wonderful. You are a goddess of healing!" He stood up cautiously, then ran to me and bussed my cheek. "A miracle worker!" He looked around. "Did I miss the talent?"

"No one's here yet," I said.

"Poor baby, you haven't met anyone yet, have you?"

I shook my head.

Freddie cocked his ear toward the door. "Well, I think your time may be arriving. Later, love." He patted my bottom and left me with my ties, or rather, Tobin Charles's ties. Usually most ties are so poorly made that I remove the label, cut the stitches up the back, iron them flat, then re-tack them. I was delighted, and more than impressed, when it appeared that Tobin Charles's ties were perfectly pressed and sewn.

I looked up; my room had suddenly become small. The talent—all six-feet-one and 188 pounds of muscle, sinew, and olive skin—had arrived. The tear sheets suggested a little bit Bond, a little Onassis, and a little bit Polo. With this man, it wasn't going to be a problem.

"I'm Wes Climes," he said, extending a hand.

I shook it. "Dallas O'Connor, stylist. Welcome to Seattle." As he laid down his bag we chitchatted about his flight, where he was from (Virginia), where he lived (Miami), and his most recent job (Istanbul). "I think they are setting up coffee, juice, and breakfast in the dining area," I said.

"I'll go check it out. Hey, who's the guy with the long black hair?"

The only man I'd seen this morning with long black hair had handed Tobin money. "I don't know," I said. "I just got in this morning, so I haven't even met the crew."

"Oh, okay," he said, and he went in search of some nourishment. I went in search of the photographer and found him looking through his viewfinder. In the time I'd been prepping the clothes, lights, cameras, and flats had been set up.

Kenneth, the photographer, was from South Africa. He guessed who I was and we spent a few minutes talking about the shot. The cruise ship, which slept probably 400, would fill the left-hand side of the frame. The tugboat, brightly red, black, and white with matching crew, would have our Tobin Charles man on it in the foreground. "I'm going to do both wide and tight shots. We'll decide the crops later," Kenneth said.

So I didn't know if we would see much of the ship or the crew. "Do you have any preferences for suits?"

He glanced up at the sky, gauging the light. We were safe; we had all day to get the shot. "If Tobin didn't tell you anything, then dress the boy and trot him out here and we'll see," Kenneth said.

"Is Tobin the art director today?" I asked. "Or is someone else aboard?"

"Kim will be the AD, I'd imagine. Between those two she's the concept man, but I don't think she'll be here today." He winked at me and tugged his huge Mark Twain mustache. "It's just you and me, girl. We would have rescheduled, except renting this cruiser is nearly impossible."

I showed him the tear sheets and he shrugged. "You've got the power," he said with a wink. "No one's here. We'll make it your call."

"Should I ask Tobin?"

Kenneth beckoned me closer. "I sent him back to Seattle

for film." I saw the two assistants helping Kenneth and held my tongue.

"Layouts?"

"It's yours, Dallas O'Connor. I'll back you up. Now go bring me a model."

For this decision-making power to be in my hands was unheard-of. No AD, no layouts, no merch designation. What did they say about absolute power? It's an illusion that will hang you. I returned to my small—imaginary—kingdom.

Wes was half-dressed, talking on his cell phone, drinking coffee when I stepped back into the dressing room. "Yes, honey, you need to do what Mommy said," he said. "I know you don't want to, but that's what big girls do. You want to be a big girl, don't you?"

He caught my eye and blushed, but kept right on cajoling. "Sweetheart, Daddy's gotta go now. You be Daddy's big girl, you hear me? Okay, bye-bye. Let me talk to your mother now." His voice hardened. "I know, Isabel, but I have to work. No. Bye."

I met his eye again. "Parenting cross-continent is hard, I've heard."

"She's been difficult," he said. I didn't know if he meant the child or the wife, and I didn't ask.

I tried the first suit on the rack, with the suggested "touches" of scarf, ascot, hat, pocket square; with deck shoes, wingtips, dress Oxfords; but Kenneth agreed with me that nothing really worked. Wes was too aggressively straight for frilly touches and too patrician for casual details. The three of us, Freddie, Kenneth, and myself, seemed to be the only crew besides the assistants. I walked back to the makeup room.

"You don't seem to be happy," Wes said as Freddie gelled his hair.

"It's not you, it's the effect they want. This suit isn't it. Hang on," I said, stepping outside to look at the scene again.

I told Kenneth my idea and he looked at the sky. "Great, let's see it before it rains."

Wes, in his boxer briefs, undershirt, and makeup, looked up when I stepped into the dressing room. "And?"

"Let's try the tux."

Chapter Four

The sun came out, the sun went in, we got mist, we got rainbows, and—a photographer's nightmare—we even got a little rain.

And we got fabulous pictures.

I'd done several things with the tux, from severely formal, with tie, scarf, and shiny dress shoes, to barefooted and unbuttoned, in black glasses and a red bandana do-rag. Freddie's visceral response to that shot wasn't repeatable, but I agreed wholeheartedly. Wes had a sexuality that attracted men and women and could be contained in a polished piece or unhinged. Either way, that $7,000 tux was going to fly out of the warehouse.

And that, of course, was the entire point.

We wrapped about five. Tonight would be a full crew at dinner; the models would be arriving tonight and tomorrow. However, according to Freddie, Richard was already checked in at the tugboat. "If his name is Richard," he said as I gathered my stuff, "why does he wear that diamond-studded initial *T* around his throat?"

"That's his boyfriend," I said. "Terrible Torinelli, a medium-sized mobster in New York. Richard got his start because Torinelli bought a European underwear company and needed to revamp the image."

"Richard got his start in underwear?"

"Even before Calvin got hold of him."

Freddie's hands twitched, as though he had gotten hold of Richard.

"You boys," I said as we disembarked.

"Your people are already at BluWater," Hope, the chatelaine, said as we returned to the boat. "Happy hour starts at five."

"They should be way happy, 'cuz it's way past," Freddie said. "Do you need my shower again?" he asked.

"Is my roommate in?" I asked Hope.

"Out at BluWater," she said, "so follow me, and let's get you checked in so you can get over there too."

Darcy Ellis, the makeup artist, and I were sharing the engineer's quarters, which consisted of bunk beds, narrow but sizable closets, and a communal shower.

I was still running late.

Fifteen minutes and the wonder of a Kiehl's shower later, I was hurrying along the dock to the restaurant in leather pants and a Banana Republic black blouse with stiletto slides and a Donna Hawk beaded choker. The hill behind the boat glistened with lights even though it was hours from sunset, and the sound of music and laughter traveled across the water.

Most pre-pro meetings take place in grim, dank office buildings with buckets of scorched corporate coffee and bushels of donuts. Not to mention *pre*-starting to the shoot. I couldn't believe how elegant this was. Out the window, lights reflected on water, the flowers filled the air with fragrance, and the clouds cleared for a starlit night. In the restaurant below us, attractive men and women mixed and mingled while drinking fruity concoctions and sampling upscale nibbles.

Better yet, those appetizers and drinks were up here as well. Quick introductions were made: Darcy, the makeup artist, had a flaming red bob and flawless white skin and was wearing a bell-sleeved, Indian-styled T-shirt with "C'mon Baby, Light my Pyre" written in script across the front, on top of a paisley print gored skirt and four-inch Lucite heels. She even had little six-armed-goddess earrings to match. She also had a cigarette.

Kenneth I'd met. Stephen was his first assistant. Nasmo King, the second assistant, was from Seattle and would be with us the whole time. We would have a third assistant—a runner—from each of the specific locations. Freddie was here for hair and male makeup.

I flipped through the books for the talent. One of Richard's photos, I'd styled years ago.

It had been a shot for The Store's most fashion-forward periodical, mailed to an elite, trés-expensive clientele. Richard, a gorgeous black man, had worn Gucci, recycled from the '70s—which was a perfect vibe for him. *Saturday Night Fever* was his inspiration.

I'd just broken up with a guy and was feeling a little blue when I met Richard on the set.

"Whatchyou so sad about?" he'd asked me, tipping my chin up. I'd been barefoot at the time, so he was actually taller. I was hemming his pants. I had muttered and made excuses. We broke for lunch and he left, which was unusual. When he came back, he had a present for me.

"This is better than any ol' drug," he said. "When your day is bad, just pop this baby."

The package was CD-shaped. I opened it and—"Saturday Night Fever?"

"No one has sung as well as the Bee Gees," he said. "And can you imagine a more '70s' hero than John Travolta? But forget about that. It's an upper. Trust me."

I'd given the CD to the assistant, and we'd listened to it the rest of the afternoon. Richard could dance, turn flips, hand-springs—and no one had a nicer smile. He gave great film. It would be a delight to work with him again.

I'd closed his book and opened Wes's. I'd seen it. Tom Fly, George, and Yvette were new to me. She was a green-eyed, five-foot-ten brunette, typical size four, shoe size nine, with long, graceful hands and a Mona Lisa smile. Her face was symmetrical, her body as lean and toned as a greyhound's.

"She was all over Paris," Freddie said, leaning over my shoulder and chomping calamari in my ear. "She's the next Gisele."

"She's the Tobin Charles muse," Darcy commented.

The film was going to be terrific; I could hardly wait.

A man in a sharply tailored blue silk suit walked in a few minutes later. His flat-cheekboned face with piercing black eyes seemed Native American, and black hair flowed down his back. He was about six feet, trim, and wore a purple French-cuffed shirt with Indian-head coin cufflinks. "I am Thom Goodfeather," he announced in a voice as dramatic as his appearance. "On behalf of Tobin Charles designs, I offer our hospitality to you and welcome you to—" I didn't understand the next few words. They sounded Indian or something, with lots of *w*'s and *p*'s.

Last time I'd seen him had been on a boat, handing Tobin cash—probably for tax purposes. Which made perfect sense—he must be in the business too. It was just my imagination that lent a sense of drama and subterfuge to the whole transaction. More likely, Tobin had paid the crew on the ship and tugboat for their use. *Dallas, Dallas,* I chided myself, *stop inventing trouble.*

Thom Goodfeather passed out a mock-up of the piece: a cover, three full-page shots, a double-truck, and four close-cropped shots on each facing page. For ten minutes he gave us a rundown of the suits, and I made notes madly. There would be twenty-six shots in all, five of which would be the "fantasy" shots. It was going to be one slick piece. I felt a thrill at being part of its creation.

"Tobin and Kim brought each of you in because you excel at the imaginative. They've seen your work and know you can produce the effect, the mood, which is all-important here. A Tobin Charles man knows who he is. He is beyond competition with anyone but himself. He's not necessarily a millionaire, but he can afford most of our clothes," Thom said with a broad smile.

The Tobin Charles man had to be pretty close to a millionaire if he wanted to afford too many of these suits.

"The fantasy shots will feature one man—our Tobin Charles brand model, Wes—and Yvette, his muse and partner. They are sophisticated people, yet charmed by life. Tobin doesn't want cynicism or sophistry, though tongue-in-cheek irony is completely acceptable."

I'd been to a lot of pre-pro meetings; rarely had anyone used a word you had to look up. Though J. Crew had used *piquant* in a recent catalogue.

"This will be an exclusive brand, for an exclusive market. Integrity is essential here. We're not just moving suits; we're building a clientele."

I wondered where the financing was coming from. If everyone else was being paid commensurate to my fee, Tobin Charles was shelling out quite a lot of dough for this ten-page-plus-cover extravaganza. I wondered who his backers were (i.e., if I'd actually get paid).

"Our clothes will be marketed in the United States, in some cities in South America, in Asia, and in the Middle

East. And since the time has finally come: an American designer for the European male, to be marketed exclusively in Paris."

I'd seen the clothes. Tobin Charles was definitely going where no American designer had gone before.

A door opened and we all turned. Thom looked over his shoulder. "Welcome home!" he said to the beauty who stepped in. They kissed on the cheeks—fashion people are fashion people, no matter where you are—and he turned to us. "May I present Kim Charles, the designer."

Kim knew almost everyone. She greeted Kenneth, Stephen, Darcy, and Freddie before being introduced to me and another latecomer, a girl of about twenty. Kim was an attractive Asian woman, ageless and flawless with a gym-hard body and gem-laden fingers. She wore head-to-toe Celine with Jimmy Choo boots.

Kim stood up at the podium and welcomed us to Seattle. "It's my adopted home," she said. "Seattle is the city of the future, a city where dreams are built."

She sounded as though she were running for public office.

"So welcome. I'll be the AD on set. Now, here is the producer."

The twenty-something girl took the podium. Dieta had been a model; you can just tell the difference between ordinary mortals and those who have been taught to move. Though she was wearing just Frankie B. jeans, pointed-toe flats and a lime green sweater, with her dishwater-blonde hair in a high ponytail and not a stitch of makeup, she was radiant.

"Hello," Dieta said with a faint Dutch accent as she listed toward the left. "I am Dieta, D-i-e-t-a. No, I am not named after Diet Coke, and I'm not the Japanese parliament. My name is not easy for you people to say, so we'll have a little class. Repeat after me. Dee . . ." She smiled at us. "Come on, repeat."

"Dee," we said, a little stiff.

"Et, like et cetera. Et."

"Et."

"And ah, like ah, so your name is Dieta?"

We chuckled.

"So, sorry I am a little late, but welcome. This will be a great shoot, with beautiful clothes, wonderful talents, and the good people at Tobin Charles." She bestowed a glowing smile on Kim. Kim smiled back. This was going to be perfect. "Anyway," Dieta said, "here is the shot lineup."

She passed around a shot list and tentative schedule.

"We have the cruiser shot, which we've already done, a river shot, desert, glacier, and cosmopolitan shots for the fantasy pictures. We will have three male models—Richard, George, and Tom Fly besides the Tobin Charles man, Wes. Also, we are very fortunate in our female talent. Yvette is wonderful and so focused. You'll like her. She has a pet salamander! Hotel reservations, car rentals, these things are taken care of for everyone. Any questions?"

Dieta leaned to the side, then righted herself. "Forgive me, I have an infection in my inside ear, so I am not grace today." She leaned forward, her green eyes wide. "I went to my master, who told me the infection is from my unbalanced *dosha*, so I will be trying to balance it."

Darcy raised a thin-plucked eyebrow at me. I didn't know what a *dosha* was either.

"Are there any questions?" Dieta repeated.

"Do we have an RV where we can leave our stuff?" Freddie asked. "Securely. At night?"

"We have the RV at each location, but to make travel easier and give you each more freedom, every person who carries gear also has a Jeep. Which you can lock. Oh, and we'll have the same driver all the time, a very nice woman," she said. "It makes it pleasant, more like a family." She smiled at us, open and sweet.

Five rental cars and an RV? They were sparing no expense.

"How many shots a day?" Stephen asked.

"Ah, well, the weather will dictate that ultimately, yes? But we are planning for one fantasy per day. The other suits will be shot around the fantasy photos in the same locations."

"But when?" Stephen persisted. "The same day?"

"You've already asked your question, Stephen. Only one is allowed," I joked.

Dieta stuck her tongue out at me. "Most of the fantasy shots will be early morning and late afternoon to get the best light, yes? So the other shots will be tucked in between, but at the same locations. Question answered?"

Stephen nodded.

"The books—oh, there, you've seen them," she said, glancing at the table. She waited another minute for questions. "No more? Very well, eat and drink, but remember to be back to the boat by call time at five A.M. We shoot at Snoqualmie Falls tomorrow and must get an early start. I see you then. We make beautiful pictures! Now I go get some sleep from my hangover."

"Jet lag?" Darcy suggested.

"No. Hangover from a layover to get over my jet lag," Dieta said with a smile. We all chuckled as she slipped out the door.

Kim took the podium again. "This feels so formal, standing here," she said.

"Sit down and have some food," Kenneth said. Stephen was already pulling a chair out for her.

"I really should—" she said, glancing at Thom Good-feather.

"He'll be here in a while," he said to her.

I assumed they were talking about Tobin. Kim smiled brightly and joined us. "Just for a few minutes. I'm still tracking down details."

Darcy lit a cigarette while Kenneth distributed menus. He

didn't look like anything interrupted his feeding schedule. "I'd wondered where Dieta got to," Freddie said. "So she's producing now."

"She was the darling of the runway a few seasons back. Every show, but she quit," Darcy said.

"Some girls can't take it," Stephen said. "Too much pressure."

"I heard she was in an accident," Kenneth said. "Lost her mum."

"The poor thing," Freddie said. "And she quit modeling?"

Kenneth twisted his mustache. "All I heard was about the accident."

"She had some sort of come-to-Buddha meeting and reconsidered her life," Darcy said. "Some psychic told her she was going to die in an automotive accident. She stopped driving the next day." She glanced around. "I was in Europe at the time, too."

"What kind of accident?" Stephen asked.

"Was she in? A moped, in Greece."

"Those little winding roads will get you every time," Kenneth said. "Sangria, everyone?"

The waiter appeared and Kenneth ordered all the appetizers and enough sangria to float the tugboat in. Kim sipped on San Pellegrino, and Thom Goodfeather, sitting back from the table, didn't eat any meat.

"I'm really into names," Stephen said to us. "Where they come from, what the story is. I confess," he said, turning to the local boy, "I've never heard Nasmo before. Is it a family name?"

Nasmo smiled. "Not really. My mother is Haitian, and I was born in Florida. She's very religious. Like, wacky religious. She goes into trances, gets messages from beyond, talks to angels. Anyway, she went into labor with me while watching church on the TV."

We all leaned forward, listening.

"She called the ambulance to get her. They came, and when they were wheeling her into the hospital, she had a vision. She knew what to name her firstborn son. She saw the letters written in the sky above her."

His amber gaze moved from one face to the other. "No Smoking."

We all laughed.

"Somehow the spelling got confused on the hospital paperwork, so I ended up being Nasmo," he said. "Na Smoking. Then we moved to Seattle and she started a cleaning business." He looked down and shrugged nonchalantly. "And she bought some stock, from one of the places she cleaned."

"Oooo," we all chorused.

"A little company called Microsoft?" Kim asked.

Nasmo nodded his head.

"Does she still have visions?" Darcy asked, blowing smoke out of the side of her mouth.

"No, now she gets massages and has season tickets to the Mariners," he said, laughing. "Microsoft is still a business client, though."

The waiter set plates of salad down in front of us, refilled our sangria glasses, and vanished again.

"What about you, Dallas?" Stephen said. "I've known a few Dallases, but they were all men."

"My parents named me before I was born."

"That's confidence," Kenneth said, twirling his mustache.

I laughed. "My mother was positive I was another boy. She already had three sons and they all had been given Texas city names."

"I'm guessing your parents are Texans?" Darcy asked.

"Completely."

"What do they do?" Nasmo asked.

"They each teach Texas history. But at opposing universities. So anyway, the birth certificate was filled out; the announcements were just waiting for my arrival date and exact measurements. Then I was born."

"That must have been a shock," Freddie said. "Your poor mother, everything is blue and then pow! Need pink!"

"It was worse than that. My mom had called me Dallas from the minute she conceived. The doctor had thought I was a boy."

"Obviously no sonogram," Darcy said.

"Yeah, they were going by was she carrying me high or low, did she crave sweets or salt, all the old wives' tales."

"And there you were," Kenneth said.

"Yep. Female."

"Did they want to change it? Your name, not your sex," Freddie said.

"Apparently they were in the middle of that decision when my granddaddy came in. He'd been widowed for a long time, took one look at me, and called me Dallas." I speared an asparagus stalk. "No one goes against my granddaddy. He's an old Irish Catholic patriarch."

"I know what you mean, girl. Rules as a benevolent dictator?" Freddie said.

"Absolutely."

"So did all of you get asked—" Darcy began, but our dinners arrived.

Kenneth cut into his lamb, gesturing to Darcy with his fork. "And your name?"

She speared a shrimp and smiled at him. "What about yours?"

"Kenneth has long been a family name," he said. "Though originally, it was Kennard, Old English for strong and bold. What about Darcy?"

My swordfish was delectable. Stephen and Nasmo were both eating steak, and Kim had refused dinner, saying she'd eaten already. Thom Goodfeather was picking nuts off the top of his salad and lining them on the edge of his plate. Each walnut half was equidistant from the last, all facing the same way. That's a Type A for you, I thought. Freddie was the exact opposite; he'd tucked his napkin into his collar and had both forearms braced on the table, ready to leap into his bowl of pasta.

Darcy shrugged at Kenneth's question. "My parents just liked it. I don't know, my sister's name is Debbe, with an *e*. I think my mother really wanted twins, so she tried to make her own by giving us similar names and dressing us alike."

"Are you the eldest?" Stephen asked, looking up from his meat for a moment.

"Yes. Debbe is two years younger."

Kenneth was married, with two children and four grandchildren, one also named Kenneth. His attitude was slightly paternal, at least when he was drinking sangria. "What were you saying earlier?" Kenneth asked Darcy as the waiters cleared the table.

"I forget," she said, lighting up. "Oh wait! Did everyone else get a third degree about outdoor sports? I mean, they asked if I could skydive! What's with that?"

I listened quietly.

"It's scheduled for the desert shoot," Kenneth said. "Though I believe only the talent is going to be skydiving. Ah, well, blah, blah, blah. Did you learn?" he asked.

"My God, I did. It was the most fabulous thing! Just falling through the air, even if I did it over Jersey. Even Jersey's beautiful before you land there. I can't wait to go back up."

Kenneth finished his glass of sangria. "Anyone want more?"

We all pushed our glasses forward.

He filled them as Darcy spoke. "Where are we going for desert? I thought the whole shoot was in Washington."

"Washington has desert," Nasmo asserted.

Everyone else, I was gratified to see, was as amazed as I had been at that information.

"I'm going to shoot the glacier fast so we have time left over to ski, so bring gear that day," Kenneth said.

"Killer!" Nasmo said. "I'm bringing a snow kayak too."

"What is the cosmopolitan shot?" Freddie asked. "Somewhere in this city?"

"It will be at the EMP," Kenneth said. "I think that's the name."

"Killer!" Nasmo said. "That is the most awesome building. We're shooting there?"

"That's the plan," Stephen said.

The servers brought dessert, but I was too full and just had coffee. Plain coffee, no cream, no foam, no milk, no froth. Joe. Plain.

"C'mon, San Antonio," Kenneth said, winking at me. "You're in Seattle. Even on the dark continent we know it's all about coffee and computers here. You can't drink just coffee, plain."

"Adding milk and flavor just makes it into another meal," I said. "It's too filling."

"Don't be so precious," Darcy said. "Sweets are required to keep women in a healthy state of mind. If you aren't going to eat sugar, then you should at least have a little in your coffee."

I smiled, undisturbed.

"Then how about a little Frangelica?" Freddie said.

My head snapped up.

"Now you have her attention," Stephen said.

"Well, I could maybe be persuaded," I said. "But not if you have to go out and get it."

"My sweetest," Freddie said, then turned to Kenneth. "What did you call her? San Antonio? How about, my sweetest Nacogdoches," he said. I had a feeling I was going to be called every Texas city *except* Dallas on this shoot. "Every Boy Scout knows to be prepared!"

"You were a Boy Scout?" Darcy asked in disbelief.

"Girl, you wouldn't believe the merit badges I received. I was an Eagle Scout, even. Then our leader left and got married, the bitch. So I ran away to New York and started cuttin' hair." As he spoke, he reached into his mailbag and produced an antique flask.

"That is gorgeous!" I said, looking at the polished silver.

"My ole pappy got it from his pappy and so on, since before the Civil War," Freddie said. "It's an heirloom."

I poured some Frangelica in my coffee, then passed the flask to Nasmo King, who examined it and passed it on to Kenneth. It was beautiful, unscratched, and engraved "To Fredrick Eauneau, 1824." And I thought he'd been kidding about his surname.

At that moment, the roar of a powerful engine drowned out the music and even the ambient noises downstairs.

"What the hell?" Darcy said, getting up. We raced to the window and watched a fast, sleek silver car with flame-red brake lights accelerate through the fence and into Lake Union.

Chapter Five

"No! No!" Kim screamed, throwing herself against the glass.

People ran toward the water from the restaurant and the pier. Kim kept wailing. Had anybody jumped in?

"What is it?" Darcy said, looking at Kim.

"Tobin! Tobin! It's his car!" Thom Goodfeather grabbed Kim's arms, restraining her. "He has that car!"

We joined the crowd racing across the parking lot. The car was almost under. I kicked off my shoes as I jumped in. The shock of the cold took my breath away—definitely not Texas.

I surface dove, opening my eyes in the murk. I couldn't see three inches in front of me.

I went up for air, to get my bearings.

"To your left, Dallas," Kenneth shouted.

Fixing the spot, I dropped down, my hands out, feeling for metal.

A door handle.

Locked.

It was too dark and dirty to see through the window, but I

banged on the glass. Maybe the driver could see me, could help me get him out. I banged again, then broke for the surface.

Sirens. Flashing lights. I was freezing.

"Is he okay?"

"Where is he?"

"Can you see anything?"

"Flashlight," I gasped out.

Someone threw one, I caught it, gulped for breath and went back down. I swam to the other side of the car and tried that door. Locked. There should still be air inside. I peered in the window, then held the flashlight against the glass. I blinked, focused on what I saw through the glass.

Ohmigod. *No.* How had he gotten this car?

I shot up. "He's hurt!" I shouted. Two police officers jumped in. I saw a diver on the dock, getting into his weight belt. Another guy, already in a wetsuit, jumped in. "He's trapped," I said. "Unconscious. Bleeding."

The diver clapped me on the shoulder and dropped down beneath the black water. The suited diver followed him. I was too cold; I couldn't feel my hands anymore. "Grab hold!" a man shouted, holding out an oar.

I couldn't grasp it, and I was losing feeling in my legs too.

Someone jumped into the water behind me and pushed me up. "Stick your arms out, baby," he said. I reached up, was grabbed and hauled out of the water.

A blanket. Something warm in a cup that curled inside my stomach and brought feeling back to my hands. My feet were soaking in hot water, my wrists were wrapped in heat strips, and my head was covered.

I whispered through chattering teeth, "Nnn–oo nn–oooo."

The scene was a mess. The Porsche Boxster had damaged several other luxury cars before pitching into the water between several moored boats and the dock. The fence was pulled down, planters were shattered, and lights from the emergency vehicles and media cast a garish, horrific look on everything.

It was fully dark, and the sounds of sirens and shouts and Kim's crying muffled the racing of my own heart.

"It's too late," Freddie murmured. "It's been almost ten minutes."

If only he had been conscious, he could have been out of there in five, but he had probably drowned, knocked out from the impact. The airbag had deflated already. I blinked back tears.

"What happened?" Stephen asked. "Why did he speed through the fence? Was he stoned?"

"No!" I snarled, then pressed a shaking hand to my mouth.

The crowd stepped back as the officers surfaced, a body cradled between them. "Get back!" the EMTs shouted, kneeling over the black man with a gold initial necklace and giving him CPR.

The crew stood in shock. "It's Richard?" Freddie gasped. "He was driving Tobin's car?"

"It's Richard?" Kim said. Her tears halted mid-flow. "Where's Tobin? Thom, did you know Richard was driving Tobin's car?"

Thom looked at me. "Did you know?"

I shook my head; not until I'd seen his initial necklace against the window when I'd looked inside the car under-water.

They lifted Richard onto a gurney and slammed the doors shut.

"He survived?" Freddie asked as the ambulance wailed into the night.

"Where are they taking him?" Kenneth asked one of the wet officers who were hurrying back to my ambulance.

"Take this," I said, handing the officer a matching heavy blanket. He stripped down to skin, teeth chattering and dropped his clothes next to mine by the wheel of the ambulance.

"Tha-thanks," he said, wrapping up in it. "Wanna help me get warm?" I didn't even look at him.

"Don't be rude," Freddie said, checking him out.

A dry officer gave Kenneth directions to the hospital.

"He's not rude," I said to Freddie. "It's the best way to beat hypothermia."

"And get close to those legs," the officer whispered to me. "It *was* rude, but I meant it as a compliment."

I guess he'd been on the force for about ten minutes; he was maybe nineteen and blond. I adjusted my blanket so it was less of a mini-skirt and more of a long sarong.

Richard.

In Tobin's car.

In the water.

What had happened? I prayed he'd be all right.

"What's going on here?" a man demanded. "Kim, talk to me."

I looked over my shoulder and saw Kim fall into Tobin's arms. "The model, Richard, I think he's dead," she said, crying again.

"She thought it was you. They took Richard to hospital," Kenneth said. "Who wants to go with me?"

"Me? Why did you think it was me?" Tobin asked Kim. His arms were around her, her face against his neck, but his hands were frozen into claws on her back and her body was tense.

"Your car," Kenneth said. "Isn't it?"

"Let's not talk about this," Kim interrupted as she pulled away. "We need to get going. Dallas, do you need medical attention?"

"No, I want to go with Richard."

Kim ignored me.

"You need to get to bed," Freddie said.

"I'm gone," Kenneth shouted as he walked away. "Have Thom and your attorneys meet me there." I looked around. The tall Native American wasn't around. Was he talking to the police? *The police. That's who I needed to talk to.*

"I'm fine," I said to Kim. "I want to go to the hospital." My teeth were still chattering.

"Are you sure you are okay?" another EMT asked me. "We have another call."

"Fine," I said. "I want to go—"

"You need a shower, and bed," the EMT guy said. "Lots of blankets. Call the hospital. You can't do anything else, anyway." He looked at the crew, standing around. "Guys. She's soaking wet, and her temperature is dropping. Get her out of here."

"Will they just leave the car in the water?" Nasmo asked.

"Probably fish it out in the morning," Stephen said.

"C'mon, Dallas," Freddie asked. "I have your shoes."

"Be careful. Stay warm tonight and call if you feel the least bit strange. And take this blanket," the EMT said. The ambulance roared off, leaving us in the cold parking lot, in the dark.

I was dizzy. Everything seemed to be underwater. *Richard.* Had I really seen Richard?

We got back to the boat and I found myself in Kenneth's quarters—which were the nicest on board. Hope ran water, Darcy spiked it with a dozen scents, and I climbed into the biggest, reddest, baddest bathtub I'd ever seen—all the time thinking, *Did I really see Richard?*

When I got out, shriveled and warm, I looked at Darcy. She was still bandbox perfect. "Was that Richard?" My leather pants hung from the shower rack. Ruined. The silk shirt would fit a cat now.

She patted my hand. "Yeah, sweetie. It was. You knew him?"

I nodded my head.

"They postponed the shoot," she said. "We'll wait and hear tomorrow."

"Have we called the cops?"

"They'll be here in the morning."

My eyes felt weighted. I saw a wall clock. It was only midnight?

Darcy took the bottom bunk and I climbed onto the top one.

I'd never even thanked my rescuer, whoever had helped me out of the water.

Just before I dropped off to sleep, I wondered: why hadn't we heard the brakes squeal? We'd seen the brake *lights,* but we'd only heard the racing of the engine—no sound of resistance.

A tap at the door woke me. I dragged myself upright. Hope stuck her head inside. "Dallas," she whispered. "The police are here to see you."

Darcy was awake but still in bed. "The hell they are! She should be allowed to sleep in! They can just come back!"

Hope looked a little surprised at Darcy's reaction.

"It's okay," I said, sitting up and throwing off the blankets. "I'm fine. I'll be out in a minute."

"Need anything?" Darcy asked. I shook my head as I brushed my teeth in the corner basin, then put on jeans and a sweatshirt, both from A&F. I closed the door quietly.

"They have coffee," Hope said as I followed her down the narrow passageway to the galley. "Do you want that or orange juice?"

"OJ," I said, testing my voice.

"I'll bring it in."

I walked across the salon and halted at the sight of a stone fireplace in the middle of the tugboat. That's creative, I thought. Very cool. I stepped into the dining room. Two uniformed officers were debating which restaurant had the best crème brûlée. They got to their feet when they saw me.

"That was quite a piece of heroism last night," one of them said as he stood to introduce himself and his partner. He wore an oxford cloth shirt and paisley tie.

"How is Richard?" I asked.

"Still in critical condition, ma'am. But his injuries come from not wearing a safety belt. He got out of the water in time."

"We're just here to get a statement," said the other officer, a heavy-set black man in a JC Penney polyester blend suit.

"Of course," I said. I told him where I'd been sitting at BluWater, what I saw, how I got to the scene.

"Now, are you a lifeguard? What made you jump in?"

I could feel myself blush. "Uh, I've been in a similar situation and—"

"Similar, how?"

"A car driving into the ocean." So I knew there was time, and air, to get him out. If he'd been okay.

He gave me a weird look. "What did you see?"

"Not much of anything. But I knew he was out. Unconscious."

"Specifically, what did you see?"

"The water was up to his shoulders, and he'd risen out of his seat."

"Floated?"

"Right. He was in the air pocket. All I got were shadows, like black-and-white film, when I shone the flashlight," I said. "But I could see he was a mess."

They took notes.

"There was blood on his face, his ear. A piece of mirror sticking out of his forehead, I think."

"What happened next?"

"I got to the surface, saw two cops jump in, with two others behind them. I was too cold, and I got out. Some guy helped me, but I don't know who."

"A professional?"

"I don't think so, but I was pretty out of it by then."

"Close to hypothermia?"

"Maybe," I said. "I don't really remember. Do you know what happened?"

"Well, we pulled the car out this morning. It should give us some clues. You say it just charged in?"

"Revved so loud it drowned out the music."

They thanked me, said they'd be in touch, and left. Dieta showed up on the walkway in yellow gingham capri pants, yellow slicker, and yellow gingham umbrella. "You are a hero," she said. "I'm so proud to know you. How did you know what to do?"

"How's your ear?" I asked.

"I'd fall over if I got on the boat," she said, twirling her umbrella. She looked like an animated jonquil. She waited a moment. "You don't want to talk about this?"

"Let's see what happens to Richard."

"Okay," she said, all smiles. "Whatever makes you happy."

"Going to sleep," I said.

"Oh, you go." She sat down on a bench, crossing her legs. "Hope and I do breathing today."

I saw Hope join her as I walked down the hallway. Darcy was asleep again. I dropped my jeans, crawled under the covers, and tried to blot out Richard's torn-up face.

I bolted awake and looked at my watch. Ten A.M. Darcy was still asleep and rain streaked the porthole glass. I got dressed in silence and crept out to breakfast. Wes was on the phone with his Miami agent, so I stole some fresh-baked cookies, then swiped the paper, and sat under the umbrella outside, safe from the rain, but reveling in the cool, fresh air.

It was going to be okay. Some reconstructive surgery and Richard would be back at work in a month, maybe two. I touched my throat, my own scar left over from a car accident. He'd be okay.

The rain continued to fall. After a while, I heard the strains of ABBA floating from the boat.

"*Dig in the dancing queen—*" an unmistakably male, off-key, voice sang.

"Freddie," Wes and I said in unison.

One by one, the crew showed up. Hope kept plying us with coffee and fresh cinnamon rolls. Kenneth finally arrived—in rain gear. "Good morning all. Well. Here we are. Due to circumstances, it's our day to see Seattle."

"How is Richard?" Freddie asked as he glanced at me.

"Still critical. Another reason to hang about."

"We are getting paid, right?" Darcy asked. "I mean, I can work in the rain."

"Everyone is getting his day rate," Dieta said, "and we have a job to do."

"I only do makeup," Darcy said. "That's it. No windows, no floors." She sat back and crossed her arms.

"So your job today is to enjoy yourselves and bond," Dieta said.

"And she doesn't mean James," Kenneth said.

Everyone groaned.

"Or gold," Stephen said.

George, who'd arrived this morning and been bent over a Palm Pilot ever since, looked up. "I don't get paid enough to listen to these bad puns."

"Gold James?" Tom Fly asked. He'd come in a few minutes ago and watched us eat, then cautiously bit into a roll.

"Gold Bond," Freddie said. "There isn't enough money, Georgie-Porgie," he said, ruffling the big blonde man's hair.

"Our taxis!" Dieta called.

Rain fell in sheets, but since Seattle's reputation is rain, everyone was prepared. It wasn't cold rain, just those spring showers one hears about, but rarely sees. We piled in.

"Hey Blondie!" the woman driver greeted me.

"Didn't know she was your type," Freddie whispered.

"Esmerelda," she started, when I didn't say anything. She pointed to her tattoo. "I picked you up—"

Freddie hooted.

"—at the airport."

"Of course," I said. "How nice to see you again."

"She's our RV driver," Dieta said, patting Esmerelda's bare, tanned, beefed up arm. "She'll be with us all along."

"Dallas has a girlfriend," Freddie sing-songed.

Freddie, Wes, George, Tom Fly, Kenneth, Stephen, Darcy, Dieta, Esmerelda, Nasmo and I stuffed ourselves in the two cars. We shouldn't have eaten breakfast. They dropped us at the Space Needle and we began our full-fledged day of tourism. By then we'd convinced Esmerelda to join us.

"After all," Dieta said, as she got out of the car, and almost fell over. "You are an employee too, for a few days, yes?" Esmerelda tossed on an REI slicker and the games began.

Richard would make this so much more fun, I thought. *Please be okay.* I called the hospital while I watched the rest of them walk through McDonald's drive-thru. Apparently they were hungry.

"Richard . . . Wilson," I said to the operator. Since he'd become wildly famous, he'd dropped his last name. It took a minute to remember it. He was still in critical condition. Across from me, the crew was loading up on drinks. Everyone carried at least two, some three. I tucked my phone in my bag and met them as they crossed the street. "Thirsty?" I asked Kenneth.

"Bringing the lads on the grounds milkshakes," he said. For an hour, we passed out milkshakes. Chocolate was the most popular, a bet that Darcy and Freddie had made while standing in line.

"So I was wrong about that," Darcy said. "A girl can be wrong. Occasionally."

Dieta sidled up to me. "I know you are worried," she said, her green eyes filled with compassion. "But . . . Richard would want you to have fun today, yes? How many times are you paid to tour a beautiful city?"

"You know Richard?"

"We were in Europe together. *'Stayin' alive, stayin' alive.'*"

I hugged her; she was right. It wasn't fair to everyone else to be gloomy. *"Ahh ahh ahh ahh—"* We laughed and joined the rest of them.

In the still-pouring rain.

Up the Space Needle—around the top—back down.

Freddie puked.

He had taken off his motion-sickness bracelets. We wandered through Seattle Center and took snapshots of ourselves in the fountain, in the rain, in our raingear; then we hopped in the monorail and zoomed to Westlake Center.

"Nooooo!" Kenneth cried as he saw the Nordstrom marquee fast approaching. "It's shopping!" We window-shopped our way to the Market. Everyone got some flavor or style of coffee, took three sips, then traded with the person to his or her right, then three sips more. We went through a lot of straws.

Why hadn't we heard the brakes? Why had Richard been in Tobin's car?

The police are asking these questions, Dallas. Let them do their jobs.

We traipsed by the fish sellers. The leading fish thrower sounded like he'd actually swallowed a microphone, his voice was so deep. George got dragged into a game of keep-away over all our heads with a salmon. Wes had Dungeness Bay crabs shipped to his mother in Pennsylvania, Darcy bought Copper River salmon for her next-door neighbor, and I stocked up on some amazing garlic-pepper jelly that would make even strychnine taste good. We took the Hill Climb, going down. It became a race, dozens of flights, eleven adults gasping and giggling, with boxes of fish, bags of candy, and bottles of marinades, heading downhill pell-mell.

In the rain.

We screeched to a halt at the red light at Alaskan Way. "Let's go see Mount St. Helen's erupt in IMAX," Wes said, "Today's the anniversary."

"How do you know that?" I asked.

"I read."

Darcy clapped a hand to her throat in mock terror. "A male model who reads. Won't *GQ* just die over that? You could start a whole new trend."

"A rage."

"A fad."

"A revolution," Nasmo said.

As if on cue, we all started singing the Beatles' "You say you want a revo-lu-ti-oon, we-ell, you know. . . ."

Wes swatted at Darcy's head and she punched his shoulder, then they both dropped into boxing stances. "C'mon big boy, are you man enough to take me?"

"I can't resist," Kenneth said, snapping shots. She was 5'4" to his 6'1" and looked a whole lot fiercer as they danced in a circle around each other.

Dieta stood behind Wes. "C'mon bruiser," she said, her accent pure Rambo. "You can comeback. Take her down."

Freddie jumped behind Darcy. "Punch his pretty little

lights out," he said with an exaggerated lisp. "Just beat those satin shorts right off of him."

We were all laughing when the movie was announced.

Somehow, I ended up next to Wes. We both sat with legs akimbo, and I swore I could feel the heat of his thigh. I leaned back and focused on the movie.

We came out of the film, quieter.

"That," Darcy said as she lit up, "was really big."

"I remember the press it got," Kenneth said. "Even in South Africa."

"Were you here then?" I asked Nasmo.

"Still in Florida."

"I was," Esmerelda said. "I was living in Yakima at the time. It went dark at noon. You couldn't drive anywhere because the ash clogged up your engine."

"Did you hear it?" Darcy asked.

"I think so," she said.

"How long did it take to clean up?" Dieta asked.

Esmerelda tugged at her dreamcatcher earring. "Months and months. I mean, it erupted several times. Sometimes the wind moved the ash west, most times east."

"Yak-ee-maw is east then?" Dieta asked.

"Over the moutains," Esmerelda said. "We swept the ash up, but it wasn't like snow, it didn't melt. There was nothing you could do with it. Finally, the city told everyone to take it to one place. They packed it down, sealed it over, and made a park."

"I understand Mount Rainier is supposed to blow next," Tom Fly said. He looked nervous. "You don't think it would happen while we're here, would it?"

Esmerelda shrugged. "Weathermaker doesn't have to blow, just let that molten core get hot enough and close enough to the surface. It would melt the glaciers and sweep Seattle into the Sound."

As though our heads were on a string, we all pivoted toward the water. Tom Fly swallowed audibly.

"So," Dieta asked after a moment, "who wants ice cream?"

We were eating dinner—I couldn't believe how many Mexican restaurants this city had—when Kenneth's phone rang.

He turned away from the table. We all fell silent. He hung up after nodding. No one looked at anyone for a moment.

While we were out, laughing and goofing off, Richard had been fighting for his life. So young, so vibrant. I closed my eyes and felt the tears on my cheeks. *I'm sorry,* I thought. *I tried, I really did. I'm so sorry, Richard.*

Kenneth spoke after a minute. "Richard . . . he . . . died at 4:27 this afternoon."

Silence.

"Esmerelda—I need a ride," I said, finally.

"Where are you going?" Darcy asked.

"The hospital," I said. "The police station, I don't know. but I have to. . . ."

I staggered back to the tugboat at ten and heard that sunshine was in the forecast. Hope had fresh chocolate-chip cookies and milk on the table. Darcy was perched on the couch's arm, blowing her smoke out the window. ABBA's "Knowing Me, Knowing You," came from somewhere, subdued.

Freddie kicked out a chair. "Where'd you go?"

I shook my head and sat down. "Everywhere. The hospital, the police station. They interviewed me again," I said.

"Do they know what happened?"

"They didn't tell me."

"Tobin called. Richard's funeral will be in New York."

"Have a cookie," Dieta said, rolling over in a breakfast chair.

"You're on the boat," I realized. "I thought—"

"She's in a wheeled chair," Stephen said. "And we'll just wheel her out of here."

"Wheel and deal," Kenneth said.

I took the cookie from Dieta. "Do you want to stay in another hotel tonight?" she asked.

Carefully, I broke the cookie into pieces. "Are we shooting tomorrow?"

"The river shot," Darcy said. "Fantasy."

"We're leaving here before dawn," Dieta said. "Do you need to think about it?"

"She's tough," George said. The ABBA music was coming from his earphone, on the table in front of him. "Besides, she gets to sleep with Darcy."

"Who would pass up a chance at that?" Darcy said, and posed lasciviously in the window. The boys hooted and hollered as she made faces intended to be glamorous and dramatic and looked like a wall-eyed fish instead. "Besides, she has to host the first match between me and Freddie."

"Which is?"

"Name That Eyebrow," she said.

They were lunatics. Not sad, not depressed. Irreverent, silly and . . . exactly where I should be. Richard would have loved them. They would have loved him. I couldn't believe it. Thirty years old, and dead.

"Sure," I said.

I was seated on a bar stool, and Freddie and Darcy sat opposite me. The crew, wired on chocolate and sugar, watched from behind them. My job was to grab a pile of new magazines, find a photo and cover all of it except the eyebrow.

Kenneth loaned me his two croppers.

Whoever guessed first, won.

Dieta was keeping score.

Tom Fly was the commentator and George was filming it all, through a tiny little video camera, for posterity.

A clock struck midnight.

"Let the games begin!" Kenneth cried.

Chapter Six

SNOQUALMIE FALLS

"They are a hundred feet taller than Niagara Falls," Darcy said. "Can you believe that? Way out here in Washington State?" She was wearing a "Fornicate U" logoed T-shirt, kangaroo-pouch skirt, and platform sneakers underneath a well-loved pashmina.

"You just say that because you East Coasters can't believe there is life west of the Hudson," I joked, watching the rush of water at Snoqualmie Falls plummet 270 feet. It was just barely six A.M. "Ya know, I get the feeling I've seen these before."

"Who killed Laura Palmer," Freddie said.

None of us said a word, but I knew we were all aware of the term "kill." Poor Richard. Killed in a car accident. The obit was in today's *New York Times*. I'm sorry, I thought again.

"That name is familiar," I said, watching the water fall, being deliberately casual. I'd seen Richard floating in the water, bloody. To everyone else, he was just a name and comp card.

He'd sung "More than a Woman" from SNF to me on the phone when he'd called one time from Los Angeles. I was supposed to be on the shoot, but had gotten on the wrong side of my boss and was punished by staying in Dallas. In August.

I sighed. I had to work. *Just forget about it, Dallas. Plenty of time to mope and mourn after this shoot.*

"Girl, were you under a rock in the late eighties? Laura Palmer was in *Twin Peaks*. The girl who got axed by her father. Whoops," he said, covering his mouth. "Guess you don't need to watch it now."

Darcy and Freddie began to sing a nursery rhyme about who eats oats and who eats ivy. "Strange how the creepiest shows are always about the most intimate relationships going way wrong, huh?" Freddie asked.

"Wasn't that when Sherilyn Fenn was doing a nouveau Marilyn look?" I asked, still trying to place this show.

"Back when she had arms," Darcy said.

"Pre-Helena," I said. Now I remembered.

"Exactly. She was almost enough to make me change teams," Freddie said.

Darcy and I exchanged looks. "A likely story."

Freddie whispered, "But y'all can't tell anyone that. I could get in trouble."

"What, the Gay Men of America Association would toss you out?" I scoffed.

"On his face!" Darcy said.

"I wish!" he said, laughing.

My cell phone rang, and I stepped away from the falls so I could hear.

"Ms. O'Connor," a man said.

"Yes?"

"This is King County Sheriff's Department, ma'am. I'm Detective Thompson. Do you have a minute?"

"Sure," I said. "Where's King County?"

"Seattle, ma'am. I'm investigating the death of Richard Wilson."

"What about it?"

"Are you alone?"

"Not really."

"Then just listen, ma'am. Mr. Wilson's death was not accidental."

"What?" I said. To my right the falls continued to fall, but instead of being beautiful, they suddenly looked dangerous. "What are you saying?"

"It was a homicide, ma'am."

"What?" The roaring of the falls filled my chest.

"Yes, ma'am. Please do not tell anyone else this. We need your complete discretion. We will need to ask you some more questions. Today."

"Uh, sure."

Tobin came down the steps from the first observation point, Dieta trailing him. Today she was dressed like a 1960s stewardess, in powder blue, complete with cat-eye glasses. "Uh, I'm working today," I said.

"Tonight then. We have some concerns, Ms. O'Connor. Please be careful."

"Careful of what? What are you talking about?"

"Ma'am, please do not mention this phone call to any of your colleagues, at least until after I speak to you."

"Why? Am I in danger?"

"We'll talk tonight, Ms. O'Connor. I don't think so. Just keep quiet."

I walked back to Freddie and Darcy. Murder? Richard was murdered? How? The glass in his head? The car?

"Putting that girl in those heels is asking for a disaster," Freddie whispered to us. I looked at Dieta's slingbacked pumps. "She's going to go headfirst down those falls."

Was that his plan? Had *he* done something to Richard?

"What do you think?" Tobin asked us, gesturing to the falls. They looked treacherous, the rocks stabbing through the frothing white water, the frigid river screaming around the curve. Slippery rocks, hook-rooted trees. I shivered.

"It's beautiful. What's the story?" Darcy asked.

"Well, this is the reason I hired Dallas O'Connor," he said, looking at me. Suddenly my hiring seemed a lot more ominous. Lots of people had done mermaids. Why me? "It's of our hero calling his muse, the river nymph," Tobin said.

"Where is the set?" Freddie asked.

"Follow me," Tobin said, leading us down a final two flights of stairs to a covered lookout point. "See that log down there?"

We craned through the morning mist to see. "That's what you're talking about?" Darcy asked, pointing to a twig on the edge of the river.

"She'll be sitting on the rock in front of that log."

"Jesus. That's a long way down," Darcy said.

"There's a road that comes pretty close," Tobin said. "And our hero will be, do you see that rock farther up, closer to that smaller waterfall? That's where he'll be." He looked at me. "Dallas, you haven't said anything."

"This could be awesome," I stuttered out. "Has Yvette arrived yet?"

"Dieta?" he said. She was already dialing her cell phone.

"When is call?" Darcy asked. "This is a fantasy shot, with fantasy makeup, right?"

"Right, it's the double-truck," Tobin said. "First we'll check in. The lodge graciously is letting us do that this morning. Then we'll have breakfast, discuss the story. Crew's call about nine-thirty, makeup and models at ten. We'll start shooting around two. Shadows start earlier down there."

Dieta motioned for us all to follow her to one of the park benches, away from the falls, so that we could hear better.

Everything was lined with flowers, pink-and-white flowering bushes, and trees. Tobin excused himself back to the hotel. "So what do you think? Does it make you happy?" Dieta asked. "Are you inspired?"

Murder was the only topic on my mind. "It's just Wes and Yvette?" I asked. *Focus.* I had a job to do. "No one else?"

"This place is gorgeous," Darcy said. "Who wouldn't be inspired?"

"Where do we check in?" Freddie asked.

"We are at that hotel there," Dieta said, pointing to a lodge-style building that clung to the cliffs, lined with those same flowering bushes, to the left of the falls. "It's wonderful. Each of you has a room. Enjoy it, because from now on you'll be bunking together. Every room has a Whirlpool spa and fireplace. Do not, repeat, do not steal the robes. If you want one, I can get it for you at cost." She looked around at us, with serious green eyes behind rhinestone glasses. "So take a look around, we have breakfast at seven-thirty, then check-in." She said goodbye and we started walking toward the trail. Freddie was ahead of us, jogging.

Had one of these people killed Richard? Why? Who? How? What did it have to do with me? Why wouldn't he answer if I were in danger or not? I was really weirded out. Had I gotten that cop's phone number? "What are those bushes?" I asked, pointing to the same flowering plant I'd seen since I arrived.

"You're asking me?" Darcy said.

"Don't you have trees and bushes up north?"

"We may have 'em, but I never seen 'em. Central Park is my idea of rain forest. I moved from Jersey just as soon as I could shoplift lipstick, then lied my way into the makeup counter at Woolworth's. My dream was to never step off concrete again."

"Unless it was Central Park."

"Right, being able to see the Plaza just makes me feel better. I know that the Marlboro man can rescue me if I shout."

"Did you always know you wanted to be a makeup artist?" I asked. *Did you ever want to kill someone?* I thought.

"No, I really wanted to be on Broadway. However," she said, stopping to do an abbreviated Rockettes kick, "you'll notice I lack a little in the height department. Put a chandelier headdress on me, and people will just try to eat dinner."

I laughed, but she really was short.

"Once I figured out how to run in heels, I had them soldered to my feet. I'm so jealous. You've obviously never had this problem."

"No. Being short has never been an issue," I said.

"So this nymph shot is the double-truck?" she asked.

"He said it," I said.

"Have you seen the dress?" she asked.

"The same Polaroid as you," I answered automatically. "Fitted green sheath covered in paillettes, with a mock turtleneck and no back."

"She is going to be gorgeous. I'm thinking a little wet look for her hair, eyes smoky, silvery lips . . ."

I closed my eyes, trying to blot out Richard's face with any It Girl's. Focusing was starting to work. "Kenneth will probably love it."

We were heading downhill still, with dappled sunshine on the pathway, birdsong in the air. So inconsistent with murder.

Had someone stabbed him . . . before he got in the car? The glass in his forehead—no, that wasn't possible. *The car.*

We went down a last flight of stairs and found ourselves on a road next to a power plant. We followed the signs through a caged walking area, then out onto a lookout across from the waterfall. It was hard to hear, so I tapped Darcy on the shoulder. "I'm going down," I shouted, pointing to the rocks below us. Who would rig his car? Why? When? Was it someone here? Though actually, Richard didn't have to know the person who killed him. It could have been just a freak of fate.

It was Tobin's car. *Tobin's* car?

"How?" Darcy yelled back. The platform was completely fenced. I watched a college kid in Skechers, cargo pants, T-shirt and pukka shells, climb over the fence. There, carved out of earth, were steps made by many feet and hands. I pointed; she nodded and we started down.

It was Tobin's car. I needed to call that cop back. I turned my back to the river and dialed. "Out of Range," it said. They're the cops. They'll know. I looked up at the cliffs that surrounded me on all sides. Tobin would be here today—the cop could wait. I'd keep an eye on the tailor myself.

"Focus on your job, Dallas," I said.

Freddie, in an ultrablue anorak, was already walking toward the designated rock. The mist was refreshing, the location amazing. I didn't know if Tobin had used an agent or just knew the state, but this was a stunning natural wonder. Not many places like this let photo crews in. We were lucky.

I crouched on the rocks, sketched the environment, and tried to understand how the proportions of woman and man against these falls would work. It was getting later, the sun inching higher in the sky.

"Breakfast time," Freddie called to us over the sound of the water. We climbed back to the hotel. Very carefully.

The breakfast room looked down onto the falls. The sky had turned gray, but the great thing about the shot was that gray was okay—almost preferred. Just as long as it didn't rain. I'd made my call and left a message. I could relax.

Darcy sat with the models, George, Tom Fly and Wes, and Dieta. She'd changed, out of respect for the linen tablecloths. Now her T-shirt read "Sasquatch," with a little bit of writing across the top, over a pair of safari pants trimmed with zippers. Downright respectable.

Not a murderer. No one was. Not here, anyway. They didn't even know Richard, and if they had they wouldn't kill him. It was meant for Tobin. I'd done my duty; I could relax. I sat down with Nasmo, Stephen, Freddie and Kenneth.

"So was he any good?" Nasmo asked Darcy.

I looked closer. The tiny print on her T-shirt read "I did." I almost laughed. Dieta came bouncing in and sat down, Freddie right behind her.

The waiters brought oatmeal loaded with butter and brown sugar, scrambled eggs, fruit parfaits, apple sausage, bacon, croissants, biscuits, and muffins—the whole of Salish Lodge's famous four-course breakfast. We ate like we'd never seen food before. Halfway through breakfast, Dieta stumbled out of the room to answer a page.

Just as I was finishing my third cup of mochaccino, a drop-dead gorgeous blonde, in fringed suede pants, halter top and jacket walked in. Her Kate Spade luggage matched her head-to-toe pink and we watched as she stood in the doorway, searching for someone. The couples who were here on romantic getaways were suddenly tense—him with looking, her with glaring.

She was tall. Blonde. Built.

Infinitely recognizable to anyone who shopped at Victoria's Secret.

I had a bad feeling about this.

"Is Dieta here?" she asked in heavily accented English. Stephen and Nasmo fell over themselves getting up and bringing her to our table. Kim, Tobin, and Thom Goodfeather hadn't shown up yet. I stood up and introduced myself.

She shook my hand. "I was told to speak to Dieta," she said. "Is this right place?"

"Yes," I said. "Who told you to do that?"

"My agency," she said. "In Stockholm."

Darcy joined me. "Are you replacing Yvette?"

"Ah yes! That is it. I am here because of Yvette. She break-ed her leg, *ja?*"

I cursed silently, Darcy did aloud.

"What? Is problem?" the girl asked. She was about nine-teen, a Nadja Auerman lookalike with slate gray eyes. From the neck down she should be illegal: a thirty-four-C, a twenty-three-inch waist, and maybe thirty-three-and-a-half-inch hips. All tanned, toned, and young.

"No, no," I said hurriedly, glaring at Darcy. "You are here in *place* of Yvette, then?"

"Yes," she said, smiling in innocence, "I am here as Yvette."

Richard had been murdered—a horrible truth that was slowly sinking in—but until this moment the shoot had been uncomplicated. Now, I had a lingerie body instead of high-fashion, long blonde on a Viking instead of the planned-on brunette gamine, and . . . breasts. Yikes—now things were officially derailed.

I would be earning my day rate and then some. "Have a seat, some breakfast," I said. "Dieta will be here any minute."

Tom Fly gave up his seat for Irma, as she was named, and conversation was stilted, with everyone, myself included, watching this Valkyrie eat. She didn't pay any attention to her audience as she consumed eggs, sausage and endless glasses of lemon water. Dieta startled us when she returned.

"That's the replacement?" she asked me and Darcy, who was now smoking next to me, in a whisper.

"Yup. Yvette broke her leg."

I don't speak whatever language it was, but Dieta and Irma carried on a long, loud conversation with lots of smiles and frowns. Dieta dialed and spoke to someone twice. We watched. "This is better than a Spanish soap opera," Freddie confessed.

"I need to get to the dress," I said. This could potentially be a disaster. Finally Dieta finished and Irma left, trailing her striped carry-on. "Where's the dress?" I asked.

"What's going on?" Darcy said to Dieta. "Didn't the agency inform you about Yvette?"

"That was my page."

"What are they thinking? She's a—"

Tobin, Kim, Kenneth, and Thom Goodfeather chose this moment to enter the dining room. "That blonde looks familiar," Kim said.

"Oh yeah," Darcy said.

"So where's Yvette?" Kenneth asked. "We need to get moving if we're going to get the light right."

"The blonde you saw, she is Yvette," Dieta said.

"The hell she is," Kim said, dialing already. "It's Kim Charles," she snarled on her phone. "Are your heads up your asses?"

The calm, smiling woman turned into a vicious, blue streak of a hag before our eyes.

"Kim," Tobin said, trying to interrupt her.

She screamed at the unfortunate agent. Then stopped. She looked at Tobin and her eyes narrowed to slits.

That look could kill.

"You did this?" she said when she hung up. She stalked to him.

"I'm outta here," Freddie said, putting his napkin down and donning his earphones. ABBA was asking if your momma knows you're out.

Darcy lit up. "This *is* better than a Spanish soap opera." I moved to get up, but she laid a restraining hand on me.

"The dress," I said.

"Oh, shit," she said, realization dawning. "Oh."

Twenty minutes after I checked in, the sewing machine arrived. My room was on the second floor, comfortably furnished with a rocking chair, a well-lit desk, stereo system, television, fireplace, bar, and, as Dieta had predicted, a Whirlpool bath big enough for two.

Pity there was no one to share it.

I could see Kim from my balcony, pacing back and forth beside the river. Tobin walked beside her. Big fight.

Thom Goodfeather brought me the dress. "Through conflict, peace and knowledge are often revealed," he said.

Whatever.

I hung the green thing up in the weak sunshine and stared at it. The front would be impossible; the hips, too. It probably would be too big in the waist. There was a knock at the door. "Come in," I called, expecting Tobin.

"It looks like a giant green condom," Darcy said from the doorway. "Jesus, do you think her tits are real?"

"I think everything is real," I said. "Including her blond hair."

"Just when you think the world isn't fair, it proves it isn't," Darcy said. "Do you mind if I smoke?"

I shook my head. "We need to rethink the look," I said. "Any ideas?"

"Her tan is all over, I think, so that's good."

Tobin knocked and came in. He halted in front of the dress, crossed his arms, and tapped his fingers against his lips. "Has she been in to try it on yet?"

"I have a call in to her," I said. "She didn't answer her phone."

He nodded.

"Is this Kim's design?" Darcy asked.

"The dress? More or less."

The question that begged to be asked was why she wasn't in here redesigning it. "She dictates," he said, almost reading my mind. "Kim's genius is that she can think up great things, draw them out, and delegate the doing part. She doesn't even sew well."

"Oh," I said. Their relationship was becoming clearer to me. "Well—"

Tobin shrugged. "You have some work ahead of you," he said.

"What happened?" I asked.

"Darcy can tell you," he said with a glare, and left.

I turned to my spy. "Yvette broke her leg last night. Irma was in California. Tobin decided it was better to go for her than to wait to find someone else."

"Well . . . time is money," I said.

The phone rang. Irma said she would come to my room and try on the gown.

"I'll get Freddie," Darcy said, skipping out.

"What the hell am I going to do with you?" I asked the dress. Thankfully, for the sake of my sanity, it didn't respond—though I could have used the input.

I was starting to feel more like myself.

"Is that what I wear?" Irma asked as she opened my door, pointing to the XXXL condom.

Only if we followed the theme of the real Cinderella story—and hacked some parts off. "It is," I said.

"My eyes will be green when I wear it."

She walked in, the heels of her pink suede boots making her about six-three. She wasn't delicate, but she was graceful. She'd taken her hair out of its ponytail and it hung down to her waist. If Malibu Barbie ever had a flesh equivalent, I was staring at her.

Freddie and Darcy burst through the door. "This will be the most fun I've ever had," Freddie said, already running his fingers through Irma's hair.

"Why don't you try it on?" I said, wondering if she was a size four with big breasts, or a deceptive size six. Either way, she wasn't a plain four.

"Ja," she said, dropping her pants and top to reveal nature as an underwire and a tiny flesh-colored thong.

"Oh dear," Freddie said.

We all raised our gazes to her breasts; big, perky, and completely tanned. A D-cup, I didn't care what her agency claimed. "Okay y'all," I said, "I'm going to need some help."

Her hips were European slim, her waist nonexistent. We started squashing her top into the dress, but it took forever because she was so ticklish. Hysterically ticklish. One touch and she was doubled over laughing. Darcy stared at her like she was a freak from Mars, and I noticed Freddie's coffee was empty and he was drinking straight from his 1824 flask.

Who ever heard of a ticklish lingerie model?

By the time Irma was in the dress, I saw it was at least four inches too short and four inches too narrow. I held in my abs for a twenty-count, thinking.

"My mammy always told me," Freddie said, "if you have safety pins, you will always have friends." He was right. A chain of safety pins across the back was one solution. Unless I butchered the dress completely.

"What shoes?" Darcy asked.

I glanced at Irma's size-ten feet. "Barefoot, I think," I said. "A river nymph."

"I need a cigarette," Darcy said.

"Oh . . . yeah," I said, making calculations and rethinking *nymph*. "Okay, take it off," I said.

"I think I need your help or it will ruin," Irma said.

"It's going to tickle again," I warned.

She giggled endlessly as we wrangled her out of it. By the time the three of us got her undressed, it was eight. I got her measurements, then banished everyone from my room, turned on the lights, and got serious about green paillettes.

At one o'clock I knocked on Tobin's door. No response. I walked to Kim's and knocked. After seeing her temper this morning, I wasn't excited to talk to her, but I needed someone's opinion and she was the designer. The door wasn't shut completely, and I could hear sounds inside.

"Hello?" I said, opening the door. Tobin literally jumped, scissors in his hand. Kim's room had a minibar, and he stood in front of the sink with a pile of white flowers. He was wearing gloves. "Sorry," I said. "I wasn't expecting you to be in here."

"Oh," he said. "I was just in my own world. How is the dress coming?"

"I came to get your opinion," I said, walking in. "I love hydrangeas. These white ones are so exquisite and almost impossible to find," I said, picking up one of the graceful white flowers. "They're beautiful."

"Kim's favorite," he said, slicing the stem diagonally.

"She's got excellent taste," I said. Maybe he was trying to woo her out of her bad mood. Which would get worse when she saw the dress.

"Yes, well . . ." he said, dropping the flower in a crystal vase and ripping off the gloves. "Shall we go see the dress?"

We stepped next door.

"Nice," he said, giving it a cursory glance. "Do you think it will work?"

"It's all I can do and preserve the silhouette," I said. "Will Kim want to approve it?"

"Well," he said, "you changed it, so it's not her design, she's not going to approve. However, if we want to get this done today, we'll make do, right?"

I nodded, a sinking feeling in the pit of my stomach. He left and I closed the door behind him.

Chapter Seven

At one-thirty I bagged the dress, collected my styling and sewing stuff, and took the elevator down.

We went down the road the power plant employees used. It stopped at a chain-link gate. From there on, we schlepped stuff around the back of the plant and down again onto the observation deck. While on set I wear a cord around my neck with a lot of my tools—scissors, lint brush, hair brush, three kinds of tape, a small bag of closures, a small sewing kit, et cetera—on it, and I carry a backpack, so I could leave my big bag on the RV.

I wore my Tarzhay knockoff Teyvas, and Darcy forsook her heels and put on some Adidas she'd bought in Seattle, shrinking almost half a foot.

Over the fence, down the muddy steps, onto the rocks.

Irma had been in makeup for two hours and looked absolutely incredible in a 1920s siren kind of way. Darcy had gotten her smoky eyes and silvery lips. I dressed Wes in a gray-with-forest-green pinstripe Super 150s single-breasted suit and vest with a slate gray shirt and a silver medallion and chain. He climbed up the rocks in sport sandals. I carried his shoes in my backpack.

Kenneth positioned Irma on a boulder in the water while Wes stood on the shoreline above her on a similar stone.

"There are two selling points here," Kim, in Katayone Adeli jeans and cashmere sweater, shouted over the falls. "One, the Tobin Charles suit is waterproof. We want it to be beaded with water to prove that point. The weave is so tight that it acts like a natural raincoat. Two, that the Tobin Charles man chooses brains over bronze. B-r-o-n-z-e," she said, smiling. "Clever, huh?"

"Here," Tobin said, handing me two tiny silver cell phones. "Product placement. A new company with better technology than any device out there. It's the equivalent of a Palm Pilot, but also with a pager, intercom, walkie-talkie, telephone, E-mail, web access and see that screen? You can watch a DVD."

The thing was smaller than my fist.

"It doesn't have any numbers," I yelled, staring at the three buttons.

"Completely voice operated. It recognizes your voice only, so if it is stolen it's useless to someone else. It also records sound. Like CDs. Hours of music you can carry with you. Killer, huh?" he shouted.

"An MP3?" I yelled.

Kim screamed, "The caption is going to read, 'Calling on Inspiration.'"

"Nice," Darcy yelled. "Give me that phone."

I clambered up to Wes and handed the other one to him. "You're calling inspiration," I said.

"No, I'm watching it work," he yelled, and patted me. The man was a flirt. He opened the phone. "Rock on. Does this thing work?"

"Only if your voice is its master," I called over my shoulder as I went back down.

"Ready?" Kenneth barked.

I nodded my head as I stepped out of the frame.

Kenneth snapped a Polaroid, then handed it to Stephen who protected it with his back as he fanned it back and forth. I counted off ninety seconds—and held in my abs—while I stared at Irma. My throat felt tight as I looked at her. This wasn't good. The dress was too small; she couldn't really move in it, though I'd given her an extra four inches in the bodice. It just didn't work.

"The shape of the girl is wrong," Thom Goodfeather screamed at me.

I stared at him. "Where is Kim?"

"I don't know, but she told me to oversee." He smiled. "Wisdom sometimes comes from the ant."

Did he moonlight writing really bad fortune cookies? I gestured to Irma.

"What do you want to see?"

"It's not right."

That was helpful. "Well, do you have any ideas?"

"Something else," he said. "Sometimes a wise man must change the direction of his craft in order to benefit from the strength of the river." He looked straight at me, his dark eyes cold. "It's the wrong shape, start over." Then I watched him, in tropical weight wool pants, shirt, and moccasins, walking away. Who the hell was he?

"Kim left Thom in charge," Kenneth said, as he climbed down to me. "What does he want?"

"Something different."

Kenneth moved Irma around so she faced toward Wes, adjusting the dress she was just barely in. I nodded at Stephen's request for another 'roid and backed off.

Ninety more seconds.

Freddie didn't like the hair, so we both went in, fussing and fixing. The phone in Irma's hand rang. We all looked at it. "I answer, ja?" Irma screamed at us.

"Why not," Freddie shouted. "What do you think, Houston?"

I glanced up at Irma's new 'do. "It's too stringy that way."

"Hmm," he said, stepping back. "You're right."

Irma laughed into the phone. "It recognizes your voice, from the phone? How cool. Okay. Knock knock."

"Who's there?" Freddie yelled.

"Move your arm," I said to Irma, arranging the train around her.

"Freddie," she said into the phone.

"Freddie who?" Freddie asked.

"Freddie or not, here I come!"

I looked over my shoulder at the originator of the joke. Wes couldn't sit down or he'd wrinkle his suit, so he was slowly turning around in a circle, entertaining Irma.

"How do crazy people make it through the forest?" she said. "They take the psychopath."

I ducked out of the frame so Kenneth could shoot a Polaroid. Ninety seconds.

I dashed up to Wes, to straighten his tie and collar. "Hair," I called down to Freddie.

We passed on the rocks. "Knock knock," he said.

"Who is it?"

"Imagonna."

"Imagonna who?"

"Imagonna kill that Injun if he doesn't start working with us."

I laughed all the way down to the rocks. Irma was still going. "What do you call a boomerang that doesn't work?" she asked. The look still wasn't right. "A stick," she said.

"Dallas, we need to shoot some of the other suits," Thom said. "Irma still to me loo—"

"Looks like a busty girl in a sparkly condom?" Darcy bellowed.

"Yes, exactly."

"The other . . . two . . . are ready to go. Are you shooting them here?" I asked.

"No, closer in. We'll be back," Kenneth said, and he and Stephen got their gear and started up the pathway. Thom would style George and Tom Fly on set. Darcy went with them.

I knelt in front of Irma. "Where they go?" she shouted.

"Catch the other shots," I responded.

"You don't like me?"

I chewed on my lip. It wasn't her fault the dress was wrong. Just bad luck. "It's not translating to film well," I yelled. This was worse than a Dallas Stars game.

"It's the dress," Freddie said. "You did a fabulous job remaking it, but—"

"Yeah," I said, looking at the Polaroid. "It's not happening." I turned to her. "How many hours of daylight left?" I called to Freddie.

"Tons."

Probably a whopping thirty minutes. "Let's go back," I said. "I can't fix this while Japanese tourists are taking keepsakes."

We trudged back to the RV and I told Irma to strip. "Hand me that duct tape," I said to Freddie.

It was so quiet up here . . . although ABBA was playing in the background. Irma sang lyrics softly. *"Take a chance on me . . ."*

It was almost four o'clock. The suits should be nearly finished and the light would be perfect for this shot. I put my Fiskars to the back seam of the green, sequined condom, closed my eyes, and ripped. Then I cut the entire bodice open. "Let's get some of those Swarovski crystals and decorate her cleavage," I said to Darcy when she came in, panting from her downhill run. "Freddie, how fast can you braid?"

"You'd think I was a sista," he bragged.

*   *   *

When the photographers came back, I heard the whistle above the sound of the water. I walked back to Kenneth. "What do you think?" I asked.

There is an internal click when you know you've done something that is visually stimulating, tells the story, sells the clothes, and makes the viewer want to know more. I have a friend who's a writer; she says it's the same thing for her. Maybe it feels that way in every creative endeavor.

"You did it," he said. "Way to go, girl."

I chuckled, blushing at his compliment as he checked Irma through the lens. Stephen held a reflector to the side, to use the light, and Kenneth gave me the Polaroid.

"Perfect," Thom said. "Now she's a nymph."

Darcy and I high-fived each other, and Freddie gave a Mardi Gras whoop.

"Okay Irma," Kenneth said. "It's all about you. Be inspiring."

"I think they're still telling knock-knock jokes," Freddie said to me. "Only now they're in German."

On the last roll of film, a rainbow filled the mist above Irma. "What are the odds of this?" he shouted. "Move, move! We can get it!"

I knelt beneath the camera. Irma was talking with the phone in one hand, the other outstretched. She seemed to be catching the rainbow's end. The dress was perfect; Darcy's makeup was stunning; Freddie's hair amazing. The double-truck was going to be spectacular.

"Thank you very much." Kenneth shouted. "Excellent."

That night at dinner, we were all high. We'd problem-solved as a team, and everyone had shone. Tobin was effusive. "As soon as I saw the way she was sitting, I knew she was a mermaid."

"Dallas is smart," Dieta said, winking at me.

"And she has a thing for mermaids," Darcy said.

"What's that famous statue," Nasmo said. "That's exactly what you looked like," he said to Irma.

"The Hans Christian Andersen mermaid," Kenneth said. "I've seen that in Denmark. You did a perfect job, even if we added the phone."

Kenneth had caught the mood completely: a little bit fun, a little bit sassy, and extremely alluring. Irma, her hair woven into a thousand platinum ropes, glittering designs on her temples, and beautifully painted "scales" on her bare breasts and torso, had been the epitome of a Lorelei. The gown had been too short and too skinny, so I'd ripped out the neck, pulled the waist down to her hipbones so she had a tail, then duct-taped her into it, and let Darcy paint anything that needed disguising. Then we'd draped ropes of hair over her supposed 34C body.

Irma had looked slick, wet, glistening, like she had just climbed up on the rock to take the phone call. Wes, of course, had been flawlessly dapper and completely dotted with mist, both of them standing with their backs to the waterfall. The contrast made it interesting. Kenneth had shot some fast film, so that the waterdrops were frozen in motion, then he'd shot slower, with color and black-and-white options on each.

"To Dallas—er, Waco!" Wes said, holding up his glass.

"Waco?" I said.

"We're never going to call you Dallas again!" Tom Fly said. "To Waco."

"To Waco!" the crew shouted, toasting me.

"To this awesome crew. Freddie of the flying fingers, Darcy, the queen of dueling brushes, and Kenneth's magic eye," I said, laughing. "That will be great film."

"The local boy said we would have it tomorrow," Dieta said. "I can't wait to see it."

"A pity it ruined the dress," Kim snapped.

Everyone looked at her, surprised. Hadn't she gotten over

her bad mood yet? She hadn't eaten dinner with us, just drank from a sports bottle and sat silently at the table. Kim wasn't having a good day.

Tobin had warned me.

"The dress wasn't the objective," Tobin said to her. "You know that."

"Of course I know that, but it was a perfectly good, exquisitely cut gown and *Wacko* just sliced it to pieces."

Darcy patted my hand. "It looked smashing. The suit will sell. Everyone will know that picture. C'mon," she said, standing up and putting out her cigarette. "It's bedtime."

"Call at five A.M.," Dieta said. "And yoga at four, if you want to join us."

"Who is us?" Irma asked.

Tom Fly and Dieta raised their hands. Then, sheepishly, Kenneth, who was a big boy, raised his.

"You're doing yoga?" Wes said to him.

"It's relaxing," Kenneth said, patting his mustache. "Besides, it's good to look at Dieta at four A.M."

We laughed and dispersed to our bedrooms. "Dallas, a moment please," Dieta called. I leaned against the wall. "Don't take Kim personally," she said. "I think her dosha is out of balance."

"Something is," I said.

Dieta looked at me a moment. "Are you sleepy? You want to get a drink?"

I wasn't the least bit sleepy; wired was more like it. "Sure," I said. "Will you tell me what a dosha is?"

She smiled and nodded. "Meet me in the Attic Bar in a half hour."

I agreed and went back to my room. Once I changed out of my work clothes, I slipped on a dress and heels and decided to take a walk. It was a clear, clean night. Not too cool even.

Moonlight shone on the water and I breathed deeply, trying to release the stress of the day. I'd done well. It was okay to enjoy that feeling. I glanced at my watch and walked around to the front of the building again.

Weird that cop hadn't called me back. I'd left another message when I'd gotten back to my room. But Tobin seemed fine. Poor Richard.

"Hey, beautiful," a voice called out of the darkness. "Can I buy you a drink?" The voice was masculine, whiskey-coated, and a little bit Southern. I didn't see anyone. "Over here, on the patio."

Under an umbrella of hanging plants, I saw a dark figure sitting alone. Only the glow of his cigarette butt and the shine of silver on his jacket showed where he was. Oh, his voice.

I grinned. "Maybe another time."

"I bet you say that to all the invitations you get from strangers in the night."

"Probably most," I said, turning toward the front of the lodge. "Have a nice evening."

"I will now. I have a girl to dream about, to write about, to sing about," he said. "Just tell me your name, so I can rhyme it."

The only thing my name really rhymes with, besides *malice, chalice,* and *palace,* is ass. "Christi," I said, knowing we were leaving in the morning.

He stretched his legs into the chair opposite him and leaned back. "You sure don't look like a Christi. Is that with a *K* or a *C?*"

The valet guy was standing at his booth, just out of earshot but close enough to run to. I was safe, even if it felt a little bit dangerous. "C."

"*I's* or *Y's?* Christy can get pretty complicated. You don't look like complicated to me."

He sat forward, a little more in the light. He had black eyes, black shoulder-length curly hair, and he was of average height and build. His hands were clearly lit and they were beautiful, carved from alabaster, next to the black of his leather jacket. I was shocked at how sexy I thought he was. And not even remotely Latin.

"We have to be careful about judging on appearances," I said.

"Yeah, you got that right, baby. Good night."

I walked back into the foyer and took the elevator to the fourth floor.

Dieta looked up when I walked in to the Attic Bar. She was curled up in a chair by the fire, sipping something dark. "And who have you been kissing?" she asked.

I blushed like a teenager. "Nobody, but I swear, there was the sexiest guy hanging out at the patio. Oh." I fanned my face. "One of those voices that just make you . . ."

"Think of tossed sheets and sweat, yes?"

"Oh yes," I said. I plopped down in the chair across from her. I'd gotten a little chilled outside; the fire felt good. "What is that?" I asked, pointing to her dark martini glass.

"Martini espresso."

"How can coffee be alcoholic and cold?" I said. "One or the other, I understand. But a martini?"

Dieta sipped it and groaned with pleasure. "Better still is a VZ."

The VC I'd heard of. "VZ?"

"Viscous Zebra," she said, pronouncing it with a short "e," like the queen's English. "It's a cappuccino martini."

"Vodka or gin?"

"Vodka, of course," she said. "The zebra has layers of cream and cream liqueur, so it has stripes, yes?"

Her martini was black, and when I sipped it, amazing. "You get completely polluted and you're awake to enjoy it," I said. "That's pretty cool."

"And it has espresso beans," she said, picking one off the bottom of the glass with a slim spoon. "I love these."

I ordered a martini espresso. "Explain dosha to me."

"It's Ayurveda," she said.

"Oh," I said as realization dawned. Ayurveda, the newest trend among the beautiful people; Christy Turlington had started a cosmetics line based on it; Donna Karan swore by her yoga; and Texas's own Nancy Kahanik, whose shoes were as sexy as anything Jimmy Choo did, served dinner parties based on the "types" people came in.

"People are three ways," Dieta said. "Three doshas. Either Kapha, Vata, or Pitta—usually a mix of all, but one is always stronger."

I nodded, wondering which type the sexy stranger was.

"Each has a different life force, something from environment. Vata is like the wind. Kapha is the earth and Pitta is fire."

I sipped my espresso martini and felt hyperalert and buzzed. A strange combination.

"Different foods, different senses, different skins and medicines: we all need something special to us."

I nodded again.

"When your dosha gets out of balance, it is possible to get sick. I get ditzy, fearful, hyperactive, and sick, full of *ama*. See, that's how I know about my ear. My dosha is unbalanced."

"I've been called unbalanced before, but I didn't realize I could blame my body," I said, finishing my drink. "So what do you do?"

"I have too much of one thing, not enough of another. So I need to do a cleansing, a *pancha karma.*"

"Like a colonic cleansing?" Those had been very trendy the past few years. Personally, I thought it was kind of gross. You did feel better, lighter, cleaner afterward. But it took a few days, after the toxins flushed through your system.

Those few days were a little unpleasant.

"Sort of. Anyway, if your dosha is in balance, you are in health. Your skin glows, you sleep well, everything is good. It's preventative, unlike Western medicine, where we only treat someone once they become ill. A really good master can look at your eyes or fingernails and tell your health."

"And yours says you have an ear infection?"

Dieta ordered another drink—I was pretty sure it wasn't good for her dosha, regardless of which one it was—and nodded. "It's been getting worse."

"You might need some old-fashioned Western antibiotics," I suggested.

"I don't take pills."

"So you think Kim is an unbalanced dosha?"

Dieta nodded. "She doesn't eat. Food is for health; all she does is drink mixes. I'm not saying they are bad, but it's not enough. Her teeth need the exercise of chewing; she needs to sit down and have the peace of a meal."

I laughed.

"What is funny?"

Alcohol was starting to get me. "Just the concept of meals being peaceful. They weren't in my family."

"You have many brothers and sisters?"

"Oh, yeah. First there were high-level negotiations for who was trading whose chores, then the swapping of favorite foods—"

"How do you mean?"

"One person liked carrots but hated peas; one person didn't like biscuits but sat next to the person who liked peas." I shrugged. "Since we all had to eat everything on our plates, because children were starving in Africa, we worked out who would clean off whose plates. Of course, those kinds of moves involved strategy, with distractions and counter distractions. It was war. Every meal."

"Your poor mother."

"Oh my mom didn't care. She would have fed us sugar and sent us to play on the railroad tracks if she could have gotten a few minutes of silence. My father, however, was a stickler for discipline. Prayers before bedtime, chores for everyone, homework checked. And we all had to eat everything on our plates."

"My parents told me also that children were starving in Africa."

"We volunteered to ship the extra, but Dad wouldn't hear of it."

"I wonder if everyone in your family is your dosha," Dieta said.

"What dosha am I?"

"Tall, medium build, medium skin—"

"Not really," I admitted. "Skin that can be dyed."

"Oh! Your tan isn't real?"

I shook my head. "Fake." Mix half a palm of Curel, half of Bain de Soleil and smear it on before bed. Wake up looking Saint Tropez in the morning.

"It's so pretty."

It was also very much the style this season. "My skin is fair, with a pink undertone," I said.

"Brown eyes, blonde—is your hair real?" she asked, looking at my head as though it were a separate piece.

I nodded. Not as real as it was when I was seven years old. It's enhanced, as my colorist Kennedy says. But still real. Dallas, Texas, after all, has more blondes than any other city in the nation. Fewer women admit to coloring though. Why should I squeal?

"You look like you came from an island," Dieta said. "Relaxed and tan, your muscle tone is good, your legs are great—"

I sucked in my stomach for twenty seconds, just from guilt. "So what is my dosha?"

"I think you are Pitta-Kapha. Color therapy is for you."

I glanced down at my black outfit. The vodka was blending her words into *Pizza, Kafka,* and *Vader.* "And what's Kim?"

"Kapha-Vata. She would benefit from hearing therapy. And smelling. She needs flowers to balance her dosha."

"Tobin brought her some," I said. "I wonder if he knows all of this."

Dieta shrugged. "When we were together he didn't, but you know, times change."

I almost choked on my martini. "You . . . are an ex?"

Dieta shrugged. "Aren't we all?" Her next drink came, and I refrained from answering.

"To balanced doshas!" she said, lifting her fresh martini. I was chewing on my espresso beans and clinked with her.

"To balanced doshas."

I staggered back to my room and slipped inside as quietly as I could. It must be almost three o'clock. I brushed my teeth and was in the middle of flossing when I heard a door slam next door.

"I can't believe you are continuing this!" Apparently I wasn't the only one awake at this hour.

"It's business, Kim," Tobin said. "What am I supposed to do, send these people home and write the experience off because some idiot can't drive?"

"You know who he was, don't you?" she said. "Torinelli's boy."

"It was an accident, Kimmie," Tobin said. "There are thousands from Richard's street Torinelli can pick up and play with."

I shuddered at the callousness—and that I'd almost forgotten what had happened entirely. Just caught up in business as usual, forgetting a murderer was loose on the shoot. Or somewhere close. Did it have to do with Richard's boyfriend? I checked my watch: too late to call that officer.

"What are you going to do?" Kim said. "The suits?

Richard's exact measurements, no time to find a new model, or—"

"Get off my ass, will ya?"

Tobin sounded tired and very New York-y. It was silent for a while. I finished flossing and creamed on my morning's tan. I turned off the light and went into the bedroom. I clicked on the nightstand light and heard Kim again.

These walls were just for show; Kim and Tobin might as well have been in my bed with me.

"Don't touch me," she said, her voice a little rougher. "I hate it when you speak so crudely."

My eyes were wide open now.

"Come on Kimmie, it's been a bitch of a day." Another long silence. I debated turning on the radio and opted to put a pillow over my head. I heard nothing for a while. I uncovered my head carefully. My eyes had just closed when I heard her again.

"Don't you have a date with Dieta? Your little Dutch treat?"

"Now who's being tasteless? You are blowing this way out of—"

"Am I? Dieta? I thought she was part of your past, your history, I believe you said. It's amazing how selective one's memory can be."

"Personally, you know she's history," he said. "But professionally—"

"Which profession, is my question," she said.

"What are you going to do about Richard?" he asked. An attempt to change topics?

"This is all falling apart, Tobin," Kim said.

"Don't say that. You're always so negative."

"It's a disaster. This whole thing. The people are weird; the timing is wrong. If we could have only waited until—"

"Kim," Tobin said, his voice a warning. "Not tonight."

"You're right, not tonight," she said. "Go to your own room. I need some space."

"Kim, you don't mean that. You're just upset over the dress—"

"Don't presume to know what I mean," she said, crying. "And don't try to touch me. Just go, just get into bed with an old girlfriend. Or is it boyfriend? What's Wes doing to-night?"

"Kim," Tobin said, his tone a little sharp.

"Either way, I have to get my sleep. Some of us work for a living."

"Don't confuse working with working out," he snarled. "One of those is supportive of your man, the other . . ."

Man? What the hell?

". . . relieves my tension," she said.

"I remember when I used to do that," he said.

Another long silence. I was sitting up now, no attempt at discretion. Could anyone else hear this?

"I don't," she said.

I didn't hear a response.

"Now you are the source of it," Kim said.

The door closed quietly and I heard footsteps go to the el-evator. Her blender turned on almost immediately and the sound of a woman weeping floated in. I couldn't listen, so I opened the balcony door to let the river drown out the sound. Then I lay down, my eyes wide open. I hurt for Kim.

Then I was asleep.

Chapter Eight

I woke to a thunderstorm. I closed my balcony door before the wind could slam it shut. Angry black clouds drenched the river and the hillside opposite. I didn't know where we were shooting today, but it wasn't going to be around here.

Ten minutes later I got a call; we were headed back to Seattle for the day. Esmerelda's RV pulled out in a half hour. We loaded the stuff we would need for the day and started the caravan west.

Once inside the city limits, my cell phone rang.

"Dallas."

"Ms. O'Connor?" The cop, the one I'd been dreading to get hold of, spoke.

"Uh, this isn't a good time," I said.

"Oh! There's a Starbucks!" Darcy said, sitting up and pointing. "Turn, turn!"

I squealed right into the parking lot. "I'll be there in a second," I said to her.

"When can we talk?" the cop said. "I appreciate you trying to keep this confidential."

"I'll call later," I said. "It's just crazy—"

"A photo shoot," he said. "I understand. But Ms. O'Connor, a man was killed. Murdered. Do you understand that?"

"I think it was meant to be Tobin," I said in a rush.

"Are you sick?" he asked.

"No, my voice is rough from the shoot yesterday. But—"

Darcy got in and showed me the drinks. "Which do you want? Chocolate Frappuccino with extra whipped cream, or a tall, skinny, why-bother latte?"

"I gotta run," I said to the cop. "But we'll talk again soon. Unless there's something you should tell me now."

"Take the latte, less fat grams and all the flavor. And keep this phone call to yourself, Ms. O'Connor."

"The latte," I said, trying to sound normal after I hung up. "I drank way too much alcohol last night."

"Like it shows on you," she said. "I'd kill for your body. A tall, lean, sex-machine. Who was that on the phone?" she asked. "Your sweetheart?"

The car phone, not my cell, rang. "Beauty and the Bitch Road Trip," Darcy answered, crossing her knee-booted legs. She wore a pleated schoolgirl skirt with a baby T that read, "That's *Ms*. Nicotine Addict to You," with dangle earrings, fishnet hose, and an armful of leather bracelets.

I laughed.

"No!" Darcy said into the phone. "Really?"

"What?" I asked. Had the cops talked to someone else?

She spoke to me. "It's Freddie. He has the poop on Kim." She lit a cigarette as she spoke on the phone.

"Poor Kim," I muttered. I'd dozed until I heard her leave at four A.M. Then I'd seen her outside, running like demons were after her on the path beside the river.

Darcy was on the phone. "But she's only five-six. My God, she must have been a cow!"

I heard Freddie mooing over the phone.

"So are they an item?" I asked Darcy. She asked Freddie.

"He said he doesn't know," she said to me. Then to Freddie, "She did? You know lipo is so cheap now it's almost easier than going to a fat farm. Best yet. You can get frequent flier miles if you charge it."

Darcy inhaled. I found myself leaning in to listen, so she held the phone between us. Freddie was in the RV's bathroom with the fan on, whispering loud enough to wake Mount Rainier. "So she found this guy who made a shake for her. Appetite suppressant, caffeine, and a little buzz, *if* you get my drift," Freddie said.

"Just like the eighties. We all stayed thin that way," Darcy said with a note of nostalgia. "All this healthiness just isn't healthy. So Kim's on steroids?"

"Maybe that makes her crazy," I said.

"Tons of them. Last time she ate a real meal was in nineteen ninety-eight," Freddie said.

"It's bad for her," I said out loud. "And it can't be true."

"Is that you, Arp?" Freddie said. Arp, I think, is a small town in East Texas.

"*Ms.* Arp to you," I said. "Why would Kim be living on steroids? She looks great."

"With all those aerobics?" Darcy said, looking at me. "She should!"

"I'm serious. Steroids are dangerous, especially for athletes."

"Oh, please," Darcy said, "her blood is probably purer than an Amish cow's!"

"Florence Joyner, Flo-Jo, dropped dead," I said. "She'd won the Olympics, and steroids got her."

"We can only hope," Freddie said.

"I thought it was some sort of heart disease?" Darcy asked. "Flo-Jo was the one with those nails, right?"

"That look was just so wrong," Freddie said. "And did you see those Seattle girls were still wearing it? I'm sorry, but gold charms on red claws are not sexy. Well, unless your clothes are Chanel," he added. "Or you're in hip-hop. Then the longer and more outrageous, the better."

"Don't forget little tiger-striped toenails," I said, winking at Darcy.

"If you're Sheena, queen of the jungle," Freddie retorted.

We were heading downhill into a curve, so I turned my attention back to the road. Darcy finished with Freddie and hung up. "So here's the story," she said. "Kim used to be a heifer."

Though I couldn't imagine it, I had guessed as much. She skipped meals, she was jealous of anyone trimmer, and she obsessed about exercise.

"She tried everything to lose weight, and couldn't. Finally got her stomach stapled."

"Ouch."

"No good. Still fat. So someone turned her on to exercise. She started seeing results. Then she got into this special shake and bammo, she's wearing Richard Tyler in size two."

"And snarling about food?"

"That's new. She used to be so nice," Darcy said. "Maybe she's a bitch because she's hungry."

"That would make me crabby," I said.

"Or maybe she's just in a bad mood because she's alive."

I darted a sideways glance at her. Surely she was teasing? I sighed. "I'm being harsh on her. We shouldn't be talking this way; she's just a human being."

"Are you sure about that?" Darcy said as she lit a cigarette. "Though that personality switch yesterday was weird. She was so nice the day before."

"Have you worked with her?"

"No, but my rep was really impressed."

"Mine too," I said.

"Maybe it's a lure, to get us to work for her," Darcy said.

"So are they married, or living together, or what?"

"I don't know. She and Tobin have been in business for a while—like a decade—but I bet before she lost weight he probably never even looked at her. A guy like that wouldn't."

"She's probably terrified of gaining an ounce." I felt sorry for her.

" 'Cuz she'd lose him?" Darcy said. "If he's that shallow, a girl is better off with an electronic carrot, if you get my meaning."

I couldn't help it, I laughed. "Well," I said, "she doesn't seem happy."

"Working with your lover could put a lot of strain on a relationship."

I parked the Jeep across from the EMP—Experience Music Project—the expensive rock 'n' roll museum. "Hey, this is why people live here," Darcy said.

Sunlight streamed down; the sky was vivid blue; the air fresh. The light reflected off the EMP's metal and porcelain sides painted in shrieking colors.

"Here's the plan," Kenneth said to us. "Four men, a lot of film. Kim, Tobin, and Thom will all be popping 'round, but none of them will be on set."

Oh, boy, I thought.

"But we need to see all of the suits we can, and pick up anything that's not going to be used in the next fantasy shots. Right, Dallas?"

"Call her Corpus Christi," Stephen suggested with a wink for me.

"Right. Corpus Christi, roll with your creativity."

"Four men?" I said, counting in my head. "But—"

"Tobin is sending another over, a local boy."

"This isn't a fantasy shot?" I clarified.

"No, that's the next shot at this place. It's too slick right now to scale the building like Kim wants, so we'll do the groundwork now, before it opens for the day," Dieta said.

"Do you mean work on the ground?" Freddie asked.

Dieta giggled and nodded. "Sometimes English still trips me."

"Let's get the groundwork done," Kenneth said. "We have a lot of suits."

The first shot was all four of the men in navy suits. One was single-breasted wool, one double, one linen and one in cashmere. I put a different pastel shirt on each man, and a London-style super-wide, pastel-striped tie. Wingtips all around, watches worn over their cuffs—another European touch—and lunch-boxes in coordinating pastels.

"Fabulous," Tobin said when he showed up, though he couldn't resist tweaking a tie or straightening a cuff. He didn't look like a man who feared for his life. Kenneth grinned at me and I got Tobin to step away. Finally.

Freddie slicked everyone's hair and Kenneth directed them into the starchiest, most businesslike poses in front of the Jimi Hendrix purple wall. All four of them in a row, starting with Tom Fly, who was the shortest, and ending with Phillip, the local model, who was the tallest, so they looked as uniform as possible.

"Where does he get his ideas?" Tobin asked me as we stood watching the models. "Do you think he would mind—"

"Yes," I said.

Next I put two of them in a fancy tan plaid with side vents and widespread-collared shirts, the other two in fancy gray plaid—basically the same suit. Kenneth arranged one shot of them against the light blue wall of the EMP, and another with two of them crossing the other two at an angle in front of the bronzed section. By now we were generating quite a bit of interest.

A horn tooted, and we all turned to watch a silver Boxster pull up.

Another one?

Richard *hadn't* been in Tobin's car?

Kim got out and drew a whistle from a few guys in black leather. Her chin moved up a notch as she pranced toward us in butterscotch stiletto boots, matching leather pants, and a suede bodysuit top she'd been sewed into.

Darcy and I exchanged glances, looked at our clothes, and started laughing. She looked like a renegade private school girl, and I was in Abercrombie jeans, beat-up Prada slip-ons, a Custo Barcelona long-sleeved T and a baseball cap. With sunscreen and lipgloss.

"How is it going?" Kim asked stiffly, dabbing her nose. Makeup couldn't hide her splotchy skin and she wore Jackie O sunglasses. Was she coming down with the flu?

"Well," Kenneth said, "fabulous, actually. We've gotten some great film. We were just about to order lunch. Are you staying?"

"I have to get back," she said. "I just wanted to check things out. That's how the suits look?" she said, glimpsing at the models against the building.

Kenneth and I smiled with pride.

"My God, that's awful."

Stunned silence.

Kenneth didn't look at me, but he took Kim's elbow and walked her away from all of us.

"What's going on?" one of the black-leather-wearing bystanders called. "This *GQ* or something?"

"Just a shoot," I said, throwing the comment over my shoulder.

"Christi," Kenneth called. It took me a minute to recognize my name du jour. I ran over to him and Kim. "Kim is concerned that the look is too staid," he said.

"With the backgrounds we're using, the contrast—"

"I don't care what you think," she snapped at me. "I designed those suits to look good, not stupid."

I felt my face go hot.

She rubbed her nose again. "You can restyle the shot, or I can drive down to Nordstrom and get someone who is used to dealing with quality to handle it."

The temptation to flip her off and walk away was incredible. It's one thing to dislike a look and discuss it. Or even say you hate it, but do so respectfully. I was a professional. I could handle criticism. But insults? Kim Charles gave the impression she wouldn't trust me to pooper-scoop after her dog. She blew her nose.

"That's out of line, Ms. Charles," Kenneth said. "If you are unhappy with the look, we will certainly change it. But don't talk—"

"Good," she said, stalking off in the middle of his sentence.

Kenneth muttered something, obviously stunned. You don't just walk away from a photographer.

"Hey hot stuff," one of the guys called to Kim. "Bet I can put a smile on that face."

She halted and stared at him, killing the fun of the moment. Then she got in her car and tore off.

A silver Porsche Boxster. Did she and Tobin have matching ones? How many were in Seattle?

"Maybe Cruella DeVil was her role model," Darcy said as the small crowd turned back from Kim to us.

"It's lunch," Kenneth said, then called it louder. "Lunch! And we're going somewhere bloody expensive," he muttered as he stormed to the RV.

"So you really are Christi," the voice from last night's dreams said. "I would have lost my life on that bet."

I turned around, but he was in the shade, so I couldn't see him clearly—just his leather jacket, a glimpse of a pale face, dark glasses, dark jeans and dark boots. My heart was pounding faster and louder than normal.

"I guess I really will have to make lyrics for Christi now."

"C'mon," Darcy shouted from the passenger side of my Jeep. "Lunchtime."

"Your crew is going to eat," he said. "Bon appetit."

I got into the Jeep and my hands were shaking. "Kenneth is so pissed at Kim," Darcy started, then broke off. "Whoa, girl, when did you get some?"

"He was there," I said.

"Who?"

I told her about the guy I'd met at the hotel, how sexy his voice was.

"You don't have to convince me of that," she said. "Your face—that's enough." She twisted in her seat to gawk at the bystanders. "Which one?"

I started the car. "Don't look. I think he's in a band."

"A band boy, oh Jesus, that's hot."

I followed Kenneth's Jeep toward downtown. "Where are we going?"

"I don't know. The newest place to be seen. Kenneth is betting it's expensive, too."

"I hope they don't have a dress code," I said, brushing at the knee of my jeans. My cell phone rang and I struggled to answer it and keep us on the road. "Dallas O'Connor."

"She's a witch!" Lindsay, my agent at Artists Alliance, said. "I'm so sorry. I had no idea. Tobin is lovely, absolutely lovely to work with. She must be bloody brilliant, that's all I can say."

Darcy leaned across and shouted at my phone, "She needs to get laid." Cell phones were the worst way to have a private conversation.

"Who's that?" Lindsay said.

"Darcy Ellis, professional smoker and part-time makeup artist," I said.

"Professional drinker too!"

Lindsay trilled a laugh. "Sounds as though you aren't terribly broken up about the dreadful things Kim had to say."

A wonderful man had been murdered. Kim's comments stung, but in perspective—I could always walk away. I had never done it before, but I could.

"She's a tight-ass!" Darcy shouted.

I handed her the phone. "Y'all talk, I'll drive." We'd hit every single red light so far. "What did you do?" I asked Lindsay via Darcy, who was holding my phone out.

"She asked for your book."

"She's seen it before."

"Exactly, and when I spoke to her before, she was the most charming, nicest person. It's enough to make Dr. Jekyll and Mr. Hyde look quite tame."

"She used to be nice," Darcy said. "Maybe it's the stress."

"Then she needs to deal with it. My talent is not there to be shat upon. Give the woman some Prozac.

"Maybe that's it," Darcy said. "Maybe she's on drugs, makes her wiggy."

I kept my thoughts to myself. Maybe I'd misunderstood the conversation I'd overheard last night. Or maybe she knew something was up with the Porsches, and Richard's death. Could she be in danger?

"Are you sure you want to stay?" Lindsay asked me. "She was quite offensive."

She sure was. Or maybe it was the flu. "Is the money the same?" I asked.

"Oh yes. I called right back and spoke with Tobin. The darling man apologized profusely for Kim's unkindness, he called it, rather than admitting she needs to be put down like a rabid dog. Oh dear," Lindsay said, realizing the extent of her unprofessional behavior.

"Darcy won't say anything," I said, looking for a place to park. "If she does, we'll tear up her cigarettes."

"You wouldn't!" she said in mock horror.

"Well, have a Bloody Mary on me," Lindsay said, "and call me if she doesn't switch back to Dr. Jekyll. Ciao, darling."

While the sun was directly overhead, we ate and drank. Kenneth claimed that since he was from South Africa, he saw no problem in a glass or so of wine with lunch. "Can't shoot for another few hours anyway," he said.

I slipped away. I just wanted some time to myself. And I had a phone call to make. Several. I sat down on a bench beneath a flowering tree and adjusted my sunglasses, then dialed my phone.

Somewhere, far east and south where the wind felt more like it was blowing from a preheating oven than a refrigerator, the phone was answered.

"O'Connor heah."

"Hi, Granddaddy," I said, feeling my eyes smile at the sound of his voice. "How are you?"

"Little Dallas? Shugah I'm just fine, cain't complain. How are you this fine aftahnoon?"

"I'm good, Granddaddy. How's the ranch?"

"Well, you know, a couple sick cows, a randy ole bull that won't pay attention to it bein' calfin' season, and eighteen days without rain."

"Nothin's changed then," I said.

He chuckled, deep in his throat. He's old, burnt teak by the sun, and still puts in ten-hour days in blue jeans and long-sleeved shirt, repairing fences, checking the range, feeding, vaccinating. He says you work until you die. That's God's way. The concept of retirement makes no sense to him at all. "What's goin' on, shugah?"

"I have some questions to ask you, but you can't tell Mother."

"She was askin' 'bout you, said you were in Washington. Drownin' in fools and politicians? Though they seem pretty much the same to me." He laughed.

"Washington State, Granddaddy."

"Ohh," he said. "Green up there, ain't it?"

I looked at the lush grass, trees, bushes. "It's emerald," I said.

"So this is costin' you," he said. "What can I hep you with?"

"It's about your favorite hobby," I said. "What's the brake system on a Porsche Boxster?"

Maybe my Granddaddy hasn't traveled much, and he isn't the most liberal person on the planet, but he knows wine, he knows guns, and he knows German sports cars. He raced Porsches forever, and he has three of them. I learned to drive a stick-shift on his 944.

"The Boxster?" he said. "Hmm . . . well, it's pretty complicated shugah."

"How so?"

"There are *two* brake systems on the Boxster."

"Front and back?"

"No, no I think it's diagonal. Right front, left rear, so you always have control."

"What about the fluid?"

"Same thing; if you lose fluid from one system, you still have two brakes—one in the front and one in the back—still working. Why, you thinkin' of turnin' in that bubblegum Mustang for a real car?"

I grinned. "Not a chance," I said. "But I saw a Boxster fail, just charge foward. Thing is, I saw brake lights, but it didn't do any good."

"That's not right," he said. "I hope the fella drivin' the Boxster was all right?"

"Uh, no, Granddaddy," I said. "He died."

He was quiet a minute. "Sorry to hear that. It's a fine car. That doan make sense."

"Granddaddy," I said, gnawing on my lip, "the car was sabotaged."

I heard him sit down, and the distant creak of an old rocker on a sun porch. For a second the sense of homesickness was so intense that I could taste its bittersweet flavor. The cool clean air and bright sunshine faded away and I felt the heat, the dry of southwest Texas. "You bettah tell me about this, Miz Dallas," he said.

"I don't know much," I said. I gave him as detailed an explanation as I could about what I'd seen.

"You think someone was after this ole boy?"

I shrugged, but he couldn't see me. "Maybe I'm just makin' it all up."

"Not about that Boxster," he said. "Those Krauts are smart. Each brake's lines woulda had to been cut."

"Would I have still seen the lights?"

"Oh sure, there'd be a little fluid left, just not enough to do a soul any good."

My call waiting beeped in; maybe the cop? "Gotta go, Granddaddy."

"You be careful, young lady. You're a precious thing to me."

Tears filled my eyes. "I love you. I will."

I looked at the local number in the ID box. "Hello?"

"So it's not Christi, it's Dallas."

"Are you afraid of light?" I asked my husky-voiced phantom. "Where did you get this number?"

"Where, or how?"

"Either, or both, would be comforting answers."

"I picked up your comp card from the RV. Your driver Esmerelda is an angel. We had lunch together, Big Macs. Anyway, we talked a little, and I saw the agency name and location. A phone call or two and if I want to hire Dallas O'Connor, freelance stylist, producer, and art director, I can."

"My agency would never give out my number," I said.

"Esmerelda did."

I was silent for a second. When had this guy shown up? Why was he talking to me? Why was I talking to him? Could he have killed Richard?

He chuckled. "Do you scare easily?" he asked in that sexy voice.

That sexy voice was *exactly* why I was talking to him. "No. I'm tough."

"I wonder. Anyway," he said. "I'm not stalking you, I just didn't want to leave seeing you again up to fate. I'm in town with my band. We have a gig tonight. I'd love it if you'd come hear us. Maybe we can even say hi, Dallas."

"I think we may be leaving tonight."

"It would be a great place for a final party, hang out with your crew."

I'd been oblivious to where I was walking; now I found myself staring at a man's wide-striped zebra suit. "Ohmigod," I said involuntarily.

"What?" He sounded suddenly alert, concerned. "What's wrong?"

"Window shopping," I said. "I take it back about being scared. I'm shaking in my shoes right now."

He chuckled. "Oh, I see. Seattle fashion isn't quite up to your standards?"

My turn to laugh. "So tell me the particulars and I'll see what I can do. And do you have a name?"

"I'm named after a different city in Texas, actually," he said. He gave me the details about the show, and we both fell silent. "I hope to see you tonight," he said. "And you shouldn't leave your number just hanging around, it's dangerous."

Yeah, right, I thought. "Play well, whether I see you or not," I said, surprised at the sense of intimacy I felt with this man whom I couldn't pick out of a lineup.

"See me."

I saw my reflection superimposed over the zebra suit: a tall blonde staring at a yellow cell phone and smiling.

We broke again at five, and my phone rang at 5:01. I'd just stepped outside to accept a richly-deserved Dove Bar latte. It was Thompson. (I'd programmed his number into my phone.)

"Where are you?" the Sheriff's Department cop asked me. "Can we meet?"

"Am I supposed to be subtle?"

"Yes."

I told him I'd meet him a few streets over and started to walk. Everyone was on their phones, trying to catch up with the other tracks of their lives. I had a half-hour. I race-walked to the civic center area and wound up across from a drug store on Queen Anne's hill.

"Dallas O'Connor?" a big blond bruiser asked me. He flashed a King County badge. "I'm Thompson. I read your statement. Thank you for your time."

He was very polite. Fastidious. And immaculately, if inexpensively, groomed.

"Civic duty," I said. "What were you telling me about"—I dropped my voice to a whisper—"homicide?"

"Have you spoken to anyone else?"

"You told me not to."

He raised his eyebrows. "Good."

He sat beside me and pulled out a narrow notebook. "I have a few questions to ask you."

"How did he die?"

"It's under investigation, ma'am."

"I'm not asking to say anything about that. I just want to know, was it from the wreck? Did he drown? Suffocate? Internal injuries? What *manner?" Could I have helped him?*

"I'm not at liberty to disclose any information, ma'am. It's under investigation. Did you know the deceased?"

"Yes. I saw him last . . . a few years ago, but we exchanged cards and phone calls. He was a very dear man."

"He was a model? Richard Wilson?"

"Right. Men's underwear, runway in Europe and Asia."

"Any possibility Richard was using drugs?"

"No."

"You seem adamant on that point."

"I don't think he was the target," I said.

Thompson unsuccessfully hid a grin. "The target?" he repeated. "Do you watch a lot of TV?"

I ignored his jibe. "The car was rigged."

"Why do you say that?"

I expained about the brake system.

He was suddenly intent. "Where did you get that information?"

"I have my sources," I said. "A mechanic."

"It was a new car," he said.

"Kim Charles has the exact same car," I said. "Maybe she shares it with Tobin. A company car or something. But that night she thought it was Tobin in the car. The car wreck wasn't meant for Richard."

"Ms. O'Connor, you are in way over your head. Let us take care of this."

I sat back.

"Mr. Wilson was killed by someone who wanted to kill him."

"How could that be? Richard was wonderful. No one would want to kill him."

"There is a possibility that it was mafia-related."

I looked at my watch; I needed to get back to the EMP.

"Why kill a model?" he said.

"Why kill anyone?" I snapped.

"Until we have some answers, Ms. O'Connor," he said, "I advise caution."

"Are you telling me that I'm at risk? What's going on?"

He stared at me.

"Do you think I did it?" My voice had risen. "That's ridiculous."

"I can't say anything else, Ms. O'Connor. But someone on this shoot could be dangerous."

That took a minute to sink in. "The people I'm working with?" I'd already gone through the names, wondering who would kill Richard and why. "Why?"

"Money? Passion? Maybe random, or someone who is anti-black, or anti-Asian—"

"What do you mean, anti-Asian?"

"These suits are fabricated in Asia, ma'am. Perhaps some fringe organization is protesting the plight of Asian workers through terrorism."

"Have you gotten a letter or something saying that?"

"We get them all the time. What we don't get is brand new cars plummeting into Lake Union filled with banged up New York mobbed-up models."

"I'm sorry," I said, standing up. "I don't know what else to tell you."

Thompson brushed at the sleeve of his jacket as he stood. "Then thank you." He handed me a card. "If you think of anything else, or if you see anything suspicious, call me at that number, day or night."

"We saw the brake lights," I said. "When the car revved. He was trying to stop."

His bulging blue gaze met mine. "He did stop, didn't he."

Chapter Nine

We wrapped at seven, and Darcy, who wasn't feeling well, decided to ride back in the RV. Freddie went with her. Tobin got shunted to my Jeep, since the models were in the others.

Mr. Anti-delegation was mine for an hour. Joy.

"Thanks for the ride," he said as he got in.

I murmured something and got on I-90. Should I tell him I thought he was in danger? Were the cops talking to him? I didn't like Thompson. But I had his card.

"Are you haunted by Richard's death?" he asked, point-blank. "It was really gutsy of you to dive down to him."

"It would have been better if I could have seen underwater." I said. "I can't imagine what happened. He flew in, how did he get a Boxster? I've never seen a Porsche malfunction before."

"What did it do? Kim has refused to talk about it, and the cops won't answer my questions. It's weird; I had just seen Richard that afternoon."

I forced myself to stay on the road. "Where? I thought he'd just gotten in."

"Well, he had. We had Esmerelda pick him up at SeaTac—he always likes a white stretch limo—then bring him to the office for lunch. We had it catered, just a couple of us—caviar and Dungeness crab, some champagne. He'd walked in talking about my Porsche, how cool it was, and asked if we could rent him one while he was here."

I had to remember all of this to tell Thompson. "He is a big-time model," I said.

"Yes, and his feelings were a little raw at not being picked as the Tobin Charles man," Tobin said. "We had to massage them. Especially since we were putting everyone up on the boat."

"So you got him a Boxster?"

"Silver. Just like mine. On such short notice, we couldn't rent it. We bought it instead. I'd just bought mine the week before, so—"

"Who called around and found that?" I said. "Dieta was working already?"

"No, not Dieta. Some Asian girl who helps around the office."

Asking for her name would be a little too curious, I thought.

"The car was delivered, but meanwhile he had taken my car to go get a massage."

"He didn't take the limo?"

"He wanted to drive. Richard could be a little, uh, demanding."

He just pushed as far as he could; he knew fame and fortune had a time limit. Poor Richard, he just didn't know how short it was going to be.

"He came back, we traded cars, and off he went to check in at the boat."

"I never saw him," I said.

"No, he ran into a friend on the way over and they went out. A little drinking, a little titty bar action." He glanced at me. "Sorry. I didn't mean to be offensive."

"It's okay," I said. "But he's gay, right?"

"Just for hire," Tobin said.

The gay men in modeling fell into several groups, my mentor had once told me: pretty boys; gay for hire, meaning guys who were really straight, but would have sex with a man if it advanced a career; and almost-men, guys who were straight but came off as gay.

"So are you straight?" he asked me.

"Uh, yeah," I responded, surprised at the turn of conversation. Tobin didn't seem fazed at all that a man had died— one he knew. "So Richard was coming back from the men's club when he went into the water?"

"I guess. Like I said, the cops won't say anything. Did you know Richard?"

I don't know why I lied. "No," I said. "But I—" I licked my lips. "I tried to save his life."

"Ah, a bond, then."

I nodded.

"Why would someone kill a model?" Tobin asked.

My fingers tightened on the steering wheel as I heard the question again. Tobin Marconi might make beautiful suits, but I really didn't like him.

"Single, then?" Tobin asked.

"What?"

"Are you dating someone?"

"Uh." I tried to order my thoughts away from murder and back to the mundane details of my sex life. "No, not for a while."

"Ever been married?"

"Yes."

"A Texas boy?"

I moistened my lips. "Mexican."

"I don't see you with a field hand. A rich Mexican boy?"

I gave him a sideways glance that I hoped was, as my *über*-proper grandmother would say, quelling. Strike two, Mr. Marconi.

"Sorry. That was rude," he said after a moment. Tobin sighed deeply. "It's nice to be out on the mountain, no real responsibilities for the day. I don't get to experience this very often."

I drove. "You ever been married?"

"Once."

Maybe he and Kim just slept together. Or maybe I had missed something, looking for intrigue behind every action. Maybe they were siblings, separated at birth. They made good suits. As long as they paid me, why should I care?

Richard's face floated in my mind. Battered. Bloody.

Why?

"How did you meet your ex?" Tobin asked.

"He came in to buy his mother perfume. I sold him Youth Dew."

"Was it love at first sight?"

Lust, definitely. Two money-making twenty-somethings with dark tans and no obligations. Trouble from the start, probably. "First, we became inseparable, and then we eloped."

"How did your family respond?"

"Irate Irish for whom divorce is a sin? They threatened to annul it. We went to Mexico."

"Do you have children?"

"No. You?"

"Two Chinese pugs."

We pulled into a gas station and I got Smartfood and Snickers cappuccino with extra foam for me and Hostess Twinkies and Coke for him while he filled up. On the road again . . .

"Were you happy?" he asked a few miles later. Surely we would be in Snoqualmie soon. This interrogation was not interesting.

"Ever?"

"While you were married."

"Yes." Blissfully so, until we moved in with his parents in Mexico City.

"Then what happened?"

We lived separate lives, me attending his mother and sisters, becoming the perfect señora, never seeing him. He continued dating, returning to me and our bedroom only once a month, attempting to get me pregnant. "Distance," I said. "We drifted apart."

"I think it happens to everyone, no matter how much you love each other," he mused.

I said nothing, just drove and sipped my cappuccino, while I listened to the weather on the radio. I really hoped that he wasn't right. I wanted to believe that love, if it was the right love, lasted forever. I hadn't seen much proof, but I was trying to have faith. Why? No clue. It took me twenty miles to come to this conclusion: I was a romantic. Finally, I noticed he was pouting. He had been pouting for twenty miles.

"This is your exit," he said, pointing. As we drove through town, I screeched to a halt. "What are those?" I said, pointing to the ubiquitous pink, white and fuschia flowering plants that made everything around here seem so lush.

"Rhododendrons."

"Oh, right," I said, driving on.

"They're the state flower of Washington."

He didn't really seem like a flowers kinda guy to me at all, but then I remembered the hydrangeas. "I used them for a wedding on the East Coast and had to import them because they weren't available in a wide spectrum of colors anywhere else but here that time of year."

"When was that?"

"What season, or what year?"

"Either."

I pulled into the valet queue and we got out of the Jeep.

"All I remember is that big shoulders were in," he said as we walked into the lobby. "Men were in vests and cufflinks. We'll meet for dinner in a few minutes," he said, and he thanked me again.

I wheeled my bag to my room, picked up the phone, but

couldn't think who to call, so I started to do some remedial work on my face.

A little tinted moisturizer, a swipe of Thong lipstick, a curl of the lashes.

I opened the curler and the white foam pad fell out. "This is dead," I said out loud. It was about time I entered the new century and got a heated one, or those tiny little Japanese ones. I settled for some khaki shadow on my eyelid and a touch of yellow in the center. I'd look more awake, anyway. A spritz of perfume and I looked better. Perfume contributes to appearance. I don't know how, but it does. Smell therapy—I wondered which dosha that worked for. I sucked in my abs as I looked at myself in the mirror.

I felt so dark. Everything seemed tainted, tinted, with fear and suspicion. Why couldn't I be light and free like Dieta? "Shopping," I said to myself out loud. "Color therapy is what you need." The Dallas uniform was black, but I thought that maybe I was getting tired of black. How many years had I worn nothing but? Dieta's yellows, pinks, blues, and lavenders were so . . . happy.

Happy was good.

And if color therapy didn't work, alcohol might.

I smiled in the mirror, then wrinkled my nose at my reflection and went downstairs. No one was around, so I wandered through the gift shop and stared in wonder at the photographs of the waterfall.

Everyone was showing up; we got a table overlooking the waterfall and ordered salads and entrees. The food appeared in record time.

"All you got is a salad?" Darcy asked, cutting into lamb.

"Do you want some of my steak?" Tobin asked me.

"Thanks, but I don't eat meat."

"I thought you were from Texas."

"I don't like tequila either," I said. "They haven't kicked me out yet."

Everyone laughed.

"So is there a religious reason you don't eat meat? Or a physical, health thing?" Freddie asked.

I shrugged. "I stopped eating it in sixth grade. It's too heavy."

"Don't you ever want to just tear into a bite of steak?" Tobin asked. "The forbidden is sometimes the most alluring."

"Uh, no," I said, looking at him for a second. Were we still talking about steak? "I don't like it. Not the texture or the smell, and definitely not the taste. And there is nothing forbidden about it. I don't *want* to eat it."

"Does it bother you when people eat it in front of you?" Nasmo asked.

"No. It's your food."

"Do you eat fish?"

"When it's fresh. I like east Texas catfish on a Friday night, served with hushpuppies, coleslaw and slices of Wonder Bread. You drive through the Piney Woods for an hour to get to some hole in the wall, and while you eat you freeze because you have a sunburn and the AC is so cold. Then you watch the stars all the way home."

"Sounds like you have deep roots," Kenneth said.

I smiled and ate my salad with three kinds of whole-milk cheeses. My cell phone rang, a Seattle area code. I excused myself to the lobby.

"Thompson here."

"I got to talk to Tobin," I said, whispering. "You need to ask him about Richard."

"We did," he said.

"Oh. Did he tell you about the car?"

"Yes." He sounded a little out of patience.

"Well," I said, "I guess that you know everything. Thanks for calling back. Sorry to bother you."

He sighed. "Be careful. Test your brakes before you go anywhere, okay?"

"I was right about the brakes?" I asked, glancing around me. No one was paying attention.

"Just be careful. Call me if anything else comes up."

I nodded mutely, not that he could see, and went back to my place at the table. Most of the crew had moved on, games in someone's room or something. I poured the wine Kenneth had been drinking.

"How can you do that?" Dieta said. "I still have a headache."

"Hair of the dog," I said, pouring her a glass.

We clinked glasses to balanced doshas and leaned back to enjoy the view. "To Richard."

"May he be dancing and singing in paradise," she said.

We drank. Over her shoulder I saw Irma and Kim come in, both wearing running shoes and breathing hard. Kim was swigging from her sports bottle. She gave us a sour look and walked away. Irma waved at us and followed Kim.

"She needs sex," Dieta said. "That would make her smile again."

"Don't we all," Freddie said, joining us. "Hand over that wine."

"So how are we going to spend the evening?" Darcy asked, sitting down and lighting up. The waiter sent her a look, but she ignored it. Tonight's T-shirt was retro with rhinestones and said "Smokin'." And she was.

"I need to go to a palmist," Dieta said. "Always, I do this before the start of a shoot. This time I didn't have the chance, so now everything is crazy and I must go."

"That sounds like fun," Freddie said. "I think I'm going to go check out that cute little depot. I always wanted to be an engineer on a train." He finished his glass of wine. "Or at least date one. Anything to get him out of those awful striped pants."

"I'm almost out of cigarettes," Darcy said. "So either I find them here, or I drive back to Seattle."

"Isn't anyone else bothered about Richard?" I asked, tipsy and out of the blue.

Dieta sat up and patted my hand. "You go with me to the palmist," she said. "We'll learn the answers about Richard there."

Darcy decided to join us; Freddie opted to skulk around town looking for his childhood fantasy engineer. Despite my tipsy condition, I remembered to check the brakes. We were getting in the Jeep when I asked Dieta if she knew where a palmist was. "Take this road," she said before we got back to the highway. "It leads into the next town. They'll have one there for sure."

"You're from Sweden," Darcy said, driving. "How do you know?"

"Trust me," Dieta said.

We drove through for coffee first. Darcy got peppermint crunch cappuccino, Dieta got a triple espresso and chocolate-dipped biscotti, and I got a Nutella-flavored espresso. Dieta started dialing her phone, then cursed it. "Every other time I try to call, it tells me the call is too far," she said.

"It's the mountains," Darcy said, blowing smoke out the open window. "I haven't been able to get my phone to work either."

"Mine's been fine," I said. "Most of the time."

"Sometimes the hour can make a difference," Darcy said.

Dieta dialed again, but the phone cut out. "Look," she said, shoving her phone in front of my face. "See? Call dropped." She slammed the Samsung shut.

The road into town ran parallel to the freeway. Schools, homes, and businesses lined it, all with beautifully manicured green lawns and flowering bushes. "I learned what those are," I said to them.

"What are?" Dieta asked, looking out the window.

"Those big bushes with the multi-colored flowers."

"It was driving Dallas crazy not to know," Darcy said.

"Why does not knowing a flower make you crazy?" Dieta asked.

"Rhododendrons. I know now."

"Stop!" she shouted.

Darcy slammed on the brakes. I looked for a victim; had we hit something? Someone?

"Back up!" Dieta said. "A palmist, a palmist!"

Darcy was swearing as she backed up. "I thought I'd killed somebody," she said. "Jesus girl, you sure can scream."

Dieta was out, already standing on the porch of a quaint little Victorian house with buckets of flowers on the steps. She pointed to a tiny sign in the front yard: a forward-facing palm with "reader" in script across it.

The door opened, revealing a five-foot-tall auburn-haired girl in homemade jeans, Wal-Mart flats, and a pink scalloped T. "I've been expecting you," she said to Dieta. But she was looking at me.

I, somehow, got to be first. My palm was sticky with slightly spilled Nutella coffee, but she didn't seem to care. "Anything in particular on your mind?" she asked me.

You tell me, I thought. I felt tired and surly. Richard haunted me. "What's my future?"

She didn't touch me, just stared at my upturned palms for a long time before she said anything. "Well," she said, her voice tolling like a cemetery bell, "it's cloudy."

Typical, I thought.

"You're about to be tested."

Wonderful.

"Because of this, you need to hold onto what you know is true. Trust your instincts. Believe in yourself—who you know you are. That's going to be tried." She moved her head, still looking at my palm. "It's all about you for a while. Have faith in yourself."

I felt chilled and slightly cheated. For this I paid thirty dollars?

I was finishing wiping my hands when Dieta came bouncing out. "You know what she told me?"

Darcy, who had gone between us, shook her head. "We were swinging in the porch swing out here. What did she say?"

"She asked me what I wanted more than anything in life, and I said happiness, peace, and joy, you know? She said"—Dieta's green eyes were wide, her ponytail fibrillating with excitement—"she said that I would find pure bliss soon. Shiva!"

"That's great," Darcy said. "Pure bliss sounds like a good thing."

"I thought Shiva was a goddess," I said.

"*He* is a god, but also pure bliss."

This was probably the reason I wasn't into Ayurveda, or yoga, or any New Age mysticism. The vocabulary bewildered me. "What did you ask her, Darcy?" I said.

"Where I could find discounted cigarettes."

"She knew?"

Darcy blew smoke in one long uninterrupted stream. "She said she'd tell me, but I would be quitting soon."

"It's not good for your dosha," Dieta said. "But I know it's fun. In fact, may I have one?"

"I thought she was pretty nervy," Darcy said, offering her pack to Dieta, "then she charged me to listen to her sermon!"

"Pure bliss," I said. "Dieta, you got the best one."

"Yeah," Darcy said, blowing out smoke as we descended the stairs. "We're jealous."

We were walking down the steps when the door opened. "Your friend is fine," she called after us.

All three of us turned.

She smiled. "He's happy." The door closed.

"Let's take a walk."

"I need some air."

"I need a cigarette."

We decided to leave the Jeep and wander around town on foot. It would be dark in an hour or so. "Let's get cherry pie!" Dieta said, pointing down the street.

"Freddie would die," Darcy said. "That's the little café from 'Twin Peaks!'"

"It was very popular in my country," Dieta said. "I must take a picture." She whipped out an Elph and we posed in front of the diner's windows. Kyle MacLachlan, who later became Linda Evangelista of the eternally-changing hairstyle's main squeeze, had made his career here as the FBI cherry pie junkie. Unglue his hair and he's Zegna's poster boy.

"I can hear the spooky music in my head," Dieta said.

I remembered the image of the girl crossing the bridge, stumbling home at dawn, the music floating in the background, something obviously wrong with the girl. She walked like a zombie, her arms held at an awkward angle. I shuddered. That had been about murder too.

We were on our way back to the Jeep when Dieta remembered something, spun around, and fell on the sidewalk.

"Are you okay?" Darcy asked.

We helped her up, brushing dirt off her knee and palm. She was white, so we sat down on the curb. "It's my ear," Dieta said, angry tears in her eyes. "Oh damn! My pants!"

Her mint green Laura Petrie pants had a gash in the knee. "We can fix those," I said. "Either get a butterfly to stick over the rip or trim them into shorts. Ten minutes, no problem."

"I want the butterfly," Dieta said. "That would be happy."

"Let's go," Darcy said, helping her up. "It looks like the rain is about to revisit us."

Dieta got up on shaky legs and I ran to get the Jeep. We drove back to the lodge with forced smiles. A few steps further, and Dieta would have fallen in the road. She wasn't safe to be alone.

* * *

Night. I stared at the ceiling. Tried not to remember Richard's face. Outside, rain fell with abandon. What's unabandoned rain, I wondered. I rolled over and put my head under the pillow.

Kim was quiet tonight. If I were still awake at four in the morning, I'd go running with her.

The digital numbers glowed at me; I glowered back.

I heard scratching at my door.

"How do you feel about a makeover?" Darcy asked, when I opened the door. "It'll be fun, give you a new party look. Hello?" she said. "Are you awake?"

Makeup artists don't often offer to do makeovers. That was giving away money. And it had to be midnight. "Just dazed," I said. My voice was gravelly.

"I know it's late," she said, as she stepped into my room. "It's just, when I get nervous I play with makeup."

I closed the door. "You're nervous?"

"Someone died, Dallas. Deaths always come in threes."

I turned on the lights. "Are you Irish?"

"Way Irish," she said. "Ellis is my last name."

Superstition was keeping her up; then again, my irrational fears were doing the same to me. "Sure," I said. "A makeover would be great."

Freddie joined us a half-hour later. "I knew I smelled Nars," he said, when I opened the door. "And I brought food. See?" he held out the not-so-complimentary basket of goodies from his room.

"You can smell makeup?" I asked. Darcy had commandeered the bathroom, putting a chair in there, and setting up her own mirror. My face, magnified five times, stared back at me in all its pre-dawn, overhead lighting glory, which is to say, I could scare small children.

"Not really," he said sitting on the edge of the Whirlpool spa cross-legged. "But I sense when someone has makeup on the mind." His smile was sad. "I couldn't sleep."

"Me neither," I confessed. "I'm glad y'all came."

Darcy's makeup spread out on both sides of me. "It used to look like this when my sisters and I played paper dolls," I said.

"I never liked paper dolls," Freddie said. "The 2-D thing just didn't work for me. I needed to touch the clothes."

"I'm visual," I said. "Just seeing that Barbie and Francie were wearing coordinated colors was enough for me."

"I'm with Freddie," Darcy said. "I had to have the real dolls. You couldn't change the hair or makeup of a paper doll."

That was true.

"Though," Darcy said, "I'll never forget the time I got in so much trouble, my parents actually took my Barbies away. Until further notice, they said."

"What did you do?" Freddie and I asked together.

"Played doctor with the neighborhood boys?" Freddie asked.

"Smoked on the playground?" I said.

"No," she said. "And you know, I didn't realize anything about this until I became a parent, but it was very sneaky."

"You're a parent?" Freddie said.

"Of three. Two twin boys and a girl."

"Two twins, not three?" Freddie asked.

Darcy smeared Vaseline on his cheek. "Next time it's your glasses."

"So location shoots are a vacation," I said.

She laughed.

"What did you do to get in so much trouble?" Freddie begged. "Tell us, I'm all a-quiver."

She sat back from me, brushes tucked over her ears, another in her hand. "I really, really wanted to stay with my friend Mary for a night, but I was too young for sleepovers. My parents had told me this at the beginning of the school year, but it was spring now and I thought I was old enough."

"Oh. I know what you did," Freddie said.

"I told my dad that my mom had said I could go if he said so—"

"—and you told your mom the same thing," I finished.

"Exactly. I got grounded for the rest of the school year!"

"Yeouch!" Freddie said. "Bet you learned that lesson."

Darcy leaned over to me again; I felt the small, strong strokes on my face. "I tried that too," I said, "but it didn't work in my family. My parents had this siege mentality that they were the embattled civilized village holding out against the barbarian hordes. We couldn't play two ends against the middle. I don't think anyone even tried after the story of Sherman's fall passed down the ranks."

"What happened with Sherman?" Darcy asked. "Look up."

"Who's Sherman?" Freddie asked.

I looked up so she could line my lower lid. "Same thing as you. Sherman, he's my eldest brother, tried to play two ends against the middle, 'cuz when my parents fought they wouldn't speak to each other. At least, not in front of us. I realize now that they must have always talked about us, and had sex. There just weren't enough months in the year for them to abstain and have that many children. Anyway, Sherman got caught and was sent to military school for a month. He came home a changed person." I shuddered. "The only way that works is when the two people who are being manipulated just don't trust each other."

"I never even tried anything like that," Freddie said. "I just didn't want to get caught wearing my mother's back-seamed stockings."

Darcy lit a cigarette as we laughed.

"How do you feel about Richard?"

Suddenly the fun, the frivolity of the moment seemed as empty and fake as a midway. "I don't want to talk about it."

"Why didn't you just break the glass?" he asked.

"What part of *she doesn't want to talk about it* don't you understand?" Darcy asked, as she turned around to glare at him. "Besides, the pressure inside and outside the car had to be the same."

Since I couldn't break the glass, and had to open the door, that was true.

"If you know that, why didn't *you* jump in?" he asked.

"I can't swim."

Oh.

"What color is that?" Freddie asked Darcy after a minute. My eyes were still closed. All I could see was Richard's face.

"I used blue and green," she said. "I think it will be a good look for Dallas this summer. A party look."

She whisked powder over my face. "Open your eyes."

"Wow," I said as I stared into the mirror. Definitely fresh and summery. My skin glowed like a pearl, with pale pink glossed lips and eyes she'd lined with bright shadows. "The turquoise mascara is a hoot," I said. "My eyes look so dark this way."

"You look like a rock star," Freddie said.

"It's the Marc Jacobs look," Darcy said, stubbing her cigarette out and waving away the smoke. "Or Oscar, take your pick."

I didn't think my room was a smoking room; I needed to check that.

Freddie looked at me. "Next is her hair. Those sideswept bangs will be perfect on her."

"Maybe tomorrow," I said. "We need to call it a night."

"Richard was murdered," Freddie said as he swept into my room, "by the mob." It was 5:30 A.M., and I was in my robe and had a towel on my hair. I'd hated to wash away my party makeup. "Sit down," he said, unwinding the towel. "Can you believe it?"

"Where did you hear that?" I asked, as I watched Freddie

comb my hair, plug in the blow dryer, and whip out a Mason-Pearson brush.

"All over the New York papers. I had a friend call me at five. He knew Richard was supposed to be with me on this job."

If the news was in New York, it would be in Texas soon. Time to start screening calls from everywhere except the ranch. "Why would someone kill him?"

"Well, you know he was shacking up with a mobster," Freddie said. "At least the *Times* said so. Maybe it was another mobster gang out to get him." He turned on the dryer and started styling my hair. "This is so relaxing for me," he said. "I just love giving a good blow job."

I rolled my eyes. "Richard, in the mob?" I asked over the noise of the dryer. It had been a while since I'd seen him . . . and I certainly knew nothing about his personal life. Yet I'd heard this twice now.

Freddie shook his head. "He was the moll. Maybe someone axed him to get a message to Torinelli." He continued to play with my hair, transforming my overprocessed straw into spun gold.

"How do they know he was murdered?" I asked.

"His Porsche was rigged," Freddie said. "I don't understand much about cars, but apparently it was pretty obvious."

Had Thompson told them? "Do Kim and Tobin know?"

"They will if the reporters figure out we're staying here," he said. "I hate reporters, especially Joan Rivers and her tacky little daughter," he said.

I didn't consider Oscar coverage to be reporting, but I didn't say anything. Why would someone kill Richard? Unless it really was something between two mob groups. That was a scary thought, but so much better than suspecting everyone around me.

Chapter Ten

DECEPTION FALLS

I felt lighter than I had in days. Freddie and I were loose, together, swilling flavored espressos and racing toward the sun for the next shot and singing *"Gimme, Gimme, Gimme a man after midnight . . ."* Freddie was doing the instruments too.

Mobsters had killed Richard for whatever reason mobsters kill people. Richard wasn't in pain; we'd miss him, but there was nothing else I could do. At least the people whom I'd grow to care for were in the clear. And I'd been straight with the police.

Today wasn't going to be a fantasy shot—just two guys in a lot of suits. Darcy and Wes were both sleeping in. Freddie would do makeup and hair.

And Kim and Tobin would both be there. It remained to be seen if that was good or bad. Kim's flu and her moods were both worsening. Thom Goodfeather had passed out headsets at breakfast, so we wouldn't be hoarse like we'd been after Snoqualmie.

When we arrived, I blessed him. You couldn't hear a damn

thing over the sound of the falls. And these weren't even big falls like Snoqualmie, but smaller ones made from snowmelt. They were wild and frothing white in some places, placid as a Texas lake in others.

"Where are Richard's suits?" Tobin asked me, sticking his head into the RV. He was in a brown nailshead suit jacket, similar to the blue one I was prepping. Underneath he wore a black polo sweater and some flat-front pants. He looked great.

"Over there," I said, my hands inside the interlining of a jacket. "Are we getting another model?"

"No, I think we'll double up the boys," he said. "It's a headless thing anyway." He put his arm around me and squeeze-hugged me. "How are you doing?"

"Good," I said, a little startled at his affection.

"Glad to hear it. See you on the set." He dashed down the stairs to the river and the falls.

Thom Goodfeather came in a half hour later and handed me a list. "Kim wanted you to have this. She'll be here soon."

I read the note in spiky, left-leaning cursive. *"I want three looks for each of the suits. Even a little frivolous, if it shows a detail or has an intriguing mood."* It was almost nice. I looked over the suits and made notes while Thom watched.

"Is that agreeable?" he asked.

"Sure."

Kenneth came into the RV a few minutes later. "Here's the story. We have upper falls, which are loud and splashy, and lower falls, and then some quiet water with picturesque fallen logs and bridges, blah, blah, blah. We'll shoot upper this morning, lower this afternoon. The light won't be really good until about four."

I had a ton of time to work with, which was good.

"So quit dawdling," Kenneth said with a wink. "Let's get to work."

*   *   *

Dieta popped in a half hour later. "How are you today?" She listed to the left, and braced herself against the door-frame.

"I'm okay today," I said. "Freddie's good company."

"Good," she said with a bright smile. "I got you some-thing. It's just little, but it might help you. I mean, with Richard and all."

"You didn't have to get me anything," I said, immeasur-ably touched. "What is it?"

She laughed and dug in the pocket of her dark rinse jeans. "It's tiny."

I opened the cocktail napkin and saw a little critter. "It's cute."

"It's a fetish."

I looked up; I had no idea what she meant. It didn't look like a pair of shoes to me.

"It's like a guardian angel, only it's Indian instead. The powers of the creature are the same . . ." she fumbled for a word. "Strengths, that the animal has. Yours is a bear, so it is everything a bear is."

"Hungry and growling?" What I knew of bears consisted of urban myths and TV commercials.

"Strong, defensive, agressive and likes honey—"

We talked a few more minutes before my phone rang. I fumbled for the button. "Thank you," I said to her.

She kissed my head and leaned her way out of the room.

I pushed down the headset and answered the phone.

"Hallo, darling, how are you?" Lindsay was great about checkup calls.

"Good."

"How's the shoot?"

"Fine."

"That's good. Are they treating you well?"

"Very nice," I said.

"Was that freakish accident with Richard anywhere around you? Did you hear about that? He drowned in a Washington lake. Extraordinary. I tell you."

I winced at her words, but then I realized she hadn't heard about Richard's death being investigated as a murder. If Lindsay, who reads the Dallas paper cover to cover, didn't know, the chances were fair that no one in my family would. And my Granddaddy would never tell. My fetish had little turquoise eyes and a fish in its mouth.

"Dallas?"

"Uh, well, Richard was supposed to be in our shoot," I said.

"What?" Her voice lost all of its casualness. "Whatdju mean?" When Lindsay gets upset, good or bad, her English heritage is obvious. "You're on a shoot where a man died? You should be getting hazard pay! This is outrageous! I'm—"

Lindsay would have been a great ambulance-chasing lawyer. She's a shark when it comes to money—and with her taste in men, women, and Milan shows, it's good that she is.

It's even better that she's *my* shark.

"Do you want to stay? Should I get you back here immejitly?"

"No, no, everything seems to be fine. But Lindsay," I looked over my shoulder in case someone had crept inside the RV and missed them. "Are Kim and Tobin romantically linked?"

"Would a hundred more a day assuage you?"

"I'm fine—"

"Would you be more fine—I mean, Dallas darling—the stress you must be under, the grief—"

"Money won't—"

"You're there, you're working despite awful conditions. I think one-fifty more might be better."

"Are Tobin and Kim together? Are they an item?"

"What? No, I have no idea. Are you switching your type to Brooklyn bad boys instead of Latino lovers?"

"No, I was just curious. Have they been together?"

"If they are, or they were, it's news to me. But wouldn't it be unusual. Designers are ordinarily quite gay, aren't they?"

"Well, some of them are married," I said.

"And your point is?"

I chuckled. "Good point," I said.

"So will another one fifty a day make you feel better?"

My shark. "Sure," I said. "How's town?"

"Bloody hot, as usual. I'm thinking of a holiday to somewhere cool, like the South Pole."

"That sounds nice, though I have to tell you that I'm wearing a jacket and boots right now."

"Ah, and think of the nice boots you'll be able to get with a nine-fifty day rate!"

I laughed. "Thank you Lindsay."

"I'm calling them right away."

"Good luck."

We hung up.

George was first, in the single-breasted tan suit. George had a sweet, sleepy, California-dreamin' look, but the body of a professional athlete. Freddie brought his hair under control and we put him on the bridge, throwing flowers down; then got a closer shot in dappled sunshine; then a last, casual shot with a straw hat and suspenders. "Shades of *Room with A View,*" Freddie said, parting George's hair in the middle and ironing it straight.

"That's perfect," Kenneth shouted. "Especially for a headless shot!"

We laughed as Freddie smacked his head. "I completely forgot!"

"We're finished here," he said, now over the headset. "The assistants will be back with lunch in an hour."

I changed George and then zipped up my jacket. "I'm going to sit in the sun till lunch."

"You're not going to get much of it, wrapped like an Eskimo," Freddie said.

"It will be nice to sit in the sun and be cold. Hand me that crossword book." We walked down to the water again.

George fell asleep on one of the logs, his hand almost touching the water. "That's the shot we should have gotten," Freddie whispered as he pointed to him.

"Right. And watch Kim kill me over messing up the suit."

"Where is she, anyway? I've never seen such no-show ADs in my life."

"I don't know, but she can stay gone."

"Forget her. Snoqualmie was genius," he said. "Pure genius."

I opened the puzzle book and sucked in my abs. I could exercise my brain and stomach at the same time. A five letter word for discomfort . . .

"This is what I pay you eight hundred dollars a day for?" Kim said, standing over me. "And your agent just tried to gouge me for another hundred and fifty. Hazard pay, she said."

I jolted awake; I'd fallen asleep in the breeze, in the sunshine. I opened my eyes, blinded immediately by sun on silver metal. "We're on lunch," I said, blinking away the afterimages of her silver Boxster.

The non-rental Boxster had gone into the lake. She *still* drove one. Was it Tobin's really?

"It's one o'clock," she said. "You should be back by now. Don't you have more work to do?"

"Kim," I said, "it's a question of light."

She looked up. "I see light. Do you have a vision problem?"

"It's exactly overhead," I said, my eyes still watering. "That doesn't make for pretty pictures."

She tapped one crocodile shoe. "Where is Tobin?"

"I don't know. Maybe getting lunch."

Muttering about larcenous agents, she walked off, picking her way in leather pants, pumps, and net sweater. She did have a gorgeous body. Pretty is as pretty does.

"Who pissed in her Post Toasties," Freddie said a minute later, sitting beside me.

"It's enough to make you believe in alien abductions," I said. "I thought she was going to demand a salute. Today, she's scary."

"Dieta says it's her dosha out of balance."

"Man," I said. "It's out of balance like the Eiffel Tower versus chili-fries—you can't even compare. She's way outta whack. I wonder what happened. She was so nice that first night, then—"

"Bammo, the wicked witch of Emerald City."

It took me a minute, but I remembered that Seattle is nick-named Emerald City. Freddie continued. "Women are so hard to guess at. You wonder why I sleep with men?" he asked.

"I don't wonder," I said. "I understand perfectly."

"Lunch!" someone shouted from the parking lot.

"Good, I'm starved," Freddie said.

"I hope they got cheese," I said, dusting my pants off and following him through the trees to the stairs. Dieta was on her way down when she overbalanced and toppled into us; her hat went flying. Freddie caught her, and I braced against the stair rail to catch them both.

"Are you okay?" he asked us.

"I'm so sorry," she said. "Is anyone hurt?"

"Are you hurt?" I said, looking up from where she'd fallen. "That was, like, six steps."

"I'm getting used to it," she said with a wan smile. But she looked a little spooked. Freddie put his arm around her waist and I got her hat then followed them up the stairs.

Lunch was mostly silent. Kim was disdainful, drinking from her sports bottle; Tobin was silent, focused on his burger; the talent and crew were all quiet. One by one we gratefully slipped back to work.

When I started dressing Tom Fly, I noticed some pink dots on his neck and chest. "What's that?" I asked, holding the shirt.

"I don't know," he said. "It just appeared."

"Hang on," I said, hanging the shirt up. I dug around in my styling kit and handed him a pink bottle.

"What's this for?"

"It's calamine lotion," I said. "It should quell whatever's irritating your skin. I'll give you a couple of minutes to put it on," I said, pulling the door shut behind me.

"What's up?" Freddie asked, looking up from his date-book. Kim was flipping through *Vogue,* watching us.

"Tom Fly has a rash," I said.

"Splendid!" Kim said, slamming the magazine down. "That's just perfect."

"I gave him some lotion," I said to her. "Sssh. It will be fine."

"Don't shush me. I knew that this was a stupid idea," she hissed. "A waste of time."

Tom opened the door wearing boxers and socks. "I can't reach my back," he said. He looked defenseless, despite being well muscled and handsome in a glasses-wearing-dot-com kind of way.

"My God, put some clothes on," Kim snapped.

"I'll go help him," Freddie said as he slipped by me.

I waited until he closed the door. I turned to Kim. "Ms. Charles."

"Your employer," she reminded me. "What do you have to say?"

"You are in the models' RV. Though I am sure you will receive the bill for it, right now it is their dressing room. They are the talent. Their comfort and ease in this situation gives you good film, which sells your suits, which pays for this RV." I stared at her until she looked away.

"You are not irreplaceable," she snapped. "And certainly not worth your day rate."

"That is your opinion. But I'm here," I said. "I have a photographer waiting for a model, so if you will excuse me."

"Where am I supposed to wait?" she snapped.

"It's a beautiful day," I said, and I opened the door. "Enjoy it."

I didn't listen to her comments, just closed the door when both pointed-toe shoes were on the first step.

Tom Fly was terrified. "She hates me. She's going to fire me."

"Then she's going to stuff you in her oven and eat you," Freddie said, *sotto voce.*

"Don't be silly," I snapped at both of them; then I looked at Tom's rash. It had been stopped in its tracks. Already it was fading. "Buy me an extra twenty minutes," I told Freddie. "No one will ever know."

A half-hour later, Tom Fly looked excellent. The suit fit like a glove; his hair was perfect; we were back on track, walking down to the set through the forest. He was ahead by a few steps, around the bend from me.

Suddenly he screamed, "They got me! They got me!"

I dropped into a crouch, running to him. The roaring of the water had apparently muffled the sound of the shot.

"Shit!" he screamed.

I skidded to a stop when I saw him. He was still standing.

"Shit!" he shouted as he took off his glasses.

"What?" I demanded. I didn't see any blood.

"Shit," he said. "A bird shit on me."

I took a few steps closer and saw a huge glob of white that started on his head, got his glasses, cheek, jacket, hand, pants, and shoes. That was one seriously efficient bird. My heart was pounding and I burst out laughing. "You said 'shit' and you meant *shit,*" I managed to say. "I thought you'd been shot by the mob, or assassinated or . . . ohmigod, you terrified me."

"What is so damn funny this time?" Kim said as she appeared like a nightmare on the pathway. We both looked at her. "God, what a slob. What's on him?"

Tom Fly patted her shoulder with his white-stained hand. "It's just a shitty day," he said.

I raced up the stairs so she wouldn't hear me howling with laughter. Tom was a tricky one.

Kenneth was shooting fast, and Stephen kept wiping the lens in a one-two step. Tobin was right behind me. He'd taken off his jacket and kept dashing in to the photo to play with the suit. It disrupted the flow completely, but he was the client, so Kenneth couldn't really complain. I ground my teeth. This was why people in my business hated the client to be around. Micromanagement.

"It's wrong; it's just wrong," Kim's voice came through into my head. "I don't like the black against the sunlit green. It's too jarring, too blatant."

Apparently, she'd decided to be the AD. And Tobin was trying to be stylist.

"Tobin liked it," I said carefully.

Where was she hiding? I looked over my shoulder and spotted her against the leg of the overpass.

"Tobin," she groused.

Maybe she was one of those women who were totally transformed by PMS. In which case, I would volunteer to go get her drugs. Anything to make her pleasant again. I touched the switch on my waist so I could talk. "Would you rather see the gray? It's less severe."

"Hmm," she said. "Fine, waste some film on this, then try the gray. The silk, I think."

I watched as Tom Fly posed and preened in front of the

camera, his fear of Mother Nature flawlessly masked, though he cast a few suspicious glances at the sky.

"Do you have it?" she asked.

"The gray silk?" I said. "Sure, it's in the RV, I'll get it at the end of the—"

"Send someone to get it now," Kim said with a dramatic sigh. "We can hold it up and see the effect." She didn't wait for my response, just clicked off.

"Denton!" I heard Kenneth call the name of another Texas town in my ear. Someone had printed a list from the Internet. "Let's try to get two frames in a row," he said to Tobin, who was in the picture, straightening one of Tom's cuffs. "Get him out of here before I do bodily harm," he whispered to me. "We're getting nowhere."

I yanked Tobin back while Kenneth shot a roll.

"Going in," Tobin said to Kenneth, as he went to fix Tom's lapel while Kenneth changed film. The photographer's wide body was growing tighter. I needed to get rid of Tobin for a while. "I need to run up and get the gray silk suit," I said to him. "Would you watch the set for me?"

"I'd rather the stylist stay," Kenneth said to me, exactly on cue.

"Oh," Tobin said, a little disgruntled. "I guess I can go get it."

"Do you mind, that would be so helpful," I said to Tobin as he left. "Is Tom's cuff bothering you?" I asked Kenneth.

"No," he barked.

He changed angles. I was crouched by the camera to check my work, when I heard tires screech. I glanced up at the road, but saw nothing. Kim didn't even look up, just kept her glasses-wearing face pointed toward the shoot. Critiquing my every move.

"Did you hear anything?" I asked Kenneth.

"Between the falls and the yakking on this head-thingy, I

couldn't hear my own heart stopping," he said. He shot another roll. "Are we finished with this suit. Yet?" he said.

"Did you get what you wanted?" I asked.

"I don't want to see it anymore," he said. "Is there another?"

"Hang on," I said as I called Tobin's headset. "How is the search for the gray silk going?"

"It's not here," he said. "Where else would it be?"

"Maybe at the lodge," I said. I thought I'd seen it this morning, but I could have been wrong. "I'll call Darcy and have her check. How about the brown while we look?"

Tobin sighed; he and Kim must war that way, I decided. "Brown on a tan man in a forest isn't going to work," he said. "Give me the navy."

Ooo, that was logical. "We have another shot," I said to Kenneth; then motioned for Tom to come with me. Kim had left her post.

"Thank you, Tom," Kenneth said.

"I'm coming up," I said to Tobin, and clicked off. Tom ran ahead of me, dodging the danger-birds who had it out for his suit.

Suddenly I heard Kim's voice in my ear, but not talking to me. "I need more money, he's getting greedy."

I tapped my headset. "Kim?" I said. But she didn't have the receiver on. Was she on her cell phone?

"No," she said. "That will just finish the job. Today, he said." She sighed. "You have no idea how tired I am of all of this."

I glanced at my watch: 3:35 P.M. on Thursday.

"Yeah, okay, I'll pick it up," she said.

What was she talking about, and to whom?

Back in the RV I stared at the rack while George stripped to his boxers and slipped on his socks. I pulled the green French-cuffed shirt, a very sedate striped tie, and the navy suit. I took him outside and tied vines through his cuffs instead of cufflinks. I made Nasmo King gather a bunch of vines and we smashed them into an alligator briefcase so that the folded edges and curling ends poked out. Then I took him on set.

"Awesome, Dallas," Kenneth said.

"Give me your shoes," I said to George as I knelt down to take off his socks.

"Let's pull back a little," Tobin said to Kenneth. "I want to see his face in this one."

"I think I may weigh too much," George muttered as he inched onto a log that jutted into the smaller stream. A beam of sunshine shot across his shoulders into the water.

"Do something with his collar," Tobin said. I angled it like a tux shirt, then tied the tie in a droopy, Western-style string tie. Then I stepped back and scrutinized the suit: no wrinkles; it draped beautifully, the lines soft yet noticeable. The little touches of ivy went with the bare feet, so while no one would actually wear it this way, it looked comfortable and elegant. George was great, laughing, smiling, playing on the log.

"Any more suits?" Kenneth asked.

Tobin looked at me. "Did we get them all?"

"We'll do the brown in the desert, you decided? So except for the gray silk," I said, "I think so." I'd even called Salish. "Darcy said the gray wasn't at the lodge either."

"That's a ten-thousand-dollar suit," Kim yelled in my face, and on my headset. Surround sound. "You better not have lost it, or we'll be paying you considerably less."

My face was hot with anger. "I'll ask Dieta," I said, escaping up the steps with George right behind me. I ripped off my headset; my ears were ringing. Dieta wasn't on the RV, or in any of the Jeeps. Not in the bathroom, not the short or long trails. Even Stephen hadn't seen her, though they rode out together.

And for the life of me, I couldn't find the gray silk suit. We were wrapped, ready to go, but still no sign of Dieta. Kim took off in her Boxster—she had a Seattle appointment to keep. "Good riddance," George muttered. "Maybe a rock will fall on her."

Freddie and I exchanged a worried look; I knew the idea occurred to us at the same time: Dieta had fallen and hurt herself.

"What do you want to do?" Kenneth asked me.

"We know Dieta didn't just abandon us. Stephen, call the lodge and have them check her room. Then ask Darcy if she's there. Nasmo, call her agency and see if she's checked in during the last few hours. Kenneth, let's you, me, Freddie, and Esmerelda walk around here, just to make sure Dieta didn't break her leg or something and is lying in the grass."

"How can I help?" Tom Fly, completely recovered from his allergic reaction, asked.

I patted his sleeve. "You keep track of all of us. George, you go walk along the river's edge." I glanced at the sky. "Everyone got your phones? We'll meet back here in a half-hour, okay? Or call George if you find her. He'll call everyone else."

Kenneth took the upper falls, Freddie the lower ones, and I wandered along the edge of the road. Traffic: huge trucks, RVs, Beetles, and every type of four-wheel-drive imaginable passed me. I walked east about a quarter of a mile, then turned around and walked west back to the parking lot. When I looked across the road, I saw a patch of brown in the very green grass.

Brown, like Tobin's jacket.

Dieta had been in violet today, with a slouchy hat. I knew that. A gray suit was missing. But—I glanced right and left and dashed across the road. "Dieta!" I screamed. "Ohmigod, Dieta!"

"Did you find her?" Kenneth shouted to me.

Esmerelda raced toward Dieta.

"Call an ambulance! Hurry!" I shouted to Kenneth.

"I was already dialing 911, looking at the sign across from me: Deception Falls."

Chapter Eleven

It was four A.M. I didn't even know what city I was in—just that it had a hospital, and I'd been here for almost twelve hours. Coffee cups lay scattered in a nimbus around me, and I'd even thought about smoking once or twice until I realized I had to go to an outside area on the opposite side of the emergency room to do so. I was too lazy, too tired, and too scared I'd be away in the moment I was needed, to try it. Freddie was sacked out across the chairs and Tom Fly had been pacing frantically for hours.

He sat down by me. "I have to leave, Dallas. I can't take this."

"Well . . ." I said. "Wake up Freddie, he can drive you to Salish."

"No, Dallas," Tom's face was ashen and his eyes were bloodshot. "I need to leave. I can't take this."

"You mean quit?" I said. "The job?" We'd started scheduled with four models. Now we'd be down to two?

"Two people have almost died, Dallas."

"One died. She's *not* going to die," I spat. I got up and walked away. Not Dieta. No. I touched the fetish in my pocket. Not Dieta.

"I'm leaving," he said, stopping me as I turned around. "I'm not asking your permission. I'm telling you."

"Why?" I asked.

"Remember earlier, when you said you thought the mob had gotten me?"

I rubbed my face. That was just today? I was wearing the same clothes. How could life change so quickly. I nodded.

"I have insurance against that. You know I'm Filipino, right?"

I had no idea. "Sure," I said. "You're taller than average, though, right?"

"An American serviceman father," he said. "From Kansas. Anyway, Thom Goodfeather is too. Filipino."

I scratched my head. "I thought he was a Native American, an Indian."

"He works hard to make you think that, but he's Filipino."

"Why would he do that?"

"There's a pretty big mafia," Tom said. "I think he vanished from them maybe."

"The Filipino mafia?" I said. I must be hallucinating, I thought.

"You can drown a person in a bathtub," he said hurriedly.

"No kidding," I said, giving him a sideways look. "Drowned in the tub?" He ignored my sarcasm.

"It's a Filipino technique."

"I didn't know Filipinos were into large tubs," I said. I didn't know they had a mafia either. "What does this have to do with anything?"

"Cars and tubs, it's how they kill people. Two things have happened with cars, already," he said. "I can't stay here. I won't. I just wanted you to know, to be careful." He kissed me on both cheeks.

"Are you telling me not to take a bath?" I asked, bewildered.

"Take care," he said. "Don't get involved in this, Dallas. The mafia isn't forgiving."

"Do you think Richard was rubbed out by the Filipino mafia?" I asked.

"Cars," he said. "It's one of their trademarks."

"What about the police?" I asked.

I saw a taxi pull up in the ER drive.

He turned to me and flashed his semi-famous smile. "I'm Filipino. I'm not worried about the police. You be safe."

"You too," I said like a robot. He got in the taxi and took off. It was 4:30 on Friday morning.

Tobin, Thom, and Kenneth had talked to the police. It looked like a hit-and-run. When it had happened was anyone's guess. Sometime after lunch, but before four. I shook my head again—I couldn't believe we were shooting fashion while Dieta was very nearly bleeding to death not fifty feet away.

Fifty feet above us, but still . . .

Why had she been up there anyway?

Nothing made sense to my wasted brain. The door opened and a nurse crossed the hallway rapidly, deliberately not looking at me. I dropped my gaze back to my black and venom green Nike Prestos.

My cell phone rang. "Dallas," I said.

"How is she?"

"I don't know. They've been in there a long time."

"How's Freddie?"

His long arms draped off the chairs, and his blue-streaked hair matched the carpet. He was gone to the world. "Drooling, but at least there's no ABBA."

"What happened? I miss one day of the shoot and . . ." Darcy sniffled. "Bad things always happen in threes."

"Don't start, Darcy," I said softly.

"I never would have thought Dieta, Dieta . . ." she sighed, then blew her nose. "We're taking today off."

"I should damn-well hope so."

"Do you need to talk about it? What did you see?"

I rubbed a hand over my face. The visuals were there; the question was, did I want to relive that moment again? "I saw a brown patch, a nailshead pattern—"

"She was wearing that?"

I thought about it a moment. "Yeah, it was Tobin's jacket. Maybe she got cold and he loaned it to her or something—"

"So you saw the print—"

"Right," I said. "I'd been looking for the gray silk suit anyway."

"Yeah, you called me. Where was it?"

I shrugged. "Still missing."

"Damn," Darcy said. "So go on."

"I ran toward the jacket, saw Dieta's hair beneath a hat, and screamed for an ambulance. Esmerelda told me she was still alive."

"Was there . . . blood anywhere?"

"Everywhere. Her hair was . . . Oh God." I swallowed the bile in my mouth. "I heard Stephen shout that the ambulance was on its way, then I went to the other side and . . ." My voice faltered. "Then I realized . . . she must have slid on her . . . face."

Dieta had been hit by a speeding car—knocked like a rag doll into the air to land in the grass. I couldn't help but recall the squeal of tires I'd heard almost two hours earlier. She couldn't have been there that long, I thought to myself. Could she?

Darcy sighed. "I can't believe they want to continue shooting, I mean, after today."

"It's sick, but it's business," I said.

"They've gone time and a half on everyone's day rate," Darcy said. "That's how sick it is. Tobin said we should hang around for the police again, so we might as well work. Do they think—Dieta will, you know, make it?"

Highly unlikely is what they'd told me, but I didn't want to even voice that aloud. "You're Catholic. Pray. Now's the time."

"This shoot is totally hexed," she said, and I heard her tears start again.

"Hang on," I said, standing as the doctor left the surgery. "No, forget it. I'll call you back."

"Are you waiting for news on Dieta Andersen?" the doc asked. Freddie sprang up and hurried to my side.

"Yes, I'm a colleague."

"She survived surgery, but it's going to be touch and go for several more days. She's not out of the woods yet."

"What happened, can you tell?" Freddie asked.

The doc looked away. "I need to talk to the police first, but it appears that a vehicle brushed against her, and propelled her a fair distance."

"Can you tell how fast it was going? How far she went? What kind of car it was?"

"As I said, I need to talk to the police. But we did find something interesting," she said, fishing in her bloodstained coat—*don't think about whose blood it is, Dallas.* "This. The victim was holding it."

I looked at a three-quarter inch thick mother-of-pearl button with a few strands of gray silk thread . . . and bloodstains. Freddie peered over my shoulder.

"Does it make any sense to you?" he asked.

I nodded. "It's from a gray silk suit." A still-missing gray silk suit.

"Do you know why she'd have it?" the doctor said.

I shook my head. "No, I don't." Or where the rest of it had gone.

"Well, you would do best to go home, get some rest, and stay in touch via phone with the hospital. You can't do anything," she said, laying a hand on my arm and smiling calmly at Freddie. "I'll be real honest though: it doesn't look good for your colleague. If she has any family, they should be contacted right away. I need the button."

"What?" I said.

"The button, I should give it to the police."

"Of course," I said, and handed it back.

I nodded again, went through rote sentences of thanks and farewell and wandered outside. The air was bracing and cool, wet-feeling without being slimy. The hospital wasn't all that big, and it was fairly quiet at this hour of the morning.

"Too late for drunk driving and too early for fender benders," Freddie said, echoing my thoughts. "Lean back and close your eyes," he said, starting the Jeep. "You're flying Air Freddie now." He backed up, then jerked to a halt. I'd already fallen asleep and bolted awake.

"We forgot Tom Fly!"

"No. He left."

"A taxi from here to Salish?" Freddie asked, horrified.

I was falling asleep again already. "The airport," I muttered.

I got in. I made my report to Tobin and the crew. I fell into bed. I slept.

"*I Believe in Angels*" by ABBA floated in through paper-thin walls. I woke up, completely alert, senses alive. I heard the low rush of the river outside. My brain was suddenly crystal clear.

Who else had a Porsche Boxster? *Tobin.* In fact, Kim had thought Richard's car was Tobin's. Dieta had been hit while wearing Tobin's jacket. She'd even had on a hat. It had nothing to do with a talented male model, or a vivacious Dutch producer; Tobin who had been in the brown nailshead jacket—he was the target.

Did Thom Goodfeather stand a chance of inheriting the company? Or Kim? Were Tobin and Kim really a couple? Was the company in financial trouble?

Blood pounded in my ears. The clock glowed 2:35. I

called Thompson—and of course, left a message. There was no change in Dieta's condition at the hospital, but she had survived twenty-four hours. They thought that was a good sign.

I dressed in record time and headed for the media room.

By three o'clock I was on the Internet. "What are you looking for?" Darcy asked after she poked her head in. "The lodge just boxed up Tom Fly's stuff to ship to him. I can't believe he just walked out." She wasn't allowed to smoke in here and she was twitchy. "Let's go to Bluefly dot com and see what they have on sale." She sat down beside me. "Dieta hasn't changed."

"Yeah, I know," I said. "I'm praying."

"Me too. How about Sephora?"

The snow had turned into cold rain in this much lower altitude, so we were all trapped inside. "You're a makeup artist," I said, finding my favorite search engine. "Why would you go to a makeup site?"

"It's not just what I do," she said, "I'm a total junkie. When I'm stressed out, makeup makes me feel better."

I got up and closed the door, giving the two of us privacy. "Someone is trying to kill Tobin," I said.

"What?" her eyes bugged out. "What do you mean?"

"The Porsche, the jacket Dieta was wearing—"

"Holy Jesus," she said, then clapped a hand over her mouth. "You're right."

"I think I need to find out who has something to gain," I said. "I mean, is it Kim or Thom Goodfeather who gets the business?"

"They're just starting out, so there can't be much to get," she said as she pushed me out of the computer chair. "But I can find out for sure," she said, typing a quick e-mail. "My boyfriend is a cop."

"Your boyfriend?" I said, eyeballing her "Pimpercrombie & Bitch" T-shirt. "A cop? Aren't you married?"

"Widowed," she said, typing furiously. "Don't say anything. My boyfriend is one of Jersey City's finest."

"Oh." I thought for a second. "Is Jersey City in Jersey?"

"Of course, what did you expect, Connecticut?" Her cell phone rang and she spoke in low, lover's tones, then smiled and closed her phone. "He's on the case."

"What did you tell him?"

"Find out where Tobin Charles gets its money, and who is the beneficiary if one of the partners dies."

"He can do that from New Jersey?"

"You would be amazed at what he can do from New Jersey," she said, with a bad girl's laugh. Definitely opposites in this attraction, I thought. "Since he's doing that, let's go drown our sorrows," she said. "Or a massage?"

"You go ahead," I said, logging off. "I'll catch up in a few. I have one more thing to do."

She shrugged and left. I went upstairs, paused outside my door, then went inside. I heard nothing next to me. From my patio I could see the river, and next to me Kim's patio. I walked into the hallway, knocked on the door and waited.

Nothing. I didn't know where she was, but she wasn't in her room.

I called the spa from my cell phone. "This is Irma Sliebensen," I said in my best fake-Swedish accent. "I just wanted to know if Kim Charles was already there?"

"Ms. Charles went in for a stone massage ten minutes ago," the attendant said. "Shall I tell her you are waiting, or have called?"

"No," I said. "I'm running late. Don't bother her."

"Certainly," the helpful person said, and wished me a good day.

I flipped through the weighty guest handbook. Stone massages were an hour long. I tied on my Prestos, tucked a pen light in my pocket, slipped on some plastic gloves from my kit and went out to my balcony. No one was around; no windows that looked at mine were open. I crawled up on my railing and held on to the wall, stretched as far as I could, and got a foot on her slippery railing.

Thank God I was only on the second floor. I jumped and landed. Her patio door wasn't locked, so I slid it open and stepped inside.

The smell of flowers was almost overpowering. White and yellow flowers; lilies, hydrangeas, jonquils, and daffodils, decorated the room. Zebra-patterned candles were scattered on the nightstands and tables, and the pillowcases were satin—kinder to one's hair than anything else—with brightly embroidered pashminas draped over the bed and chair.

In the little bar area, a box filled with sealed envelopes, presumably Kim's protein powder, a water-cooler-steamer dispenser, and stacks of bottles of San Pellegrino, left only enough space for a shiny portable retro-style blender.

What was I looking for? Ten minutes' search proved she had taken her purse, with her phone, daytimer, and everything else. The bathtub's edge was littered with products, both those supplied by the hotel and a sampling of high-quality stuff Kim had brought. I looked in the closet, her suitcase, the cabinets, and found nothing.

A quick glance at my watch showed me I was doing fine on time. Where else to look? Maybe I was completely wrong, but my instincts were jumping up and down. Kim knew what was going on. I froze when I heard footsteps at the door. I raced to the patio and flattened myself against the wall.

There were groups of kids walking along the river's edge in brightly colored raingear. No way I could avoid them seeing me jump onto my patio. Please, don't come out here, I prayed. Quietly. The door slammed and I counted to fifty; was she in the room or out?

I peeked around the edge and saw no one. The window that separated the Whirlpool spa from the bedroom was open, so I could see the complete room. No one was in there.

Another bunch of white blossoms had been delivered. Delicate bells of Lily of the Valley in a narrow, clear vase. Had room service brought them? Who else had a key card?

"Mommy!" a kid screeched outside. I glanced out and saw a horde of children around one who had fallen on the ground. Twenty people suddenly grouped at the base of the window. I was in the center of the room when I heard the sound of a key card in the door. I ripped off my gloves and grabbed the vase.

"Dallas? What the hell are you doing in here?" Kim asked, as she stepped inside. "Why wasn't my door locked?"

"Room service," I said. "They uh, brought these to me by accident. Uh, and I, uh, started to rearrange them before I realized they were for you. So I, um, called housekeeping and they let me in."

"I hate those things," she groaned, dropping her purse on the floor. "Why Tobin keeps sending them to me, I just don't know."

"I thought you liked them," I said.

"I hate them. They're grim. Funereal." She leaned against the door, trim and lean in gym clothes, her eyes closed.

"Have you told him you don't like them?"

She gave me a woman-to-woman look. "Once I told my boyfriend—a well-connected, up-and-coming politician, that I hated the roses he gave to me. He bought them at the grocery store and they were frozen. They'd died as buds. It was to encourage him to spend a few dollars more and get fresh flowers, from a florist."

"He never gave you flowers again," I guessed.

"Never."

"Ah. Well. I see your point." Though—Kim and Tobin had some issues. I wasn't even going to think about it. I should definitely leave out the front door. And not take her flowers with me.

"Damn," she said. "Dieta. It's so unreal that I can't remember it happened."

"I know what you mean," I said.

"It was meant for me," she said, moving to the bar, wiping her nose. Her skin was still splotchy.

I set down the vase. "What are you talking about?"

She got chilled water from the dispenser, poured it in the blender, then ripped open a pouch of powder and dumped it on top. In seconds of whirring, it turned brown, deceptively chocolate.

"Kim, do you think someone is trying to—"

She started crying, braced against the counter, her head down.

"Come sit down," I said, motioning her to the sofa her room had instead of a rocking chair. She followed me, sobbing.

"He hates me. The car—he said an exotic Asian beauty should have a sports car. And at the shoot . . . I'd just spoken to Dieta, then walked back down to the shot. I went over the highway so I wouldn't interrupt Kenneth."

I had seen her leaning against the overpass. There wasn't any other way she could have gotten there, besides walking through the shot—and she hadn't.

"I think someone was supposed to get me, but got Deita instead."

What had she been wearing? This was brain Twister. "Have you told the police?"

"Dallas," she said, and looked at me. Her makeup was streaked and the light wasn't forgiving. "I think I'm . . . I'm . . . losing my mind. I fly into these rages and . . . why would the police believe me? I'm not in control of myself. I don't dare eat. I think he's trying to kill me."

She started to cry again. "I'm so scared . . . there's no one I can trust."

Color me blown-away.

"Why . . . do you think it's Tobin?"

"Who else would want me dead?" she asked.

Oh lady, that's a long list.

"He'll get the business. He can design if I'm not there. He's always wanted to."

I sat back; her words were penetrating. "He killed Richard?"

She nodded. "I think so. He thought it was me in the car."

"How could he have hit Dieta?"

"Paid someone, I'm sure. He would want to have an alibi when . . . I was hit," she whimpered. "Since it was supposed to be . . . me–e–e–e."

I handed her some Kleenex; her nose was really running. "Do you have any proof?" I asked.

She stood up and walked over to the chocolate protein shake. "The police wrote off Richard's death to the mafia, and Dieta . . . that's just a hit and run. Happens all the time." She swigged her protein drink, then set the blender down. "I'm going to get in the shower."

"Okay," I said, moving toward the bar to rinse out the blender cup.

"Don't worry with that," Kim said. "Some little maid will be by to wash it."

"I'm standing right here," I said.

"Whatever," she sighed, and went into the bedroom. She turned on the fan and I heard her close the window. I waited until the shower sounds were inconsistent—a human body moving beneath the water—and grabbed her cell phone from her purse.

Menu.

Calls.

Log.

Outgoing.

Thursday. 3:35 P.M.

The Seattle number came up and I memorized it before I dropped the phone back in her bag. As I opened the door, I looked back. This was my last chance at her room. She turned off the shower and I closed the door behind me. Quietly.

My head was spinning.

It was driving me crazy. Where the hell was that gray silk suit? I grabbed my Jeep and headed north. I couldn't believe forty-eight hours ago I was happily pressing—and now Dieta was in the hospital. They still didn't know anything.

As I parked at Deception Falls, I noticed mine was the only vehicle. It was colder today. I zipped up my coat and stepped outside. I could see why so many fairy tales and horror stories started in woods. The menace of them was tangible to me right now. "Focus," I muttered to myself, as I looked more closely at the ground around where Dieta had been found.

I walked the paths, looked in the shallows, among the rocks, by the bridge . . . the forest had consumed the gray silk suit, and hadn't left a thread of evidence. I wandered in and out of the trees, maybe the wind had carried it . . . but there was nothing.

And I didn't see it with Dieta, when we'd discovered her. Yet she'd had the button. Why?

Distinguishing footprints was impossible. There had been all of us, two EMT guys, two local cops, a few tourists—I gave up. As I was trudging back to my car, I heard another vehicle approach. I recognized Thompson's car. He pulled to the side of the road and got out. I waited.

"Good afternoon," he said. He was as letter perfect as ever. If he ever got money, he could be dangerous.

"Hey."

"Why are you here, it's about to rain," he said, opening his umbrella.

"A friend of mine was struck here yesterday," I said. "She's in the hospital."

"I know that," he said. "The doctor called us, I thought I'd check it out. It's a gray suit that's missing, I heard?"

I nodded.

"You looked around?"

I gestured at the wealth of nature. "I wish you luck. Please, call me if you find it."

"What happens if I don't?"

I smiled. "I get a ten-thousand-dollar deduction on this job."

He walked me to my car and I waved as I drove away. It was starting to rain in earnest. I cranked up the radio and hit seventy. *Please, let him find it.*

Back to my room. No change in Dieta at the hospital, nothing from the police, nothing new at all. Darcy wasn't in the bar and everyone else I ran into was wrapped in his own world.

I knocked on Darcy's door and she opened it, a mask on her face, her hair in foil, her hands wrapped in plastic, and her toes in drying position.

"Sorry," I said. "I thought you were going to be drinking."

"It's detox," she said. "I thought I'd try a positive approach first. I'm pretending it's one of those places where life is so stress-free I don't need a cigarette every five minutes."

I flopped down on her mammoth bed. "I've never been to one of those places," I said.

"You should try them," she said. "There's one just downstairs."

I picked up her room's teddy bear. He had a vest and bow tie. Mine was a country bear, with a cowboy hat.

"What do you think of our home away from home?" she asked, gesturing to the room. "Nice for a prison, huh?"

"How long are we here for?" I asked. There was a knock on the door. I glanced at her, then went to answer it.

"Dinnertime," Wes said. "You two coming?"

"Did I eat today?" I asked myself.

"It's supposed to be awsome," he said. "Saturday night fills up quick."

Darcy appeared at my elbow, her hair wet but clean, the mask gone, her toes in sandals. "I'm game," she said. "There's a dress code, though, right?"

We agreed to meet in fifteen minutes—dressed. Everyone else seemed to be on the same schedule.

The meal was divine. A delicate Asian salad or flavorful fresh herb and potato salad; marinated vegetable tart; grilled swordfish with some sort of sauce, or cheese-stuffed chicken with couscous. Fresh crescent rolls, sourdough bread or Parkerhouse rolls; and for dessert, crème fraiche with berries, fresh pear-and-apple torte or chocolate mousse. We ate until movement was impossible for us.

"Replete," Kenneth said.

"Gorged," Stephen said.

"They're gonna kill me for Thanksgiving," Freddie said.

"Aren't we going to have a cheese course?" Irma said. She was apparently fully recovered from her debilitating migraine episode.

"That's just not right," Darcy said. "When the model eats more than the photographer."

"I'm a Viking," she said. As though it were an explanation.

Wes had eaten hardly anything—he was more calorie-conscious than anyone. The waiters hovered about.

"I think they have this table reserved for the second seating," I said.

"Attic Bar?" George asked.

One by one, we begged off and returned to our own rooms. I sketched for a while, wondering about Kim's accusation of Tobin. Dieta was the same at the hospital. Thompson was probably on a date—he hadn't called.

On the possibility that I was losing my mind, I decided to

go look at the merch room we were keeping at the Salish Lodge. Really, it was just an extra storeroom where we'd wheeled the rolling racks. The desk attendant let me in, and I locked the door behind me and looked through the plastic bags of suits. I counted browns and blues, blacks and grays—and counted again. I unzipped the hanging bags and looked at them. The gray silk was back. "Impossible!" I shouted. "Thank God."

"Where have you been?" I asked it. "I bet you need a new button now." My eyes teared up at the thought of when I'd last seen the mother-of-pearl button, stained with Dieta's blood. I pulled it out of the bag and opened the jacket; spares were kept inside. "Was it the left or right that lost a button?" I muttered. The right side had three buttons; so did the left.

I must have miscounted. I counted again: three and three. *Was* this the gray silk? I checked the tag—the number matched. I looked inside at the spares. Whoever had replaced it had obviously resewn it.

They were there.

Stumped, I leaned against the door and stared at the suit.

"Am I going crazy?" I asked it.

I dug out the loupe I carry in my backpack and looked at the buttons. It didn't take long to find the replaced one. It had been done well, but not with the same weight silk thread. Okay, someone had found it, and . . . the button was the one I'd seen at the hospital. I'd swear it.

My hands were shaking now.

I took the jacket off and looked at the inside to see if it was the same suit. "I'll be damned," I said. The careful slow machine stitching that I'd seen in twenty-four suits had been replaced by nice, neat, orderly handstitching.

I sat down on the floor and turned the suit inside out, checking every seam, every twist of binding . . . the suit had been taken apart. Then restitched. It had lost a button, then it had been resewn. In a rush I hung and bagged the suit, then slammed out of the room.

The meal I'd had was sitting in my stomach; my brain was on a roller-coaster. I needed to calm down, to stop thinking. Tomorrow was work. The desert shot. Call at 6 A.M. In my room I threw on some tights and my Prestos and closed my door behind me. I started walking, then I ran a little too, over the covered bridge, down the main street of the town. To my right remnants of a defunct train hulked in the darkness. I jogged past the new depot that advertises tourist rail trips. A gas station, grocery store, all-purpose deli and coffee shop were dark. The faint glow of rhododendron blossoms was visible against the dark foliage.

There weren't many lights on this road. It was haunting. The music from *Twin Peaks* was in my head again. Could Kim be right? Was Tobin trying to kill her? Pretty stupid way to do it. Better to catch her on her early run.

I turned around and realized that the Salish Lodge, much to my dismay, was on a hill. I sprinted upward, fueled by fear. By the time I reached the hotel's front patio I was hot and sticky. I did some wall stretches; I was safe. It was okay.

My imagination needed a leash. Surely I was wrong about the suit. But I know my merch, I knew it had been tampered with. Why reconstruct a ten thousand dollar suit?

"If it ain't Miz Christi?" a soft, slightly Southern voice said from the darkness. A whiskey-laced voice that made me suddenly aware of having breasts and soft lips, of sweat dripping down on my back and the stretch of muscle in the backs of my legs. "My prayers have finally been answered," my phantom said. "Though you don't look like you want that drink tonight, either. Don't you know it's dangerous to be out so late?"

"Or early," I said. Was he mafia? A hit and run driver? A mad tailor?

"Never know who you might meet." His voice was still sinful. I watched the glow of his cigarette butt. He was sitting at an outside table, the fragrance of hanging flowers mingling with the tang of tobacco.

"I better go in," I said.

"You better."

He leaned foward and the light fell on his hair—black ringlets—and his eyes, dark and heavily lashed. His hand shielded his mouth, and I saw that the nails were long and oval. Not manicured, which I find gross in a man, but cared for. His other hand, lying on the table, had neatly trimmed nails.

"Guitar?" I guessed. My voice sounded strange to me.

He grinnned, just a little, and though I couldn't see his smile I saw the twitch of his lips. "You a music fan?"

"Yeah, of course," I said. "What do you play?"

"Whatever you want to hear."

"That leaves a lot of room for interpretation."

He stabbed out his cigarette and for the first time I saw him. He wasn't pretty—he looked a lot like Edward James Olmos, the guy who had been the head honcho on *Miami Vice*—but he was sexy as hell. I was sweating and it had nothing to do with my run.

"If you don't drink alcohol, how about some coffee?" He crossed his feet—black alligator cowboy boots. I fell in love.

"It's almost two A.M."

"I couldn't be happier," he said.

Happy. *Dieta*. I looked away, embarrassed at how quickly I'd forgotten she was alone, in the hospital.

"Hey," he said softly, leaning out to catch my gaze. "It's okay. I'm just a guy sittin' here. You won't hurt my feelings if you don't want to stay. You're probably tired after getting all lathered up out there. Go get some sleep, baby."

I shook my head. "I don't want to sleep."

He pushed out the chair with his foot. "Then hell, baby, sit down." He looked at me again: black eyes, hard face and more compassion than I'd ever seen on the countenance of a beautiful man—almost like he knew. "Can I do anything? Bring a smile to that pretty face?"

"Where's your guitar?" I asked, looking at him again. He grinned a little, lit a new cigarette and reached behind him to retrieve a beautiful amber-colored acoustic guitar.

"Spanish," I whispered. "Play me Spanish guitar."

He plucked the strings and I leaned back and stared at the starry sky. It was poignant; Falla's mournful music. I slouched down in the chair and watched his fingers on the strings. He used his nails instead of a pick. Sometimes he played so furiously that his hand was just a blur of white motion.

He stopped in a rush, and bent his head to light another cigarette. The sky was getting brighter. Call at 6 A.M.

"Get some sleep, baby," he said, not looking up. Just a mass of black curls. "I'll see you around."

Chapter Twelve

I t was a silent RV. We were riding all together—the shoot was on some property that only Esmerelda and the photographer's two Jeeps had permits for. I got on last; I'd just called the hospital.

"Is she going to be all right?" Irma asked.

"Every day is better," I said. Which is word for word the non-answer I'd gotten from the doctor.

I glared at Darcy—not a word about deaths coming in threes.

"I will think good thoughts to her," Irma said.

George had on earphones and electronic bings and bips came from his seat. Wes was stretched out in the back. Stephen, Nasmo and Kenneth were driving behind us with our equipment. I turned the tiny figure Dieta had given me—"A fetish besides your one for shoes," she'd said—over and over in my hand. How could we have missed hearing the accident?

I mean, we heard it, but we didn't hear its *significance*. How did we miss that?

God, please let her be okay, I said. I knew from Kreg that internal injuries were the deadliest. *Please, not Dieta. She de-*

serves so much. The fetish was a minuscule bear made of gypsum, with a pink shale fish in its mouth. "Successful," she'd said. "And he's big, he'll defend you. He'll help you go after what you want. Rooarr!" she'd growled like a bear.

Kim thought the hit and run had been meant for her?

Tobin poisoning her? Was she trying to throw off suspicion?

The sun was starting as a bright line on the eastern horizon. Darcy snored across from me, sitting cross-legged and wrapped in her ratty pashmina like a swami. I needed to ask her if she'd heard from her boyfriend. Freddie had been staring at the same photo in *Allure* for at least ten minutes.

The gloom was contagious and the RV ate miles and miles while I watched the signs pass. Cle Ellum. Ellensburg. Yakima.

"We're going home for you, Esmerelda?" I asked.

She smiled, her dreamcatcher earrings swinging as she turned to me. "We're stopping a little east of the town. The government owns property around there. Watch what happens once we get through this valley," she said.

The mountains had given away to a Shangri-La plain that was brilliant green, laced with silver, rushing streams. I glimpsed a road into the town, and pastures with glossy-coated horses, then we were climbing again.

Cypress windbreaks protected the hilltop houses and barns, with orchards in front and back. We went downhill and around a bend. We were in a different world.

"Whoa," I said.

Freddie stuck his head over my shoulder. "Are we still in Washington?"

Desert, miles of brownish gold dirt, dotted with cactus and shrub, edged with multi-colored mesas, fell before us. I turned in my seat. "An hour ago we could see snow," I said.

"Look over there," she said and pointed. "See that mountain?"

A white peak poked through the haze.

"And over there?"

We turned southwest, and saw another peak.

"And if you turn almost completely—yes! It's out today."

Freddie and I craned our necks. "That's PhotoShop," Freddie said. "You can't fool me."

I'd seen pictures of Rainier—hell, I'd been in Washington for a little more than a week. I'd have to have been blind not to. "That's amazing. It looks like a postcard, pasted on the horizon."

"Can you see why I love this place?" Esmerelda enthused. "It's got everything. Rivers, ocean, city, country, mountains, beach—"

"Any beach where you dare not go nude for fear of freezing your gents off, is not my idea of a beach," Freddie said. "It's beautiful here, but until a Barney's opens, I just can't relocate."

"City boy," she said. "You all might want to start shaking," she called to the snoring passengers. "We're almost there."

We exited the freeway and drove past an open gate that said "U.S. Military Reservation: Authorized Officials Only"— Freddie and I raised eyebrows at each other—and up to a guard gate.

"Good morning," Esmerelda said.

The guard grunted, looked at her paperwork, and opened another gate.

"MUNITIONS TESTING," was just one of the signs.

Esmerelda stopped the RV. "Welcome to the desert!" She turned off the engine, and we walked down the steps and outside, in various stages of waking up. The air was sharp; we could still see our breaths. The sun cast a glow on the sand that surrounded us.

"You're going to wish you wore shorts," she said, getting

off the RV and setting up a table and coffee carafe, boxes of bagels, donuts and croissants. "It'll be in the eighties today."

"I thought I was going to be in the woods and mountains when I packed," I said. "I didn't bring shorts."

"That's okay," Freddie said. "Just walk around in your undies."

I gave him a weird look. "You're gay."

"Doesn't mean I don't appreciate a pretty pair of legs."

Wes had discovered the food and was picking at a bagel. Irma was fully engrossed in slathering her croissant with butter. Darcy had poured some coffee and was enjoying her morning cigarette, her eyes narrowed against the sun.

I knelt down and opened my purse. Sunscreen, lipscreen and sunglasses. I'm from Texas—I'd take this stuff to the North Pole. By the time I'd finished slathering on my various forms of protection and donning my trusty Dallas Stars cap, the two Jeeps were pulling up.

Tobin, Kim and Thom were behind them in a third Jeep.

In five minutes, we were sitting down at a long table underneath a tent and preparing to have a breakfast of eggs cooked to order, sausage and breakfast breads. The best part was the cappuccino frother someone brought.

Sated, we sat back. Kim stood up. As usual, she hadn't eaten anything. She looked like hell—apparently she hadn't slept last night. "The news from the hospital is okay. Dieta hasn't worsened." She pressed her lips together in an effort to keep from crying. "She hasn't improved either. I'm so sorry," she said, then she sat down.

Tobin stood up. "Today's shoot is going to be hard, we realize that. However, we are all professionals. We'll shoot Polaroids in an hour. Dallas, meet me in the RV."

How many people had been talked to by the cops and told not to tell, I wondered. Why should I think I was special? Should I say something to Tobin? Was he the bad guy or the good guy? Poison your wife, lately? What if he was innocent?

Work, I thought.

Everyone scattered. We were professionals. We did this for a living and we were very, very good at it. The mood was subdued, but we would get good film today. Just hang on, I thought to Dieta. Just be okay.

I separated my plastic and paper into the appropriate garbage bags, and took the steps into the RV in one jump.

"How are you?" Tobin asked me as he searched my eyes.

"I'm a professional," I said. Was he scared? Guilty? *Just work, Dallas.*

"Glad to hear it. Okay, here's the feel. I want that suit and that suit," he said, pointing to some plastic-wrapped clothes I'd never seen before.

I looked at the tear sheets. "I didn't know you made safari clothes."

He grinned. "No one else makes them, and more Americans take desert treks and safaris than ever before. I've got the market cornered."

Safari, slash combat, slash military had been a very hot look this spring. I'd bought Moschino's jungle camo skirt, but for the cut more than the pattern. "I'll do it," I said, plugging in my iron and steamer. "What about Irma?"

"Kim will be in," he said. "She had an idea last night, and worked on it."

Was that why she looked so bad? Not from worry, but from work? She was schizo anyway—why did I care? "Great." She was scared, too.

Focus.

He left and I started on the linen shirts and khaki linen pants with detailed pockets and CoolMax lining. I'd stripped off two layers by the time Kim came in. "Looks excellent," she said, touching the sleeve of one of the shirts. "I've never seen linen look so sharp. What's your secret? Do you starch it to death?"

Death.

No, I thought.

"Water and weight," I said. "I have the heaviest iron of anyone I know."

She looked at it. "It's ancient."

"It was my grandmother's, back in the days when cotton sheets were pressed with liquid starch." When servants did that kind of work.

"No wonder your arms are so well-cut," she said, hefting the 20-pound thing. "This is a workout by itself."

I chuckled politely. "What's Irma wearing?"

Kim sat down and leaned forward. She almost looked like a teenager, in sunglasses, her hair in a ponytail through a baseball cap. She wore running tights and a jacket today—no stilettos or leather. She was truly beautiful when she smiled. "The mermaid gown inspired me," she said. "I must apologize. I was so mad, but not at you. That gown had been designed for Yvette, the model we were supposed to have."

"Of course, right."

"Then Tobin . . . well, that's water under the proverbial bridge. What you did is dress the girl for the picture, instead of making the picture for the dress. As Tobin said, it's not about the dress in this, it's about the feel. So I did something."

I resisted looking at my watch, but time was flying and the sun wasn't going to wait for us. "A dress? May I see it?"

She stepped into the living area and brought back a plastic bag filled with tea-dyed linen.

"Uh, does it need to be pressed?"

"No, this outfit—" She pressed the button at her waist and I saw she was wearing her headset. "I'll be right there." She clicked it off. "Darcy is doing Irma's makeup. I'll get Irma dressed. I know time is racing and you have a lot of linen suits to deal with. I just wanted you to see the concept."

"I, uh, can't wait to see Irma in it," I said. "See you on set in"—I looked at my watch—"twenty minutes."

Nasmo dropped off a suitcase after she left. "New accessories."

I'd finished unpacking boots and belts when Wes, or rather, Lawerence of Arabia, walked in. "That's a serious tan," I said. "What's going on out there?"

He turned down the Dixie Chicks—they weren't loud, but combined with the rumble of the RV it was deafening. "Hear that? It's a camel."

I switched the button on the steamer with my toe and lifted the curtain on the window. "There are four of them!" I'd never seen real camels. I'd never wanted to, either.

"Yup," he said.

"Goats, too."

"The sheep are grazing out back," he said, leaning across my back. "Behind the animal wrangler's trailer."

"On what?"

He shrugged. "Dirt? Those scrubby plants?"

"I guess."

"What do you get when you call four bullfighters in quicksand?"

I raised my eyebrows.

"Quattro Sinko."

"That's nice," I said. "Let's get moving."

Somewhere, outside, the lyrics of ABBA floated in. "*Money, money, money—*" The day was gaining momentum.

"I must be in Egypt," I said when I arrived on the set. "This is incredible." A tent, luxuriously appointed with pillows and rugs, brass and copper pots, even incense, was pitched with the camels and the desert in the background.

A brilliantly colored seven-foot-tall Egyptian coffin stood in the center of the wall.

"Look at this," Darcy said. "You won't believe it." She opened the lid like an armoire door and the creature inside opened her eyes. Slate gray, in a Nordic face.

"Ohmigod! This is amazing!"

"You like?" Irma said from within her wrappings. Kim had constructed a bodysuit, and covered it in strategically draped linen bandages. The outfit showed Irma's shape, the tautness of her gold-dusted belly, but it smothered her breasts, which gave her a completely different look. Darcy had outdone herself cosmetically. I didn't even begin to guess all she'd done. "You look . . . incredible."

"It's even better once they get the lights," Darcy said. "Her face is dusted in gold, too."

"Let's go," Kenneth called.

Wes was in khaki and white linen, the part of the archaeologist. The shot, the shot we had all waited for, was when he stared out past the camera, and the "mummy," glittering and exquisite, looked at him from her upright coffin with unquenched desire.

I knew Kenneth had caught it on film.

I smiled to myself. This was why I was a stylist; for a fleeting moment I made fantasy appear real. And let's face it, there's way too much reality in this world.

There were sillier pictures, too: Irma with crossed eyes, or when she looked side to side, like those black and white cat clocks. Wes playing Gene Simmons, Wes inside the coffin and Irma jumping rope . . . if only Dieta were here.

Then the boys were in the act. Linen suits, riding boots, camels, turbans and a vest that got eaten right off George— by a goat.

Kim just laughed and we broke for lunch. The caterers

hadn't arrived yet, but it was too hot, too bright to shoot. "We're also waiting for the helicopter," Kim said. "So rest until then." She smiled brightly and pranced off.

"She's schizo," Darcy said.

"Bi-polar is the term," Freddie said. "Bi-polar clothing taste too, apparently."

"Those little tights are still Prada," she said. "I'm impressed she's not stumbling around out here in a pair of Manolos." She lit a cigarette and leaned back with a sigh that was almost indecent.

Wes had stripped to fitted boxers and tank and was playing hacky sac with George, Nasmo, Esmerelda, and the local runner. I excused myself, picked up my phone and walked away from the camp.

"I'm calling to check on Dieta Andersen?"

"Just a moment. Which room please?"

"Maybe ICU, or perhaps she's been moved?" I said. ABBA, but this time on the hospital's Muzak, floated into the desert. I knew the lyrics after this past week: *"S.O.S. The love you gave me—nothing else can save me—"*

"She's still in ICU, ma'am."

"Is her doctor there?"

"I'm sorry. The doctor is in surgery now. Can anyone else help you?"

"Does anyone else know anything?"

"The police were here, you might call them."

"Great. Which police?"

She was quiet for a moment. "I don't know. Let me see if I have a card."

She was gone a moment more. "Detective Thompson, ma'am," she said in a completely different tone.

"Thank you." I hung up.

I stared at the phone, thought about redialing, but didn't.

A streak of dust was headed our way. Lunch, I assumed.
I trudged back to camp.

"It's a fiesta!" Freddie said as he walked past me, a rose
in his teeth. The tables in the mess tent were covered with
Mexican blankets, baskets of chips were set out in som-
breros. "How's the guac?" I asked Wes, who was going to
sweat his tan off if he wasn't careful.

"Onions," he said.

Kenneth walked in behind me. "Esmerelda claims they
have the best salsa in the world. I'm here to test it, though
I suppose I should let you go first, Ms. Cut-'n'-Shoot."

"That was a pretty inclusive list of Texas towns," I said
as I dipped my chip.

"Drum roll," Darcy called. "The professional is tast-
ing."

The CD paused in the first bars of "Fernando."

"Oh. My. God," I said, then got a new chip and dipped
again. "Oh Darcy, hand me one of your cigarettes. This is
amazing."

I don't know if the Mexican restaurant usually catered
for photo crews, but they watched with wide eyes as we
devoured everything in sight: tamales, enchiladas, tacos,
fajitas, migas, empanadas, beans—black and refried—
rice—yellow, and Mexican, queso, ceviche (my fave),
and . . . flan.

"I am sated," Kenneth said. "That was the best meal
I've eaten in America."

"Probably not America," George said. "The U.S."

"Yeah. They might do better Mexican food in Mexico,"
Darcy said. "It's just a guess. Though my boyfriend says
the best Italian he's ever had was in Jerusalem. How weird
is that?"

"How weird is he?" Freddie said. "The best Italian is in
New York."

"What's the difference between the black beans and the mushed-up ones?" Irma asked me.

"Fat," I said. I had half a flan left and I wanted to eat it, emotionally. It wouldn't bring Richard back from the dead, and it wouldn't heal Dieta, but it would give me such a sugar high that I wouldn't care. Bad nutritional theory, but probably why a lot of people were overweight. "The mushed-up ones are fried in fat. The black ones are cooked in broth."

"The helpers made a picnic for me, after the shot," she said. "I'll be careful which ones I eat."

"It's like anything else," Darcy said. "The fattening ones always taste better." She threw a chip at Irma. "Not like you have anything to worry about."

"I usually only eat breakfast, and lunch, then have protein shakes for dinner."

"Like Kim," Nasmo said. "Speak of the devil."

Kim walked in wearing glasses, then suddenly acted as though she were blinded by the contrast. She was being funny? She walked up to us. "Freddie. I have a challenge for you."

Freddie, who was leaning back with his hands over his belly, the first button on his CK cargo pants unbuttoned, and eyes closed, said, "Speak."

"Name This Eyebrow." She held up a book, and we all craned forward.

"He's the undefeated champion," Darcy said. "You can't win against him."

Freddie sat forward, leaned his elbows on the table and templed his fingers. "The black and white photo means nothing." He squinted at the photo. "It's the artificial arch of the 30s and 40s."

Kim held the book in both hands. She was smiling, smug, but not superior. The Nice Kim. Maybe she was losing her mind—could Tobin do that to her? How do you make someone go crazy? "I'm not going to give you any hints," she said.

"I don't need any hints," he said. "It's dark, on fair skin."

I stared at my flan. Of all desserts, it's the least evil. I'd get high enough to get through the afternoon, then crash tonight. Tonight, when hopefully I would receive the news that Dieta was going to be fine.

"It's not Claudette," he said.

I glanced at the photo.

"Not Myrna."

A moment on the lips, forever on the hips. Eating to feel better was a losing battle.

"Not . . . Norma."

We exchanged glances, those of us who were awake. The mercury had risen to about 86—a rude awakening after 50s and 60s the past few days.

"It's Drew Barrymore made up to look like a starlet."

Kim's mouth dropped. "How do you do that?"

"I'm an eyebrow genius," he said, winking at her.

She sat down beside me. "I'm challenged now. I'm going to find an eyebrow you don't know. What are the rules?"

"Must be a published picture of a famous woman. A photo, though," I said. "Models, movie stars, politicians?" I asked him.

"Some wives," he said. "Barbara older and younger, I could do. Chelsea, Hillary, Laura, and most of the Senators. I just have a hard time remembering their names. I know their states. I can keep track of them like aged Miss Americas."

We all laughed.

"While I'm trying to find a photo he can't identify," Kim said, "Tobin is off getting the chopper."

Kenneth started awake. "Chopping?"

"Helicopter," Irma said.

"The final shot will be at sundown, both sleekly attired, at dinner, with the chopper on that dune over there," she said, and pointed to an impressive striped hunk of dusty rock. "We'll start setting up about five. We're going to put some cots in here, if anyone wants to take a nap." She got up. "Or, have a piñata."

"A piñata!" Darcy cried.

"What is this?" Irma asked. "A pin-ya-tah?"

I laughed. "Sure, why not? Before or after naptime, kiddies?"

"Before! Before!"

"Dallas," Kim said, "I need you to go into Yakima and get some flowers for the shot."

As I climbed into the Jeep with Esmerelda, I saw Wes run outside for a baseball bat to beat the piñata with. I looked at my list from Kim. "Okay," I said as Esmerelda tore off toward the gate. "I need lilies."

"What kind of lilies? Aren't there a bunch of kinds?"

"She's going to hold them, so they'll probably be Calla," I said.

"Funeral flowers?" Esmerelda asked as she waved at the guy at the checkpoint.

"Yeah, I guess. How did we get permission to shoot in here?" I asked. "That's having some serious connections."

"I don't know," Esmerelda said. For some reason, I thought she was lying. We pulled on to the highway. "How are you doing, about Dieta?"

"I'm thinking good thoughts," I said, then I chuckled. "But I think this shoot is making me crazy." Just like Kim.

Esmerelda laughed. "Join the crowd!"

"No, I'm serious," I said. I told her about the suit.

Missing, found. The button. "The absolutely strangest, weirdest thing is that the stitching inside is different."

Esmerelda didn't say anything; I guess I didn't expect her to.

I stared out at the desert, not traditional sandy dunes, but mesas and scrub.

"Different from what?" she asked after a few miles. "Is there a difference in stitches?"

Poor thing, I spent the rest of the trip explaining about stitch lengths and widths, the different types of stitches and finally Tobin's stitches. "Every fifteen stitches, there's an aberration. Not on this. Every stitch is exactly perfect with the other. Someone tore up the coat. That's why I think I'm going crazy. Why would someone do that?"

We exited to Yakima.

I hadn't seen so many Spanish signs since I'd been in El Paso. Yakima was a little Mexican town, a couple hundred miles from the Canadian border. We drove through a downtown that I'd seen in the IMAX, buried beneath ash. She pulled into a large parking lot. "This is supposed to be the best wholesaler on this side of the mountains," she said.

I climbed out, stripped down to my tank, khakis, Prestos and a wide choker. Inside, I blinked and took off my hat. Kim's AmEx was in my hand, and I saw at least four different types of lilies at first glance.

"Buy some flowers?"

"Uh, yeah," I said, walking up to a window. I placed my order and watched as she bustled around. Esmerelda was talking to some stocker in the back with a goatee and beer belly. I made my first offer in the bargaining game.

The salesgirl counter-offered as she pulled out a pot of Easter lilies. To me, these were funeral.

I considered it while she got Tiger lilies and trimmed the

stamen off—the pollen would ruin clothes. I could Magic Marker the ends, if need be. I made a second offer and looked at the peonies—flowers we just didn't have in Texas. Their edges were rippled like lace and the colors were breathtaking.

The woman put on a pair of gloves and grabbed the Lilies of the Valley. She turned around to dump the water in a biohazard container, complete with a skull and cross-bones emblem.

Biohazard.

What was a biohazard? Flowers weren't dangerous.

She poured some water from the dispenser and dumped it into the vials for each of the flowers. "Be careful with this," she said. "It'll give you contact dermatitis. It's toxic, like rhododendron."

"Ohmigod," I whispered. "That's it!"

"Are you all right?" she asked, handing me the flowers.

I nodded, scrawled a signature on the receipt, and ran out into the street.

Biohazard.

The sun was moving into position when we returned, and the camp was scrambling. Irma's look had to be changed completely. Darcy had scrubbed her face before lunch—not that Irma hadn't gotten to eat—and she'd do her cosmetics again.

Freddie was playing with her hair. "I'm so tired of the ponytail," he said. "We've done it low and casual, high and sleek, messy and any height, and this year it's all about low and polished. But it's the same thing. Hair, pulled back to look like a horse's ass. I just don't understand."

I patted his shoulder. "That's why you are a genius hair designer and will come up with some new twist on a ponytail."

"Hmm . . ." he said, playing with Irma's flaxen lengths. "A twist . . . could be interesting."

I walked through to Darcy's makeup area. Wes's tan had streaked and she was matching the stripes with foundation. "How far is he?" I asked.

"'Bout ten minutes," she said. "Then he's off to Freddie."

A half-hour, then.

I knocked on the RV door and Kim opened it. "How was it?"

"I thought you wanted Calla lilies, but then I wasn't positive and I couldn't get your phone." Tobin popped up behind her. They both looked disheveled. And relaxed.

Probably not a good time to discuss his poisoning her.

"Sorry," she said. "I'm sure it's perfect, whatever it is."

We, all three of us, walked out to the Jeep. I revealed the plethora of lilies.

"Which do you want, or do you know yet?"

"I want you to look at the dress," she said.

Tobin put his arms around her waist and smiled down at her. They made a handsome couple. *Couple of psycho freaks.* "Kim finished this dress a month or two ago, and loaned it to . . . well, I don't want to name-drop," he said, looking at the blushing designer. "But you saw it at the Oscars."

Most anything that fit a starlet wasn't going to fit Irma. Not again, I thought. I don't have enough duct tape.

"It's good to see things walk down the red carpet," Kim said. "You can tell where they need modification. I did the dress in black, and it should have been white. It's hanging up in the RV."

"Okay," I said, as we walked back. All three of us. "Shoes?"

"Do you have any of those Grecian sandals?"

"Gladiator boots," I said. "For the EMP fantasy shot."

"What color are they?"

"Black with silver grommets."

"Hmm . . . Irma's a ten?"

"A full ten."

Her stomach growled. She slapped it. "Excuse me. I haven't gotten a chance to eat today."

"There's food in the tent still, I think."

"I don't process solid food well," she said. "I need to grab my cooler and drink my shake, I just haven't gotten to it."

I looked from her to Tobin. Should I warn her?

"Producing is hard work," she said.

"She's been doing Dieta's job," Tobin said.

"Don't make yourself sick," I mumbled lamely. "I'll see you on set."

"Nothing beneath this?" Wes said, looking at his bare chest.

"Aren't you glad you shave," I said.

"I wax," he said. "I'm a carpet if I don't. This is sexy?"

It was the most daring of the Tobin Charles suits. And the most expensive. "That's cashmere," I said. "The whole damn thing."

It was three-buttoned and fit better than a glove. More like a sock. Wes wiggled his hips. "It's snug."

"Too much?"

He shook his head. "Where do you wear something like this?"

The buttons were embossed, buffed gold. "Cruising for chicks?"

"Hanging out with the coolest of the cool," Darcy said. "Heya Waxahachie—"

I turned. That was a Texas town I recognized. Former home of the SuperCollider. "Yes?"

"Does she have a high-necked thing? Her hair is . . . well, you won't believe it. But a turtleneck will mess it up."

I pointed to the dress.

"It looks like a wet dishrag."

"Shut up," I hissed.

Darcy clamped her hand over her mouth. "I forgot. The winds can change."

"Kim's great today."

"She got laid," Freddie said behind her. "We were banging on that ole piñata—"

"And he was bangin' her," Darcy said.

"It'll look good on," I said, dragging the conversation back to work. "I think her hair will be safe."

Darcy and Freddie tripped out and I stepped back. "Are you going to be able to breathe?" The exquisite food had added a little to the exquisite model.

By five o'clock, the shadows were long.

Irma's hair was indeed twisted. And braided. And in a ponytail. It was as elaborate as her dress was simple. "It reminds me of the Eiffel tower. If it were made of gold," I said.

"Any lunchboxes for this?" Freddie whispered to me.

"Indiana Jones and the Temple of Doom," I said.

"You have that?"

"In storage," I said.

"Do you collect them—"

"Austin!" Kenneth called. "Fix it."

I stepped into the shot and rearranged the metal vase so it didn't reflect Kenneth's crouched figure.

We stood around, waiting for the light. The tent, the piñata, the cots and chairs, were gone. Even the camel dung had been retrieved and disposed of elsewhere. When we left, no one would know we'd been here.

Except for the tire tracks.

Darcy had just lit a cigarette. "The sky looks like my two-year-old got hold of it," she said. I looked up. Streaks of red and orange were splotched with yellow and purple.

"Polaroid!" Kenneth called.

I crouched beneath the camera, to see what he saw.

A woman in the foreground, her dress a column of wheat-colored silk, asymmetrical and jagged-edged. A man standing beside a perfectly set table in nothing but cashmere. In the background, against a blood-red sky, a helicopter waited.

My phone rang. Normally, I would ignore it, but this was the hospital number. "Cover for me," I whispered to Darcy. I ducked away, turned my back to the shoot and answered. "Dallas O'Connor."

"Ms. O'Connor," a voice said. "I regret to inform you—"

Chapter Thirteen

"Dallas?" Kim said, and touched my shoulder. "Are you okay?"

The shot. My job. My responsibility.

If I told them that Dieta had died, the spark that had finally caught here today would die. The film would show it. There was nothing anyone could do. A few hours weren't going to make any difference. The ME wanted to look at Dieta's body anyway. Dieta had never woken up. She didn't know she was alone when she died.

"Fine," I said, amazed at how fine I sounded.

We worked through the sunset, screaming, brilliant colors and two beautiful people who moved toward each other in a super-charged atmosphere. I hadn't worked with Yvette, but I couldn't imagine her being better. Irma's fair coloring was grounded by her earthy body, and Wes's darkness seemed that much more mysterious and elegant.

God, I sounded like a Barbara Cartland novel—they were the only romances my grandmama had allowed me to read at her house.

"That's it!" Kenneth called as the last fingers of light crept away. "Great work!"

Irma walked over to me. "Get me out of this dress, I starve for Mexican food."

Wes was unbuttoning his jacket. "This baby is hot to wear."

I took the jacket.

"What do you call a cheese that isn't yours?" Irma asked.

"I don't know."

"Nacho cheese."

We climbed into the RV and they handed me their clothes then they raced out to raid what was left of the food in the coolers.

"Hey Dallas," Wes called to me. "What do Eskimos get from sitting on the ice too long? Polaroids!" He laughed. I shut the door.

Dieta was dead. My hands were trembling as I fought to get garments on hangers. Through blurry vision I checked for spots or holes the models might have made. Both outfits looked fine. I brushed the suit gently, then pulled out plastic bags from my stash and covered everything.

ABBA sang through the speakers, *"The gods may throw the dice, their minds as cold as ice. And someone way down here, loses someone dear."*

"Blondie, the food is going fast," Esmerelda called. "You want me to grab you anything?"

"No," I said. "Thanks."

She stepped up into the living room. "Are you okay?"

"Fine," I lied, my back to her. "Give mine to Irma. She's starving to death."

I cleaned up the room, brushing sand off shoes, collecting dirty clothes in a bag, repairing and replenishing . . . Dieta was dead. I put my hand to my mouth. It couldn't be. How could she be gone?

I didn't hear her climb on board, or sit beside me. "What's up?" Darcy asked.

I turned to her; she read my face.

"No, it can't be."

I nodded. She wrapped her arms around me. We both cried.

Freddie found us like this, put his arms around us. "Why are y'all crying? It makes you look older," he said. "It actually ages—"

"Shut up," Darcy said softly. "Dieta's gone."

He crossed himself, then hugged us again.

By the time the RV pulled out, everyone knew.

Irma sat in the very front seat; she said she didn't feel so good.

"It's the Mexican food," I said, utterly drained. "Sometimes it can be a bit much."

"Now you tell me?" She looked a little green, even beneath her masterpiece makeup and hair.

"Here," I said. I handed her some Tums. "You'll feel better in no time."

George, Wes, Freddie, Darcy and I sat in the back and spoke softly. There was no real thread of conversation; I think we just thought out loud, each person in turn. "Two deaths," Darcy said. "That means someone else will die."

"That's superstition," I snapped.

"Superstition because it happens," Darcy retorted.

I didn't say anything else. This just couldn't be real.

"What happened with those cops?" she asked. "Have they found who hit her yet?"

"I don't know."

"Plans have changed," Esmerelda's voice came over the loudspeaker. "There is snow in the pass, so we will be heading directly to the next shot location."

"What! We don't even get to sleep?" Darcy shouted.

"We'll be staying in a location east of the mountains," Esmerelda said in a calm, airline-attendant voice. "Thank you."

"I could have used the spa tonight," Freddie said. He looked haggard. The circles beneath his eyes matched the streaks in his hair. We'd waited to hear about Dieta. And now we knew.

The rest of the ride was silent. Esmerelda turned on the heater. ABBA played softly in the background. *"The winner takes it all . . ."*

"Where are we?" I asked, jerking awake. The RV had stopped. I made my way forward—it was in idle, both driver and passenger doors were open.

"EMERGENCY ROOM" was written in rainy red letters across the windshield.

I zippered up my jacket and jumped out.

"Ma'am, you can't leave your vehicle here," someone in scrubs and a coat said to me. He was smoking, moving back and forth to stay warm.

It had gotten cold.

I ignored him. "Did you see—?"

"Blond girl, helped by a bigger woman? Yeah, they're checking in."

"Dallas!"

I turned around; Freddie had poked his head out the door like a jack-in-the-box. "What's up? Why are we here?"

"Move the RV," I said. "I'll find out." This better not be Darcy's number three.

I met Esmerelda as she was walking out. "What's going on?"

"Oh. Irma got sick, I think she should stay overnight."

"The Mexican food?"

"She must have an allergy. She broke out in red patches,

and her skin got clammy. Then she complained of a head-ache. She went hot, then cold." Esmerelda shook her head. "Whatever she's allergic to, it's severe."

"Is she going to be okay?"

"She checked in for the night. The doctors want to observe her."

I looked around. "Where are we that she can just *walk* into an emergency room and get help?"

Esmerelda laughed, put her arm around me and walked me out. "This is one of the benefits of living in the country."

I stopped. "Where are we going?"

"Kim, uh, made arrangements for us to stay in a lodge, a little further up the road. Irma will be fine. Just needs a stomach lavage, to get rid of the . . . allergens." She nudged me. "Come on. You didn't get any sleep last night; you worked hard all day. Irma will be fine."

"She'll be alone," I protested.

"Have you ever been in a hospital? She'll have more company than if she was at a party."

"Are Kim, or Tobin, coming by?"

"They took the chopper ahead of us, to be at the lodge when we arrived. I may see if they want me to drive them back here. Really, Irma just needs some sleep."

Guilt about Dieta was driving me. Irma had an upset stomach, or an allergy. She'd be fine. I wasn't like Darcy; I didn't have superstitions.

"Okay."

A half hour later we pulled into a parking lot.

"Where's the hotel?" Darcy asked from her passenger seat.

She had a point. Small lights, like affixed fireflies, wove in and out of some two-story buildings, but there was nothing noticeably hotelish. Kenneth knocked on my window. "Start unloading," he said. Then he looked beyond me to Darcy. "No smoking anywhere around here," he said. "Not in the buildings, or on the grounds."

"No smoking!"

Her curses were cut short by Kenneth's firm, "None, Darcy." They stared at each other for a minute of heavy silence. "You can smoke all day tomorrow," Kenneth said. "We'll be on location."

"We're shooting tomorrow?" I asked.

"We can't go across to Seattle," he said. "We might as well. We're here." He didn't sound enthusiastic.

"Where?" I asked, unlocking the doors.

"Somewhere with snow," he said. "Breakfast is in that building there," he said, pointing to our left. "See you at 6:30. Get some sleep."

I looked at my watch. It was 9:30. All I wanted was a bath and bed.

I was struggling with my bags a few minutes later when a shape appeared out of the night. "Help you?"

"Thanks Wes, I think I've got it."

"You say that, but it's rock beds from here on," he said. "You can't roll your luggage. What section are you in?"

"Don't you mean what cluster?" Darcy snarled. "This looks like Stalag 13."

Wes's hand covered mine on the backpack, so I slid it off and let him carry it. "The food is great," he said to us. "Four fork, they promise."

"How do they expect me to eat when I can't smoke. My God, eating is all I will do! Last time I tried to quit smoking I grew to a size eight."

She was about a size two now. "I want a drink," I said. Dieta was dead; it didn't seem real.

"This way," Wes said, guiding us. "The good news is wine is offered at dinner, but we missed dinner."

"What do you mean—Jesus, where are we going?—we missed dinner? Can't we just order? How do you know all this?"

"I checked in with Kim and Tobin. Dinner is in a cafeteria. It's open for an hour for each meal."

"Do they give us milk and cookies before tucking us in?" Darcy growled as we found our way to the cabin.

There was no moon; I couldn't see anything. No ambient glow from a nearby airport, no lights from the neighbors. Blackness. The setting of a Freddy Krueger movie.

Dieta was dead.

Wes unlocked the door and we stepped inside. Plywood ceiling soared above us, pegs for clothing lined the room, there were two narrow twin beds, two nightstands and everything was very . . . rustic. "Who decorated this place? The freakin' moose from *Northern Exposure?*" Darcy asked, swearing.

"Welcome to Lounging Lizard Lodge," Wes said.

Darcy threw her bags on one of the beds and went into the bathroom. A sink with a mirror faced the beds. That was it for decoration.

"Rough day," he said quietly.

"Yeah."

"You okay?"

"Better off than Dieta," I said. I rubbed my face.

He brushed the hair back over my shoulder. "I'm not sharing my cabin, well actually, I am, but it's the local boy and he's at his girlfriend's tonight. He thinks the buildings will collapse."

Darcy opened the bathroom door. "Well, there is certainly no danger of us getting vain around here. There's no mirror in the john. Oh, here it is," she said, washing her hands. "I'm starving. Where can I get some dinner?"

"There's a little German town," Wes said.

"And the name of this German town?"

"Leavenworth," Wes said.

"That sounds about right. Can we smoke in town, or are our freedoms being taken away everywhere? What the hell is this place anyway?"

"It's a retreat," Wes said.

"My God, if I want to retreat, I'll go to the Phoenician," she snapped, then threw her purse on her shoulder. "Are you coming with me, Dallas?"

I shook my head. "I'm going to bed."

Her gaze flickered to Wes. "I bet. I'm taking Kenneth's Jeep. I'm outta here."

She slammed out of the cabin.

The door banged, shocking me out of a deep sleep.

"I swear to God, this is Jonestown!" Darcy shouted. I leaned over the stairs.

"What are you talking about?" I asked.

She screamed; I screamed. "Who's there! Dallas, where are you?" she shouted.

"Keep it down in there!" someone shouted from next door.

"Up here," I said.

Darcy looked up, "How the hell did you get up there? I'm going to the john. Be careful if they offer you Kool-Aid," she said, and slammed the bathroom door.

I put my head under the pillow and went back to sleep.

The sound that woke me was the worst alarm I'd ever heard. It honked endlessly. I fumbled outside my covers for the nightstand to silence it, but I couldn't find anything.

"Shut the damn thing up!" Darcy yelled from downstairs.

"It's yours," I shouted back, having opened an eye and realizing I didn't have an alarm. I heard stuff moving on the table downstairs, then a crash. Still the noise continued.

It rushed past my window and was gone. I looked after it,

blinking in the sunlight, dazed at the sight of a mountain growing out of my window. "It was a bird," I said.

There was a moment of silence, and I thought Darcy had gone back to sleep. "A what?" she said.

"Like an alarm clock bird," I said. "It flew right by me."

"A bird like that should be extinct," she said. "Oh, I would kill for a cigarette. Damn Kenneth, and damn Tobin for picking this place. It's kindergarten!" she shouted at the top of her lungs.

"Shut up Darcy!" someone shouted from close by. Either the walls were paper thin, or everyone had great hearing.

"Jesus, what time is it?"

I looked at my watch; I was still wearing it with my khakis and wife-beater. I hadn't made it to the shower last night. "Six."

"When do we go?"

"Seven."

"An hour before I can smoke. Oh God," she said.

I was dozing when she woke me up. "Are you hungry yet?"

I opened my eyes and she was standing on the step, looking into the loft. "This is cool. Where'd this come from?"

"We just didn't see it," I said. "Can I sleep some more?"

"Sure thing," she said, patting my leg. "It's 6:30, so you have fifteen minutes."

I jerked up, then realized she was dressed, showered, wearing a new offensive T-shirt and everything. "I bet you love Ted Nugent," I said and rolled over again, pulling the blankets over my head.

My internal alarm shrilled and I dragged up, ducked my head and looked out at the day. Snow covered everything; cotton pads and Q-tips is what it looked like. I stuffed my feet into my sneakers, zipped up a jacket and stumbled outside.

Where the hell were we?

A lot of little cabins clumped beneath the shadow of a mountain with a beetle-killed forest. I followed a pathway that led past empty dirt plots with "Plants in Therapy" signs; frozen cement fish ponds in the middle of the cabin groups and birds. Red and orange and yellow and black.

I guessed the lizards had gone south for the return of winter.

There were cars in the parking lot. Some of them were crew cars, even. But no one was around. I crossed over to the dining hall/meeting room complex.

Through the glass doors I saw Darcy, standing almost at attention, a tray in her hand. I stepped inside and saw she was part of a long line—a cafeteria line. The room was decorated in wood and wool; no music played; and the line moved with mechanical precision. I tapped her on the shoulder and she jumped, then spun around.

"You're here!" she whispered.

I nodded. "Breakfast?" I asked, gesturing to the line.

"Only for ten more minutes," she whispered.

We were standing in line before cereal and yogurt. "Granola?" a wizened lady asked me in a decidedly German accent.

"Yes, please," I said.

"Yogurt mit berries, or mit-out?"

It took me a moment. "Uh, mit, please."

A bowl of cereal and a bowl of yogurt were handed to me as I moved on down the line. Another elderly woman, this one with a hairnet. "Ekks Benedict or banana nut vaffles, or boat?"

I made a decision and was passed on to the meat guy, then the bread woman, the coffee girl, and finally the juice boy. The meal looked incredible despite the fact that it was on putty-colored plasticware. I joined the rest of the crew, who were solemnly stuffing food in their mouths, at a table overlooking an icy rushing creek. As soon as I sat down, the breakfast bar closed. Ten minutes must be up.

No one spoke, but we groaned in delight. Everything was amazing: waffles so fluffy they almost floated; coffee that was roasted on the premises; fresh yogurt with hand-picked blackberries; scones, muffins, and squeezed-while-we-watched juice.

"This," Darcy said, sitting back with her hands on her stomach, "is the best breakfast I've ever had. In my whole life. Ohmigod." She opened her pack of cigarettes. We all jumped at the shrill of a whistle.

"Verboten!" one of the wizened ones screamed. "No smoking! No! No! Is verboten!" Three of them descended on Darcy—one screaming, one whistling, and one actually swiping the package of cigarettes.

"Alright, already!" Darcy shouted back, standing up so they had to look up at her three-inch-platform advantage.

"I'm just going to sniff them."

We groaned.

"I'll go outside."

"No outside," one of them said. "No smoking. None."

"Not smoking," she said. "Just sniffing." She turned to Kenneth. "I'm just going to sniff them, until we get out of here."

He stood up and hitched his cargo pants up. "Darcy, with the weather . . . we're not shooting this morning."

"What!"

"But really Darcy, missing a few wouldn't hurt you."

"That's what you think," she muttered. "Give me back my pack," she said to the little person.

"No, verboten," the person said, marching off after Kenneth.

Cursing, Darcy followed them—the paunchy photographer, the three Munchkins and her package of cigarettes, held out by thumb and forefinger like a particularly offensive diaper.

When they'd all left, Nasmo leaned forward. "Where are we?" he asked. "Berlin?"

"Not Germans, Austrians," Wes said. "There's a difference in their accent."

"Why are we here?" I asked. "I thought we were shooting today?"

"Weather," Stephen said. "We're socked in with snow. The pass is closed."

"What do you mean, closed?" I asked.

"The only places to get across are snowed under."

"It's May."

"We're in the mountains."

"It's the new millennium!"

"The snow doesn't care."

I turned to George. "There's no technology for dealing with snow? We can check the soil on Mars, but we can't move the snow?"

His sleepy expression made me feel as stupid as I realized the question was.

"I can't wait to get out of here," I said. I got up and walked out.

Dieta was dead. Was anyone doing anything about it?

I was dozing when my phone rang. I jumped up and ran for it—a south Texas call.

"Dallas shugah, this you?"

"Hi Granddaddy?" I said. "Is everything okay?"

"Yup, hot already. Honey I been thinkin' 'bout that Boxster question. Did you say the car just charged forward and the brakes didn't stop it?"

"Yeah."

"To disable the brakes would be mighty awkward, since you need somethin' like bolt cutters. Those are big, and pretty obvious. Not the best way to set about sabotaging somethin'."

"Oh," I said. "I guess I was just being silly." This was the least of my heartaches.

"However, it would be pretty easy to stick the throttle on that car."

I picked up the edge of the bedspread and draped it over my shoulders. "Stick it?"

"It would rev so high and fast that brakes wouldn't even matter."

"How long would that take to fix?"

"'Bout three minutes."

I sucked in my breath.

"'Course, sometimes all you have to do to disable a Porsche is look at it funny. They're sensitive cars, for being German."

I laughed. He used to joke that he had three Porsches, so he might have one for a ride somewhere, if he needed it.

"Did they know he would be driving that car?"

"I think they did, Granddaddy," I said, "but—"

Someone knocked on my door. Then again, more forcefully.

"I gotta go, Granddaddy."

"You be careful."

"Love you," I said, then shut the phone and slithered down the ladder.

Wes stood on the threshold.

"What's up?" I asked.

His eyes were rimmed with red. "Do you need a friend?" His lip trembled. "I do."

I nodded, then I don't know what happened. I was wrapped in his Cool Water-scented embrace; my face and hands felt numb. Next thing, we were sitting on my futon in the loft; I had a glass of wine in my hands, and I still didn't believe it. "Tell me it isn't true," I whispered.

He pushed the wine to my mouth. "Drink it," he said, reminding me vaguely of Father Ralph who would say the same thing at Communion. "All of it," Wes said, confirming the feeling. I drained the glass and he poured both of us another. If I kept drinking, I wouldn't remember; it wouldn't be real.

"She's gone," someone said. Him or me, I don't know. I just started crying.

"I don't think she felt anything," I said. "According to what I was told, she never even regained consciousness. The doc said it was a miracle that she didn't die at the site." I felt sick at the memory of her face. Her wrecked face. That she'd been able to breathe that way—God, I couldn't think about it.

"It's okay," he whispered, pulling me into his arms. "She's better off now."

I absolutely loathe it when people say that.

The light moved across the snow-covered mountain.

"There was no hope," I said. "Maybe if it had happened in front of a hospital, or we'd found her sooner, but," I shrugged, "it just happened."

"Was she crossing the road?"

I sat up a little. "I don't know," I said. "I can't think of any other reason to be on the other side from the shoot."

"Maybe she didn't want to interrupt the shot? She was going to climb down on the far side? I've thought about it all day and that's the only answer I came up with."

"No answer is good enough," I whispered. I was so tired.

"Is the suit still missing?"

"No. I found it at the Lodge."

"Darcy looked for it, but I guess she didn't recognize it," he said. "That's why you're the pro."

My brain was exhausted, but my body was jumpy and I kept twitching.

"You remind me of my dog when she's having nightmares," Wes said after I jerked for the fourth time.

"Is that your way of calling me a bitch?" I said, a stab at humor.

He laughed; the vibration rumbled against my head.

"What kind of dog?"

"An antique basset hound," he said. "When I was a little boy I fell in love with the Hush Puppies dog. Finally I got one. Had her since . . . oh, since I was in high school."

"She *is* antique," I said. The alcohol was taking over. I was willingly slipping away.

"We can get more comfortable, if you want," he said.

"Isn't there someone named Isabel?" I murmured as I snuggled in deeper next to him, feeling empty and warm. Anesthesia, in a way. I let myself fall asleep. I didn't want to let go of my haven.

Bam!

We both froze. It wasn't a shot; I'd recognize that. But I'd rarely heard a door slammed quite so forcefully. This plywood palace wasn't terribly soundproof or solid. I hated to think that every word I'd said had been heard by the whole crew.

"You lying son of a bitch! Why did I ever trust you? Believe in you? You—" The sounds came from next door.

"Sounds like Kim and Tobin," Wes said. His hand cradled my head. "Go back to sleep."

I listened to Kim's ranting. What had changed since the smiley happy people holding hands in the desert? If Tobin was responsible for Dieta's death, I wanted to nail his hide. For Richard, too.

"She's been yelling a lot," Wes said. "Probably Tobin."

"I wonder what holds them together," I mumbled. "Opposites attract?"

"Do you think opposites attract?" he asked. "Or do you think a relationship works best when the people are more alike?"

"I don't know," I said, closing my eyes again, speaking softly. "I'd hardly use them as an example of a relationship working."

"As a partnership it seems to be perfect. He's hands-on; she's a delegator. Or do you mean they're involved?"

"They're separated," I said. "Have been for years." That much I'd gotten from Darcy's boyfriend.

Wes chuckled. "Nice try at sidestepping the question." He was whispering, too. "What about opposites attracting?"

"I guess I've always been drawn to my opposite," I said a few minutes later.

"You ever been long-term with anyone in the business?"

"No. Have you?"

He chuckled. "No, definitely not."

"So your wife isn't in the business?"

"No. But my daughter is. She's six."

I smiled. "Following in Daddy's footsteps?"

"Maybe," he said. "If it makes her happy." He touched my hair for a few minutes.

"No kids. Single."

"Poor guy," he said. "How long since you broke up?"

I didn't think about how he knew, or why, I just saw Alejandro's beautiful face and deep-dimpled smile flash before me. And I heard the words of our last conversation in my head. *"I want you for every day, Dallas. Live with me; see if you are happy here. That's all I ask."*

"I can't, Alex. I'm sorry. I love being with you, but I can't; I just can't."

"Then I'm very sorry, Dallas, but I can't bear to see you anymore."

"What happened?" Wes asked.

"We had one of those 'get on the plane or get out of the airport' conversations," I said. "I didn't want to get on the plane, and he was ready for takeoff. He wanted children, a family. Neither of us were getting younger, so it was time to get out of the airport."

"Those are hard topics," he said. "Were you living together?"

"Give up my own house?" I said, half-joking, half-serious.

"Are you crazy? I finally have *my* bedroom that I don't have to share with anyone."

He laughed. "How do you feel about children?"

"I don't even have a dog," I said after a while. "I can't keep my lawn alive. To want and to be ready for are not the same. Someday." We were quiet for a while; so were Kim and Tobin. "Are you breaking up with your wife?"

"She got offered a job in Hawaii."

"Wow. How incredible."

"Well," he said with a sigh, "I got accepted to art school. Not in Hawaii."

"Tough choices."

"She hates my travel," he said. "When I met her, I was a waiter with no ambition."

"And now you're a model and an art student?"

"Yeah," he said ruefully. "It wasn't part of her plan."

"What about your little girl?"

"Do I keep her with me, hire a full-time nanny, or let her grow up in Hawaii?"

"With another full-time nanny?"

"I wish I could not care," he said. "Just be a house-husband, or Mr. Mom, or whatever the word is, but I can't. It's not enough."

"So you understand how your wife feels, then," I said. "About her career, ambition."

"She's good at her job," he said. "But not for more than an hour with my daughter. She's just not made to be a real parent."

I winced for this poor woman. "That's harsh."

"She's a lot like Kim. She hires people. A cook, a gardener, a personal shopper, a personal trainer, a maid. If there is a way she can give someone money so she doesn't have to dirty her hands with actual labor, she'll do it. She's only interested in the end result."

"Where do you find all those people," I wondered aloud.

"If you pay enough, you can get anyone to do anything," he said. "Just look at TV."

"I don't watch TV," I said.

"I don't turn it off," he said. "I can't stand to be alone. It's great in a hotel room."

"Do you think you and your wife will compromise at all?" I asked. I was more than half-asleep, but something he said was gnawing at my brain.

"No," he said. "She left for Hawaii this morning."

"Where's your little girl?"

"At summer camp."

"Isn't it a little early?" I asked.

"Yeah," he said. "I want to get home and take her away from there. It's not fair of Isabel, but . . ." He didn't say anything more, and I didn't want to know any more. I closed my eyes again, enjoying the feel of his fingers in my hair, rubbing against my head.

"What does a stylist get a degree in?" he asked.

I was awake now, on the defense. "Uhh, I didn't get a degree."

"Oh. I guess I thought—your parents were college—"

I sat up, pulling away, stretching my back. "Yeah, they are, and it was completely expected that I would go. I was registered and everything. I even went a semester or three."

"And? What stopped you?"

Protectively I touched my throat, my turtleneck camouflage. "I was in an accident my senior year of high school. It shook me up pretty bad and I guess I couldn't concentrate after that. Not for a while."

"What kind of accident?" His hand was on my neck, the crook of my shoulder, his fingers interlaced with mine. His touch wasn't invasive, just kind.

"Automotive."

"Weather or —?"

"Drinking and driving."

"A drunk hit you?"

"No," I said, looking down at the comforter whose mono-chrome pattern I could just barely see. "My date was plowed and took down a telephone pole with his graduation present Corvette. A piece of glass almost ended me. I spent eighteen months in PT."

He whistled. "Physical therapy?"

"Right. I tried to go to school after that, but I didn't have a clue what I wanted to do. I had lousy study habits and I—" I sighed. "I was so scared of being dead that I only wanted to live, you know?"

Wes chuckled. "I know exactly."

"LIVE with big capital letters, so I moved in with one of my sisters, who had a place in El Paso, and started working at an upscale department store."

"That's nice."

"It fit in with my party lifestyle," I said. "I don't think I ever made it to bed before two A.M. Anyway, I met a guy; we got married; I tried to make it work for five years; then I left and moved in with a different sister, got a job in the floral business."

His fingers touched the beading on my choker. "The acci-dent. That's why I've never seen your neck?"

I bowed my head. "I didn't realize you were looking," I said.

"You can have surgery, you know—reconstructive."

"I know."

"How was your boyfriend?" Wes asked.

I closed my eyes, trying to forget the day, ashamed of my craven wish to put it all behind me, to pretend it never hap-pened.

"Dallas?" Wes prompted.

Two words, that's all it would take. I never told anyone

this story. Sure, about my part as the victim of the accident, but nothing about the rest of it. My secret. My scar. Confessing this was admitting to the weakest part of me. Opening a door, letting someone in. Letting them judge me, without knowing all the facts.

"It's okay," Wes said as he drew me back into his arms and kissed my forehead. "You don't have to tell me. Just be."

We were falling asleep, propped up on pillows, tear tracks drying on both our faces. I reached up and covered Wes's ears with my hands; then the words slipped out, just for me, mingled with a deep sigh. "He died."

Chapter Fourteen

The afternoon sun woke me. Wes had left already—which was good. Where Darcy was, I couldn't imagine. I leaned over and dialed my phone. Maybe Thompson knew something new.

"Out of Range," it said.

My language wasn't pretty. I fell back on my futon and looked at the sky.

Someone banged on the door, then Darcy fell inside, stomping her feet. "We're shooting this afternoon," she announced. "Leaving in fifteen minutes."

We were professionals. We scrambled.

Irma was stunning in a full-length white mink coat and turban—Kim had pulled some strings to get it. From my kit I'd created a chain metal bikini out of 1960s garage sale belts, to go with enough white diamonds to satisfy Elizabeth Taylor. If you keep layering simple diamond necklaces, the look eventually becomes very elaborate. The off-duty policemen were sitting in the helicopter, watching me watch the diamonds. I'd snatched Wes's amber aviator sunglasses for

Irma and loaned him mine. Irma's hair was tucked somehow and it looked chin-length. Freddie was extremely gifted. She looked way sassy.

You'd never guess Irma had recently spent hours in the hospital with a blinding migraine and stomach upset. Of course, that might have had more to do with Darcy's amazing makeup than any health issue. Irma stood on the front of Wes's skis as they swished a few feet down the moutainside, then posed, then swooshed a few feet more. The snowfall was fresh. We were trapped on this side of the moutains because of it.

Jon, our local-local boy, spent all his time sweeping the footprints out of it.

"Don't worry about it," Kenneth called. "I'll just fix it in PhotoShop."

"Why didn't they do this whole thing in PhotoShop," I asked. "A helluva lot cheaper."

"And warmer," Freddie said, blowing into his hands. "Baton Rouge boys just don't ever grow accustomed to this frigid northern weather."

"New York winters are cold," Nasmo said.

"Honey, I spend winter in Miami with supermodels and old farts. Why are we out here instead of in a virtual world?" he asked Kenneth.

"Something about authenticity," Kenneth said. "The Tobin Charles man is the real thing."

Wes was in a spectacular winter wheat double-breasted suit that cost a meager ninety-five hundred dollars. We did one shot with overcoat and black cashmere mock, another with a white silk Euro-collared shirt and a final one with a gold dress shirt and a narrowly striped wide gold-and-black tie. It was striking and sensational, all of it.

In one shot Wes was offering her a martini, in another, a diamond bracelet. In what I thought was the best shot, she was on his shoulders, with a dove in her hand, both of them laughing, the sky brilliant blue behind them, the moment tense with emotion. And animal attraction. They were a dynamic team. This would sell millions.

Dieta would be so proud, I thought; then I remembered that she was gone. Did everyone else feel this way? I touched my tiny bear, feeling the jab of the pink fish through the fingers of my glove. I blinked back tears.

"That's it. Thank you very much," Kenneth said.

Wes walked by me and kissed me on the cheek. "Hang tough," he said. Had he seen the tears in my eyes? We rushed Irma into the helicopter and into another coat, Wes right behind her. Kim took off with them, back to the airport with the couriers for the diamonds and the mink, so they could meet their return flights. The guards had been in the 'copter the whole time. Wimps.

As quickly as we could, we packed up the rest of the gear and boarded the second chopper, almost overloading it with weight. By the time we landed, it was dark. Another drive back to the lodge of the lounging lizards, because travel across the passes, either Snoqualmie or Stevens, was impossible. Still.

Shivering, sweaty and now sniffling, we tromped into the cafeteria for our five-course, five-star meal. Copper River salmon, filet mignon, steamed asparagus with some creamy sauce, several salads and Tiramasu.

I excused myself to call Thompson. He actually answered.

"Dieta is dead," I said.

"Ah, yes, the hit and run."

"Who's investigating that? No one ever called me to ask questions or anything."

"That would normally be under the jurisdiction of the highway patrol," he said. "However, given my prior involvement, I'll be overseeing that investigation too."

"Are you actually going to do anything this time?" I blurted.

His voice was chilled. "Ma'am, I understand you are upset. Law and justice must move in proscribed paths. They're not always fast."

"Do you know anything about who hit her?"

"It was a hit and run. The officers are following up several leads. Thus far, I'm sorry to say, they have nothing solid."

"I think there may be a third killing," I said.

"How is that?"

"I think the designer is being poisoned by the other designer, on the fashion shoot."

"What makes you say this?"

"I used to be in the wholesale floral business," I said. "I sold to florists and wedding people, grocery stores, and whoever wanted flowers."

He couldn't have sounded more bored. "Yeah?"

"It was around Easter one year, I was on the road. I'd just checked into a Motel 6, when I got paged. I checked the number and saw it was one of my best customers in Tyler. I called back. She was upset because one of her small-town customers was threatening to sue."

"Over flowers?"

"I asked why, and the florist said because the woman's cat had died after drinking the water from the flowers."

"What are you talking about?"

"I had a heart-to-heart with Kim Charles. She's convinced the deaths were intended for her, and that someone is poisoning her. I think I know how."

"Is Kim dead?" That got his interest.

"No, no, she's fine."

"Then what are you talking about?"

"Lily of the valley. It's got such a potent poison, that even the water it's kept in is dangerous."

"The water's poisoned?"

"In grade school, did you ever dye carnations? For St. Patrick's Day or something?"

"Yeah, I guess I remember that."

My hand was clenched on the fabric of my pants. I knew I was right. "The way you dye them is to pour the color in the water, because it's absorbed through the stem."

"You're saying it works in reverse, too."

"Yes. The water looks clear."

"How does it taste? Wouldn't it be bitter?"

"That's the trick with this," I said. "The reason why it's worked. She mixes the poisoned water with a protein powder. The heavy flavor of chocolate and artificial sweetener would mask any flavor. Kim gulped that stuff; I doubted she had any tastebuds left."

"What about when she just drinks water? She doesn't notice?"

"It's not just water. She carries around San Pellegrino bottles everywhere. She drinks it, throws it away. New one."

"I can't believe in this day and age there are people who don't recycle."

I glared at the phone. "But the water she uses with the protein powder is different. It's from a water dispenser she carries everywhere and leaves on her minibar."

"Anyone could poison it, then?" He was a little less skeptical.

"I guess, yeah."

"Hmm," he said. "It's an interesting theory, but Ms. O'Connor, there's no crime."

"Does someone have to actually die before you care?"

He was silent a moment.

"Sorry to bother you," I said, pressing the End button so hard it almost stuck. What had Dieta said about Western medicine—it just dealt with sickness? It wasn't preventative? "Western law seems the same way," I said to my empty room.

I'd tell Kim—but how would that information go over? Was Tobin her lover or her enemy today? There wasn't even anything to hit in here. I paced back and forth, glaring at the furniture from IKEA.

I didn't have a Stairmaster, so I climbed up and down the ladder until I was sweaty. I was still mad. My phone now claimed it was Out of Order. I threw on a jacket and stomped outside into the snow. The cold took my breath away.

If the cops weren't going to do anything, then I would. *We would.*

I marched past "Plants in Therapy," headed for Kenneth's cabin.

The crew was there, slouched on sofas and chairs. ABBA had been forsaken for some Indian flutes and everyone was well on their way to being blotto.

I walked in on Darcy's oft-repeated line:

"Someone else is going to die." She ducked a pillow aimed for her head. "I'm not being negative, but deaths come in threes."

"I'm out of here before it's me," Freddie said.

"I'm sure we'll be cutting it short and going home," Kenneth said. "The guts have kind of gone out of this thing."

"Have you talked to the cops, Dallas?" Stephen asked.

"Yeah," George said, bereft of his electronic toys since he'd run out of batteries. "Since you found both bodies."

"Neither were just bodies when we found them," Irma said. "Both were alive."

"You weren't even there," Nasmo said.

"I heard about it."

"Yeah, I've talked to the police," I said. I wasn't going to sit down. I wasn't going to drink. I was going to get sastisfaction.

"If the mafia got Richard, did they get Dieta too?" Nasmo asked.

The Filipino mafia? Or the Italian one? Was this about a conflict between the two?

I turned on Tobin. He'd just stepped out of the bathroom. "Why kill a model?"

"I am so damn sick and tired of hearing that. 'Why kill a model?' Why kill anyone? Or if you're going to kill, why not a model? Models aren't some strange, alien beings who move among us. You of all people should know that."

"What, models are people too, Dallas?" Wes said.

"Why kill a producer? Why kill a designer? Why kill a stylist? We're all people! With lives outside of what we do." Okay, maybe not really true in my case, but still. "Darcy isn't just a makeup artist. She has kids, she's been through trials and triumphs, she has a family and knows the stuff of life beyond mixing colors and working with lights."

The were all staring at me.

"I hold *Sex and the City* personally responsible for this anti-model bias," I said. "It's just crap."

Tobin excused himself in the face of my wrath and I slammed the door shut behind him.

"Good job," George said. I couldn't tell if he was serious or sarcastic.

"Shut up and have a VZ," Darcy said. "Do you want some nicotine gum?"

I paced as I held my drink. "I don't know why the cops aren't doing anything," I said. "I talk to this one guy, and he takes notes and sounds earnest, but . . . Well, Dieta died."

"Is it a serial thing?" Freddie asked. "Picking off different components of a fashion shoot?"

"I'd believe the mafia story more," Kenneth said.

Irma opened a bottle of water and added it to her Vox. "Ohmigod," I said, sitting up. "Irma. When you got sick, was it the Mexican food?"

"I don't know. I guess so."

I looked at her water again. "Tell me, did you drink from Kim's sports bottle that day?"

Everyone was looking at me.

"No, of course not—no, wait. Ja, I think I did. Just a quick sip because I hadn't taken my vitamins that day. Kim and I use the same . . . how do you say . . . produce."

"Product?" Darcy said.

"Yes, product. The package, we both get it from—"

"That doesn't matter. After you drank from it, when did you start to feel sick?"

"Kim's protein drink is poisoned?" Kenneth asked. "Is that what you think?"

"I took a sip after we changed, then she gave me the rest. We got in the van right after," Irma said.

I hadn't been paying attention to her, but it couldn't have been two hours later that we checked into the hospital. I stood up. "I'll be back in a minute."

The darkness was illuminated with snow, and the reflections of the firefly lights. I wove my way next door along the pebbled paths to Kim's and knocked. She opened it in peignoir and mules. "If you wanted to talk to the crew," I said, "now is your chance."

I looked beyond her and saw the room was set up very close to the way it looked at the Salish Lodge, minus the view and luxury. Zebra candles, colorful pashminas, and her stash of protein mixes, bottled water and giant water dispenser. In addition to her usual hydrangeas, she had vases of all the lilies from the shoot and a jar of cut rhododendron. Jonquils and daffodils stood on the bar.

An absolute buffet of toxicity. "Have you had any of your protein drink?" I asked her.

She shook her head. "I was getting ready to, but I wanted to shower first. I just got in from my evening run."

"The water," I said. "It's poison."

"That's impossible!"

I was sick of hearing these exclamations. I pushed past her and looked at the dispenser. It was about half full. "Do you change it yourself?" I asked, looking at it. How would you get poisoned water in there?

"No. Tobin usually does."

"Oh, I bet," I muttered. "Do you have any gloves?"

"What kind?"

"Plastic, preferably."

She went into the bathroom and came back with Nice n' Easy haircoloring gloves. I would have pegged her as a salon woman. They were very thin plastic, but maybe thick enough. I lifted the jug off, spilling a few drops on the counter top. "I don't know what kind of poison it is," I said. I needed to call Kreg and ask him. "But it will affect skin."

Her eyes were wide, her face ghastly white.

"I'm not sacrificing mine," I said. "Give me your hand."

She stared at me.

"The poison was in the drink you gave Irma. She got immediately, horribly sick. From one drink. You must have built up an immunity, but . . . don't you want to know?"

She looked at the bottle.

I got in her face. "The whole crew is back at Kenneth's. Tobin just left. This is your chance to tell your side, ask for their help. If Tobin killed Dieta and Richard, then they will want to know. But if you don't learn if this is or isn't poison, if you don't tell them what's going on, then they will hate you like they have all along. A spoiled, petty, bitch."

I peeled off the gloves, put on my leather ones and walked to the door.

"Dallas! Wait!" she said.

I turned around. She pulled the top off the jar and poured some water over her hand.

In seconds it was red, irritated.

"Get your coat," I said.

*   *   *

The party had picked up. Name That Eyebrow had turned into a drinking game.

They froze, glasses halfway to their mouths, when we walked in.

Tobin wasn't here.

I held up her hand; it was beet-red with tiny white blisters. "This reaction came from what you drank, Irma. This is what Tobin has been feeding Kim in her protein shakes. It's probably what her stomach looks like." I had no idea; I was appealing to the dramatic side of this very drama-loving group.

"How did Richard die?" I asked Kim.

We hadn't had any discussion on the way over here—I was flying on fury and she better keep up with me.

"Internal injuries," she said.

"What happened to cause those?"

"Did we stumble on *Law & Order?*" Darcy asked. I threw a glare at her.

"The Porsche was rigged."

"Was it Richard's Porsche?"

"I thought it was Tobin's—and mine. We share one."

"What about Dieta being hit?"

"I'd just talked to her and walked down the far side, back to the shoot . . . I think he hit her by mistake. And this . . ." She fell apart, looking at her hand. "Tobin did this to me? He's trying to kill me?"

I looked at the crew.

"Let's kill him," Darcy said, banging down her drink.

Chapter Fifteen

"That bastard," Kenneth said. "Dieta died by a mistake?"

"Call the police," Freddie said. "Quick, before he gets away."

I held up my hand. "I've told the cops. They aren't going to do anything. Not enough proof. It's a domestic case, until someone is dead. Then it is worthy of their attention."

"I can't believe how bad the cops suck," Darcy said. "The guys you talked to, what about their superior officer? Get him involved."

"Guys?" I said. "No, I have one guy who maybe calls me back after eight calls. It's just not a priority."

"He doesn't have a partner?" she asked.

"Well, I can only talk to one person on the phone at a time," I said. "But no, not that I know of."

"That's weird."

"Every state is different," George said. "What are you suggesting we do, Dallas?"

Kim had stopped crying and was listening, her hand held in front of her like an offering—or a trophy. I didn't trust her, but I couldn't dispute the fact of her hand. "We're going to be here at least one more day, right?"

I looked from face to face: Kenneth's blustery one, Stephen's narrow one, George's sleepy but sharp blue eyes, Irma's beauty, Darcy's fire, Nasmo's caution, Wes's olive perfection and Freddie's ageless bones. "I want to scare him shitless. Then we'll get a confession. George can tape it. We'll walk in and present the cops with their case. We'll make it so seamless that they'll have to prosecute."

George smiled.

"Darcy, Freddie, go get your makeup kits. This is going to take some doing."

The Lizard Lodge's breakfast trough was deep and everyone arrived exactly on time. "After you left last night, Tobin," Kenneth said, "we decided we should hold a wake for Dieta. And Richard." He cut into his Eggs Benedict. "It's going to be at Kim's since she has the most room."

"That's very nice," Tobin said. "Dieta was a dear girl." He looked at me. "I'm sorry I offended you, Dallas. This has been trying for you."

I heard the palmist's words. *"You'll be tried."* I shook away the eerie mist and drank from my coffee cup.

"What time?"

"About two. Wear bright colors and be prepared to listen to ABBA," Kenneth said.

As soon as he left, the crew went into action.

"This reminds me of Halloween," Freddie said.

I turned to my own job, my own memories. Halloween was huge in Dallas, especially among the gay, lesbian and artistic communities. On Halloween night, Cedar Springs, a huge street, is closed down to become the strip. The most fantastic costumes parade there.

What a casual observer doesn't know is the months and weeks of preparation that go into them. Lunchtime at photo shoots is spent pouring over Polaroids and costume designs so they will be just perfect.

Truth to tell, most people I knew were too worn out by Halloween to enjoy it. I wasn't sure about the enjoyment factor this afternoon, but there should be some satisfaction.

George set up a series of cameras in Kim's plywood palace. Nasmo and Stephen fiddled with the lights until they were exactly right. Most of us missed lunch, but everyone was dressed and ready by 1:30.

Tobin walked in at two, and Freddie followed him. "Come on, I swear Darcy, you'll be late to your own funeral," he called.

She ran in, flushed from the cold. "My winter clothes are not the ones to wear to this par-tay," she said, stripping off her jacket to reveal a T-shirt with "Let 'Er R.I.P." over orange and pink capris.

I had on the party makeup Darcy had suggested a week ago, with my brightest clothes—a gray shirt and gray pants. I hadn't had time to go shopping. We'd decorated the place with crepe paper flowers and streamers. The Lodge had been persuaded to make petit fours with multi-colored lizards on them. Colored Dixie cups, the point of the whole thing, were stacked next to the water cooler.

George played bartender, Freddie played DJ, and the scene was set.

"To Dieta," Kenneth said, raising his espresso martini.

"To Dieta," we echoed. No one said anything for a minute; this was very real. She was lost to us forever.

"I spoke to the hospital," Tobin said. "She had an organ donor card." He looked into my eyes. "Her heart went into the body of a sixteen-year-old drunk driving victim as soon as Dieta was pronounced dead."

"When is she being shipped back?" Stephen said.

"I think her body has already gone," Tobin said.

I covered my face for a second. The temptation was to just

leave. The laughing, smiling, color-loving girl was now hollow and taking up space beside someone's luggage. I wasn't sure if I was going to throw up or cry.

She would be so blissed to know she'd saved a life. *Shiva.*

Goosebumps rose on my arms.

"She was color, you know?" Darcy said, "The personality of color."

"I miss her at four A.M.," Kenneth said. "She was so positive, such a nice person to watch the sunrise with, even if I did have my knickers halfway up my arse every morning."

We chuckled, then fell silent.

"I miss her laugh," Freddie said. "She made you sound like you should join in, even if you didn't know what was funny."

"She wanted everyone to be comfortable," Wes said.

"You wanted to smile with her," I said. "She was contagious."

"To Dieta," Stephen said, raising his VZ.

"To Dieta."

"She knew how to live," Irma said. "Let's party about that."

So it began.

We danced. Tobin and Kim were great together, spinning and twirling. He didn't ask about her Michael Jackson glove or her wig of multi-colored dreds. They laughed—you'd almost believe they liked each other.

Kim was a damn good actress.

Freddie and I two-stepped, then Nasmo and I waltzed and Kenneth and I jitterbugged. George had just started "Saturday Night Fever" when Nasmo, appreciably sweaty, walked over to the dispenser and got some water.

He drank the cup full, then another.

No one was supposed to look at Tobin.

"Hey!" Tobin shouted to Kenneth a few minutes later. "Don't dilute the VZs with water! Have some tonic or something."

"Nothing refreshes like cold water," Kenneth said.

Tobin's eyes got wider. He'd eaten his spiked petit fours.

One by one, we drank the water.

George put on ABBA and got his cup.

"Waterloo" began.

Kreg had said, when I woke him up the night before in the middle of concocting our plan, that the only visual side-effects of convallatoxin, the glycoside that was the poison, were excess saliva, red, splotchy skin, dilated pupils and vomiting. "Of course, there are headaches and nausea, stomachache, coma . . . but those aren't visual. What are you doing, Dallas?"

"A home movie. Thank you. Love you. Bye."

Darcy lay down on the couch; she had a headache. Irma went to the bathroom and retched loud enough to hear over the brass players in the song. Kenneth's face turned red and splotchy and he began to drool.

Tobin looked around in panic.

Kim picked a fight with Stephen over which piece of cake was whose. George fell over on the sound system, conveniently hitting the "repeat" button on cheerful "Waterloo." Freddie threw up violently on the floor. I collapsed on a chair.

Tobin was the only one left standing.

"How does it feel? You've won the war," ABBA sang.

My eyes were shut, and I couldn't hear much besides Tobin's nervous mumbling.

"Waterloo, knowing my Fate is to be with you, whoa-whoa."

It would play three times after the last body fell. He didn't know it, he was hallucinating from his "special" petit four, but the lights were changing. We counted the choruses, the times it repeated. Tobin made noises, but we'd sworn we wouldn't open our eyes.

Waterloo's last word.

"Why did you kill me?" Kim screamed at him.

He shrieked in fear.

"And me?" said Stephen.

"And me?" asked Kenneth.

"And me?" I said, raising my face with opalescent make-up. Under the lights, it was almost all he could see. A skeleton face and undead body.

We advanced on him; he was scared, relieved, uncertain, and just where we wanted him.

Darcy clicked the handcuffs around his wrist and George killed the music.

Tobin was on the ground, ankles taped together and surrounded by the enemy.

"What . . . what do you want?" he asked.

I knelt down, and leaned into his face. His eyes were dilated, but he wasn't drugged by much. "You're going to tell us every detail about how Richard and Dieta died in your attempts to murder Kim."

"I didn't have anything to do with it!"

"Read him his Miranda rights," Stephen said. "We want to be able to use his words in court."

"Court?" he shouted. "I didn't do anything!"

"What about the water? The poison you've been feeding me?" Kim asked, ripping off her glove. "You've been doing this to me?"

"I can explain!" he said. "Let me go."

"No way," Darcy said. "You're going to tell us everything first."

"I don't know anything! You have to believe me."

We looked at each other, as though considering.

"Nah," we said in unison.

In a group, laughing and singing "Waterloo," we walked Tobin to his cabin next door. Stephen and Nasmo were going to clean up Kim's place; they'd be over shortly. Besides, it was almost dinnertime.

Darcy and I changed in our room. When we got back, Freddie, Kenneth and Kim had stripped Tobin down and restrained him. "I'm starving," Kenneth said. "I don't want to miss dinner."

"Oh, he's not going anywhere," Darcy said.

Tobin was in the bathtub in his cabin, naked, his wrists taped together and to the shower head, his hairy legs taped to the bathtub, bathroom wall and the spigot wrapped in tape between his knees. Then more tape crossed over his chest and belly, pinning him to the wall.

He wouldn't be going anywhere without leaving a lot of hair behind. "You know what I'm thinking, if he doesn't talk?" Darcy said to me.

I nodded. Tobin watched us with huge eyes. His mouth was taped too. "Yeah. If he doesn't talk, we'll give him the Brazilian."

Freddie spun around—he was a man, but he knew. "Only as a last resort," he said. "That's wicked."

"He killed Dieta, Freddie. He'll get a bigtime lawyer who will have the charges dropped to conspiracy to commit murder or something. He'll get twenty and walk in five. He'll live in a prison with a TV, time to design, and even a little romance. He's not going to suffer unless we make him suffer." Darcy gave Tobin a look that should have soldered him to the spigot. "We're the only justice he's ever going to see."

I guessed that Jersey City boyfriend was a little sore at the legal system and Darcy had listened to his rants.

"Get changed," I told Freddie. "We need to put in an appearance at dinner."

*   *   *

The snowfall had affected the trough, but not a lot—and in my favor! They'd had to pick a lot of vegetables so they wouldn't freeze, and as a vegetarian, I was in heaven.

"Dying really improves your appetite," Irma said.

"The resurrection part," George said, "actually."

They exchanged a look. Amidst murder and mayhem, romance bloomed? Irma was trés IQ-ey for a model, despite her penchant for one-liners, and George seemed like one of those quiet rivers that runs deep. Who knew.

Kim had come down with a headache, so she took some bread and went to her cabin. She'd be over later. That was part of it: we all had to be guilty.

"Just like Death on the Orient Express!" Irma had said last night.

"I think it's Murder," Nasmo said.

"And there's quite a difference between a death and a murder," Kenneth had offered.

"No one is going to be murdered. Not even to satisfy Darcy," I'd said. "We're just going to do what the police can't . . . won't. I don't know. That's it. Eveyone has to participate, though. From this point on."

I was the eldest girl—once my sisters were old enough, I'd been the ringleader. "Instigator," was a word we'd learned early in my family. Usually with my name attached.

I dove into my artichoke souffle.

"This is the best food I've ever had in my life," Darcy said. "Look, my pants are too tight already."

"If they combined the tugboat with the kitchen—" Nasmo said.

We interrupted him with "Hear! Hear!"

"No one would ever leave," Kenneth said.

We ate dessert, which was heavy on fruit and light on

chocolate due to the pass closing, drank another four cups of coffee, and meandered back to our victim.

Tobin had tried to move, but the tape stuck to every little hair on his Mediterranean-heritage body. "You have to change rooms," Darcy said. "We don't all fit in here."

Tobin started screeching through his duct-tape-covered mouth. There was only one way out of that much duct tape.

"Cheer up," Irma said. "You do this to models all the time, to give us cleavage."

"Nasmo, Stephen, help me?" Freddie said.

The rest of us left, and Darcy and Irma ran outside to see how well sound traveled out here, even through tape.

George turned on music to torture by. "It's Dead Can Dance," he said. "I thought it appropriate."

It was as surreal as the rest. We set up a snack bar, some drinks, and tried to ignore Tobin's muffled screams. He sounded as though they were putting him through a wood-chipper backwards.

Eww.

Finally, Tobin hobbled out held between the men. Wide swaths of hair were missing from his body.

"How did Dieta's accident happen?" I asked.

Irma and Darcy came in, stomping off the snow and shivering. "Temperature's dropped," Darcy said. "Expecting more snow tonight."

"It's spring," Freddie said. "I couldn't bear to live with such disorganization in my weather."

"Oh, it's weird for here too," Darcy said. "They have late storms, but this is *really* late." Her gaze flickered to him. "Anything?"

Tobin had been allowed to have his underwear, but he looked beaten already.

I shook my head. "We're going to have to go through with our plan."

"Not the Brazilian," Freddie said. "Let me work with him a while, but you have to give the man a chance. His heart is still pounding from seeing us die."

"Did you hear him scream?"

They both shook their heads.

"I'll go get Kim," Kenneth offered. "Maybe she knows the questions to ask."

Chapter Sixteen

It was ten o'clock. We'd drawn the drapes. Tobin sat in his underwear, in one of the IKEA chairs, his hands with permanent-marker-painted nails taped behind him. One leg was taped to the chair's leg, the other was on a portable ironing board so Freddie didn't have to lean over much as he ripped the strips of linen from Tobin's leg. Linen affixed to melted wax.

Kim sat opposite him. "What happened with the cars, Tobin?"

"You know!" He said. "You were the one who was there! I had nothing to do with it."

Freddie pulled a little of the tape. Tobin hissed in pain.

"It's always worse when they do it slowly," Darcy said to me as we watched from the bar. "My girl just gives me a glass of wine, tells me to hang my head over the edge, and rips it one big strip."

"The first time is the worst," I said. "I thought I was going to cry."

"On my first bikini wax, I did cry."

"Have you Brazilianed?"

"I'm a coward. Besides, the only place I'd go is booked a year in advance."

I shuddered. On the theory that anticipation is the worst part, that could be heinous.

"Are you getting this?" Irma asked George, who had the video camera.

"There's not been much to get," he said. "This guy isn't talking."

"Have you been poisoning me?" Kim asked Tobin.

"You don't have any proof."

She waved her hand in his face.

Freddie tugged the strip some more.

"I thought torture would be less tedious," Darcy said. "This is boring."

I stepped forward. "This isn't working. We need to up the ante. Freddie, do you have bleach?"

When Tobin saw his white eyebrows and lashes, he screamed. "Yes!" he said to Kim. "Yes! I admit it! I've been trying to get rid of your bitching ass for at least a year! You quit eating, so I couldn't poison you that way. I had to think of something else."

"Is that when you hired a killer?"

"What?" Tobin said. Either he was a great actor, or he really hadn't thought of that before. "Then I'd just have to kill him, so there wouldn't be a trail."

"Oh." Apparently that thought hadn't occurred to Kim.

"Who rigged the car?" I asked Tobin.

"I don't know, I swear I don't know."

"Another color, Freddie."

"I always wanted to try a peacock feather look," he said. "Everyone out. *L'artiste* must work."

We left the bathroom and Kim sank onto the sofa. I'd ask how she was, but it was a patently stupid question.

Darcy and I played a modified Name That Eyebrow with Irma, George, Kenneth and Nasmo while Stephen napped.

Tobin's shout of horror snapped us to attention.

Freddie peeked out the door. "He's ready to talk. To Dallas."

"Bring him out here," I said. "Everyone else can go watch cable."

"There's a TV?"

"All this time, we could have watched TV?"

"Hockey!"

"What's tonight? Is *Friends* on?"

They raced up the stairs. Tobin walked out to me. "That does look like a peacock," I said to Freddie. Tobin's roots were green, blending into turquoise, blue, violet and tipped with gold. "I have a friend who shoots for a salon contest," I said. "He's always looking for wacky things to do."

"I'm not allowed to compete except on the international level."

Oh. I looked back at Tobin's hair. I could see why.

"Talk to me," I said.

"I'm not hiding anything, Dallas," Tobin said. "We talked on the ride. Do you remember?"

"I remember you didn't tell me that you and Kim were married."

"We aren't, not really. We had a justice of the peace ceremony, then lived together for only six months. It didn't take long to realize we were much better partners than lovers. We just never got around to the paperwork of divorce. And we never found anyone else. I don't consider myself married."

"Hmm. How did Dieta die?"

He shook his head. "I would tell you if I could, but I don't know. I was on the shoot, you saw me. You had to send me to the RV to get rid of me. I wouldn't hurt Dieta. We'd been lovers."

"You were trying to kill Kim, and y'all had been lovers. That logic isn't convincing."

"Kim . . . I just hate her," he said. "I couldn't take it any more. She's hard to kill."

"You've poisoned her with lily-of-the-valley water?" I asked.

"I've poisoned her with everything I can think of that will look natural. I've read more books on poison than you can imagine. But she doesn't eat!"

"So you decided to run her over, or into the lake."

"No! I didn't have anything to do with either of those, I swear."

I didn't like Tobin, but . . . I was beginning to believe him. "Then how did they happen?"

"Kim's after me," he said in a whisper. "It was my car—"

"She's been driving it all over," I said.

"We share it. We've only had it a few days. She told me to take it to the meeting, said it would give the illusion that we were wildly successful."

"Fake it till you make it?"

He nodded. "Dieta had gotten cold on the shoot, and I loaned her my coat. That's when she got hit. Kim hired someone to kill me. That's her way."

I looked at Freddie. His expression was serious. I knew he was thinking the same thing: had we screwed up? I looked back at Tobin, suddenly understanding the reasoning behind the witch trials. "Give him a Brazilian. We'll see if he's telling the truth."

"No, no, I don't know anything else, I swear!"

Freddie sighed. "I'll go mix more wax."

My phone rang. The caller ID was Thompson. "Ms. O'Connor," he said in a rush. "I think we need to see each other. Talk about the case at length."

"I'll be back in Seattle in a few days," I said.

"No, no," he chuckled nervously. "It's strange, but I'm already on your side of the pass. I was going to go skiing when the snow came and I underestimated the severity of the fall."

Tobin was blubbering; I was afraid Thompson could hear him.

"Well," I said. "I'm at this little camp. I could meet you in Leavenworth for breakfast."

"Excellent. Uh, I look forward to it. Get some sleep, it's already late and you're still answering your telephone."

Was he my father? "Yeah, you too," I said, and hung up.

I heard the microwave humming as Freddie melted the wax. Tobin's legs were so tightly flexed he was going to snap the chair. The high of finding out the truth, and extracting justice for Dieta, had passed. Now I was tired, frustrated—

A knock at the door. It was almost two o'clock. I cracked the door.

"Heya Blondie," Esmerelda said. Since she'd heard we were stranded here, she'd gone to visit her family in Yakima. I guessed she'd just gotten back.

I slipped out the door and closed it behind me.

"Party going on?" she said.

"We found a TV, nothing big," I said. "It's kind of late. Who did you want to talk to?"

"You, actually," she said. "I saw that guy, the one from the EMP? He's in town, with his band. They're about to play their last set. You want to go?"

The sexy-voiced stranger. "I don't think so, it's late."

"Then . . . can I come in and watch the movie with you all?"

She was welcome, we liked her a lot, but she wasn't a partner in crime. "Actually," I said. "I think the movie is almost over."

"What was it?"

"*Murder on the Orient Expresss,*" I said. "But I'd love to

get some coffee. Why don't we walk over to the dining hall and see if there's any left over?"

"Sure, get your coat. I'll just stick my head in, say hello."

"Uhh, I tell you what—they're really into the movie, that fabulous conclusion"—I'd never seen it, but it was the first thing I'd do when I got home—"you know how that is. Wouldn't want to interrupt them. I have to go to the bathroom first, so I'll just do that, grab my coat and meet you at the dining hall. How's that?"

"I don't want to wait there by myself," she said. Grumpy.

"I'll be right over, I swear," I said.

She looked back at tme. "Okay. Five minutes, or I'll come get you. So you'll be safe walking across the grounds."

"I'll be fine," I said. I waited until she was on the path before I stepped back inside. Freddie was stirring a bowl of wax. He'd put tape over Tobin's mouth to keep him quiet.

I grabbed my jacket. "It's over."

"I heard."

"Keep him taped till dawn," I shouted up to the mob watching *I Love Lucy*. "Party's over. Go home now!" Then I raced over to Freddie, kissed him on the mouth. "You're the best," I said.

"Torquemada was my hero," he said dryly.

I grabbed my jacket and fled down the path.

I'm not sure if it was the sleep of the just, but I was deep into it when I heard the blast. Large caliber. Handgun.

Silence.

"Dallas," Darcy whispered from her bed. "Was that a gunshot?"

I slid down the ladder and threw on a coat. "A .357. I think."

"Holy Jesus," Darcy said. "Are you going out there?"

I stuffed my feet into my boots and ran out the door.

Kenneth had a ski jacket over his night shirt. His white calves glowed like the snow. "Kim's, I think."

"Tobin?" I asked.

"What's going on?" the campus cop said, sliding to a stop in his golf cart. "Who fired a gun? Guns are not permitted—"

I ran away from him, up the hill to Kim's cabin. No lights were on. I ducked down in front of the porch. "Kim?" I called, and ducked again. I didn't want to get my head shot off for her.

Darcy caught up with me. "Freddie has Tobin with him. He didn't do this."

Lights were coming on everywhere. Kenneth, Stephen, Nasmo and Irma joined us in the bushes. "The back door is open," Irma said. "George saw the curtains moving."

As a group, we mounted the stairs.

Kenneth turned the knob on the door and pushed it open. I turned on the light.

Kim's blood was spattered over the zebra candles, the white lilies and the hardwood floor. Kim herself was the centerpiece on a backdrop of bright red blood, eyes staring at the ceiling, black hair fanned around her.

I touched her wrist and noticed the small hole in her chest. My words confirmed what we'd all known in the silence of the room.

"She's dead."

Thompson came to meet *me* for breakfast instead. He spoke privately to the local cops and they started taking orders from him. "Jurisdiction," he said.

"That's funky," Darcy said to me. "He did this in Deception Falls, too?"

"First come, first serve," I said.

"I guess that's three," she said.

"Where is Mr. Marconi?" one of the cops asked. "Which cabin?"

"Oh shit," Darcy whispered. "We're busted."

He looked at us. "Show me, please?"

Kenneth was talking to the owner/manager of the facility, and Irma, George, Stephen and Nasmo were all giving accounts of what they'd heard and seen.

We knocked on the door and Tobin opened it. The cop introduced himself and did a good job of keeping his reaction to Tobin hidden.

Darcy and I failed at that. "Oh no," she said.

Freddie popped up from the sleeping loft. "You called?"

The cops were trying to keep us apart, but there were more of us than of them.

They took Tobin aside to tell him about Kim's death—he knew, of course. "What did you hear, Mr. Marconi?"

"Uh, nothing," he said. "Nothing at all."

"Were you sleeping?"

Freddie giggled and waved at him from the loft. "If you must use a euphemism," he said. "*Actively* sleeping."

Tobin blushed bright red. Since his head had been shaved sometime between two A.M. and now, 5:30, he looked like a tomato. I trusted Freddie; something was up. I was going to play along.

"You were with him?" the officer asked Freddie.

Freddie wandered down the stairs in Prada pants, his slender, but well-muscled torso nude and shining with oil. The top button on his pants was undone, and we couldn't see any underwear. "I was right with him," he said. "It wasn't until a crew member knocked on the door, banged really, at four, late-ish four, that we got out of bed."

Or that he'd gotten Tobin freed from the tape, the dyed hair, et cetera.

"Okay, thank you, sir."

"Do you know who did this?"

"Looks like a robbery, ma'am. The place was tossed, her purse is missing, some jewelry."

"She had four-carat stud earrings," Tobin said. "She never wore them, but she kept them."

"Thank you, sir, I'll make sure and mention that." He backed out of the house and suggested we stay in the area for the day.

Darcy pulled back the curtain to watch him walk away. "Nothing like a man in uniform."

I turned to Tobin and Freddie.

Tobin glared at me and stormed upstairs. He dumped Freddie's clothes over the loft's rail. Freddie threw on his blue anorak and left with me and Darcy.

The place was crawling with police. Dawn was just breaking.

Kim was dead now, too.

This was just too confusing.

"I'm going back to bed," Darcy said. She didn't even moan about a cigarette. Freddie waved as he walked to his cabin. We waved back.

"Good idea," I said, following her. Thompson would wake me up when he wanted to talk.

"I wonder who blew her away, though," she said.

I thought about the things I'd heard and seen. It seemed that maybe Tobin had been telling the truth. The only thing—not that it wasn't big, but it was the only thing—he'd done, was poison her. She, on the other hand, hired people.

She suggested a hired killer.

Had the killer killed her? Why kill your meal ticket?

"I feel numb," I said, as I climbed the ladder.

"It's going to be okay now," Darcy said, crawling under her blankets. "No one else will die. Superstitions are true. Death comes in threes."

Chapter Seventeen

"This is from a different mystery," she said as we walked across the compound.

It was almost dark—we'd slept the day away. No one mourned Kim. That's a sad life, I thought. Her parents would, surely, somewhere. Had they been told?

"We've been summoned to the drawing room while the master detective tells us everything and ferrets out the murderer," Darcy said in a dreadful English imitation.

"I can see you dressed up for the occasion," I said. She was wearing a T-shirt with "The Marlboro Man's a Fairy" in glittered script across it. And it was pink.

"In honor of Freddie's sacrifice," she said. "Having to pretend his taste is as bad as *actively sleeping* with Tobin."

"With a little time at the gym," I said, "Tobin could really make that shaved head look work for him."

The crew was in the library, which consisted of left-behind paperbacks and aged theses on subjects or topics no one had discussed in fifty years. Thompson's shirt was so starched you could cut cake with it.

Kenneth sat on a chair, sedate in a sweater and corduroy

pants. Nasmo was in a baggy long-sleeved T and baggy jeans. Wes was decked out like an athlete, as was Irma. Esmerelda wore a Polartec jersey over her normal tank, and dreamcatcher earrings. Stephen's shirt was pressed, if a little big for him. And I was in . . . black. Head to toe.

Color therapy, I thought. It was going to be my new style, my lasting tribute to Dieta. For Richard . . . I didn't know what to do. Meanwhile, I wore what I had. We were the last to sit down, squeezing between Nasmo and Irma.

"Where's Tobin?" someone said.

"He's not going to join us," Thompson said. "I think that's best."

Could we get sued for dyeing his hair and waxing his legs? I had a feeling we could. Not to mention feeding him a tiny bit of marijuana. I didn't know who'd had it, and I was glad I didn't know.

"You're a checkered crew," he said. "It's been a very dangerous shoot, hasn't it?" He referred to his notes. "Richard Wilson, model, dies of internal injuries in a car accident in Lake Union. Dieta Andersen, dies of injuries sustained in a hit and run accident. Now Kim Charles is blown away in the middle of her rented living room, at 4:30 in the morning." He looked up. "I've spoken to all of you individually during the past week or so."

A few surprised grunts; I'd guessed as much. Why single me out?

"All of you agree there is no logic, and there doesn't seem to be. You were watching two events take place. One, Tobin Marconi was poisoning his wife, slowly. Two, she had hired a killer to kill him."

More surprised reactions.

"Unfortunately," he said. "She hired a bargain-basement killer with a nasty crack habit who she found online. He rigged the wrong car, because she didn't know Tobin had got-

ten another one for Richard. Tobin's car was supposed to be
the only Porsche Boxster in the parking lot. It would even
have dealer's plates. She thought there was no way the murder could go wrong." He shrugged his shoulders. "In order
to establish an alibi, she was out of town all day, and came
from the airport by taxi. She left Tobin a note, to take the car.
He did. After Richard picked up the brand-new, rigged car.
Tobin drove to the restaurant in his own Boxster."

No wonder I hadn't been able to figure it out. Kim hadn't
known about the new car. Who bought it, then?

Thompson continued, "Then the killer struck the wrong
person in a brown jacket." He shook his head. "I don't know
why Kim invited him here this morning, but the phone call
was easy to identify on her cell phone. We guess they argued
about money—"

"*He's getting greedy.*" Who had she been speaking with?
I'd memorized the number, but I'd never called it.

"Maybe she refused to pay him, I don't know. He decided
to kill her, then take what he could."

"Have you caught him?"

Thompson smiled. "She got what she paid for. He left
huge footprints all over the place, he drove a beat-up car that
left an oil trail. We picked him up in a bar just outside the
other side of town, trying to score a hit." Thompson closed
his notebook. "He told us everything."

That was it? Dieta was dead because of a mistake? It's one
thing to be an accident, but to be dead because some idiot
was too dumb to tell a man from a woman? My mouth tasted
bitter.

Thompson sat down. "There's something else I want to
discuss with you," he said. "When we were gathering evidence, we found this. I think you might want to watch it."

A videotape. Darcy grabbed my hand; we were going
down.

The images were clear, if a little skewed because the camera had been placed beside the light fixture in the bar area, looking down at a weird angle. ABBA sounded weak as it floated into the speakers, and our voices were exaggerated. We were designed to die, draped over the furniture and floor.

Tobin stood in the middle of the room, his face ashen. He clutched at a cross necklace around his throat, his mouth working but soundless. He turned and stared at each of us in turn. He spun around again.

Then he walked back to the bar. Was he going to try suicide?

"That ratbastard!" Darcy cried as she pointed at the screen. "He's stealing my credit cards!"

I hadn't even thought about it; we'd piled our purses, knapsacks and bags in one corner, to the far right of the camera. Tobin went through each piece individually. *Unbelievable.*

Thompson turned off the video. "Check your belongings," he said. "And don't worry about the rest of the tape." He looked at us. "There was a little justice there."

"It's a thousand dollars a day. One more day," Lindsay said. "Plus a nice ticket to a Mexico resort." I was packing as she was talking.

"Three people died," I said.

"Deaths come in threes," she reasoned. "Besides, they caught the man, right?"

I sat down on the bed. "I hate Tobin Marconi."

"Understandably, darling, but this is for the company. Thom Goodfeather promises you will leave with a check for the full amount. He just needs that last photo for the brochure. You know how it is, the pages. One of them cannot be blank."

"Why isn't the company out of business?" I said. "Who got it?"

"No one, darling, three-way partnership. Kim's shares, or

whatever, will be divided equally between Tobin and Thom. It's a lot of money, darling. One more day. A police officer is going to be on set with you. Thom described the shot. It would be stunning—"

"Okay! Okay," I said. My one weakness is I despise being badgered. Lindsay knows this well. I looked out the window at Seattle. We weren't at the tugboat—I was sorry about that. We were in a Euro-style boutique hotel, and we were the only Americans. "Is everyone else staying?"

"I don't know, darling. You won't regret this, Dallas. I'll pick you up at the airport myself and take you to dinner. Oui-We? Palomino? Café Pacific? I have an in with the staff, I can get us a table."

I sighed. "I'll call you when the thing is over," I said. "And Lindsay, that damn check better not boomerang."

"He says he'll do a wire transfer, if you feel more comfortable. Just call me and I'll do it."

My shark. Who gets twenty percent.

"Great. Talk to you later."

A knock. I opened the door. *"If you change your mind—"*

"No more ABBA," I told Freddie. "Are you staying?"

"Absolutely! I always wanted a little St. John's getaway."

"I got Mexico."

"They probably were sending us to the closest exotic location from where we live," he said. "Darcy got Cuba."

"I hate her. She's staying too?"

"Between morbid curiosity and flat-out greed, we all are. George even, but just to be close to Irma, I think."

"This is going to be on the EMP?" I said, remembering the complete and total lack of any straight line.

"Yes. Extremely dramatic."

"I just hope it doesn't rain," I muttered.

Chapter Eighteen

Definitely dramatic, I thought as I stood on the curved aluminum skin of the EMP. It curved and rippled like ocean waves frozen in time. "Is she ready?" Kenneth asked me over my headset.

"Are you okay?" I asked Irma. She was going to stand on top of the building, her twenty-foot parachute cape stretching out of the picture, revealing the simple halter front of her minigown, the fishnet stockings, and Gladiator boots. Freddie and Darcy had had a blast doing her makeup and hair. Her wig was Day-Glo pink, and short; her lips were velvet purple—she was the goddess of rock 'n' roll.

Below her, in head-to-toe black sharkskin, mesh shirt, and shades, Wes stood on the roof of the monorail car that ran through the building. In a perfect world, Kenneth would catch Irma dropping the mocked-up "guitar" into Wes's arms. It was going to take all day because the real monorail ran every ten minutes and we could only shoot in between.

Tobin, the sadist, had designed the shot. But he didn't want anything to do with us—he was resting comfortably in jail, and refused to come out—and Thom Goodfeather was afraid of heights. Consequently, in order to do *my* job, I was going to slither up and down with mechanical ascenders, clamps that climbed up and down the rope, to check on Wes below, and Irma above. Maybe the shot wouldn't need much styling. I hoped.

Rock climbing was for climbing on rocks, not on Frank O. Gehry's newest, slipperiest and snazziest piece of art-cum-architecture. The reflections of the metal building were crazy: silver on fuschia, pink on blue, red and green and purple all over each other.

A little glaze of glamour remained, but mostly I just wanted this job done, over, so I could go home and get back to my normal life, where corpses didn't show up every ten minutes.

It took a few shots before Kenneth was happy with the setup; meanwhile, Wes's monorail kept retreating so the real monorail could work. Three shots, then a six-minute break. Getting one roll of film was going to take forever. I'd anchored Irma to the roof to keep her from flying away. The end of the cape was rigged to a crane above us, and when it filled with air the first time, it almost lifted Irma off the roof. On the first break, Esmerelda and I cut huge gashes in it, so the wind could flow through it. "What's the difference between a bad golfer and a bad skydiver?" Irma asked me while I readjusted her duct-taped breasts.

"I have no idea."

"A bad golfer goes whack, damn. A bad skydiver goes damn, whack."

Not the most comforting of thoughts when one is stories off the ground.

The real monorail car zoomed by. Our monorail car zoomed out.

"Straighten your tie," I shouted to Wes. I stood up, straightened the hem on Irma, then moved behind her and billowed the cape.

"We're on film!" Kenneth shouted.

A gust of wind caught the edge of it perfectly and I ducked out of the way. Twenty feet of it blew up, twisting to show the purple and scarlet sides.

Maybe the glaze of glamour wasn't completely gone.

We had a Vietnamese lunch catered, and ate while we talked about which of the fourteen thousand drive-thru espresso stands had been our favorite. We were so brittle, we were about to crack.

"Definitely Jack and the Bean," Wes said. "The foam on that cappuccino was art."

"I liked that little Java Haus, or whatever, right before we got into suburban Seattle," Stephen said. "I'd never seen peanut brittle as a coffee flavor before."

"Now you know the reason why," Irma said.

"You don't even drink coffee," Darcy cried. "You can't vote!"

"Ah, but I love espresso beans, and the best ones were at—what was the little gas station in that flat town?" Irma said.

"Cle Ellum?" Stephen said.

"That's certainly the only flat town I remember," Darcy said. "And even then, it was surrounded by mountains."

"I don't remember that," Nasmo said.

"The best beans," Irma said. "That is my vote."

"The best name was Ooo La Latte," I said. *Tres chic, n'est pas?*"

"I don't know, Horton Hears A Moo with that purple Dr. Seuss cow was pretty cute," Freddie said. "I even took a picture of it."

Kenneth stepped back inside. "Well, are we ready to do this?" he asked.

For the afternoon, Kenneth set up across from Irma, who

was now sitting on the edge of the building, her legs miles long and crossed, her cape exchanged for a dangerous zippered leather jacket I'd picked up in my travels. The label had been ripped out, but I'd recognized vintage Zandra Rhodes even without it.

"I love the bag," Freddie said to me.

"It does work, doesn't it?"

"You have a thing for lunch boxes, don't you? Where did you find it?"

"I bought that off a kid who was flying home to the East Coast. He got on the plane in Sex Pistols Forever garb, but then he came out of the bathroom, his hair combed down, a plaid shirt, and Hilfiger jeans with his Doc Martens. He was trying to stuff the lunchbox into his backpack when I told him I'd just buy it," I said, remembering.

"You think I'm a freak, don't you?"

"Nah. Freaks don't try to make their parents happy," I'd said. "You aren't compromising, you're just keeping the peace."

"It's my little sister's graduation. She's valedictorian and the smartest thing you ever saw. She could do calculus when she was, like, in seventh grade. I just want her to be, well, happy. If my parents aren't bitching about how I'm dressed, it will be her day, like totally."

"I'll give you fifty bucks," I said.

"No shit?"

"It's original art," I said. "A punked out Little Mermaid lunchbox. It's cool."

"No way!" Freddie said. "I saw those in a store, somewhere in New York. They were rave. The private school kids were snatching 'em up. TDOC, right? That's the company."

"Are you serious?" I said, smiling.

"Yeah, were those the kid's initials or something?"

I heard the kid's Bostonian accent in my head. We were

about to land and he turned to me. *"You really think that's cool? The lunchbox?"*

"I wouldn't pay you if I didn't think I could use it. It's very cool."

"What's your name?" he said.

"Dallas O'Connor. I style fashion photos."

"No shit? Oh, man, I must be under a Saturn moon." He raised his Nantucket Nectar to me. *"To Dallas O'Connor. My muse."*

"Are you two going to work or what?" Darcy called.

Freddie cursed as he slithered across the roof. He finally got level with Irma and straightened her wig, dusted her with more powder, then wriggled his way back.

"Oh, God, I've got to get to the gym just as soon as I get back to New York," he said. "My arms are killing me."

We shot a few more rolls, Irma changed position and Wes changed position. "Now let's get them both on the monorail roof," Kenneth said. Carefully we inched Irma to the rope, then down to the roof of the train. I hopped down after her, straightening Wes's jacket, smoothing Irma's skirt. Kenneth shot a Polaroid.

"Going to film," Kenneth called.

I needed to get out of here. The rope dangled.

"Film!" he shouted.

I grabbed the ascenders and started up, making a ladder of the ascenders and climbing it until I reached the curve of the building. I had one hand on the aluminum roof when my foot stirrup slipped and fell. Time seemed to stop. The rope slipped.

I threw myself at the building as the rope slid down like a waterfall beside me.

"Dallas!" someone shouted. I grappled for a hold on the building, but it was smooth, like glass. Only the lip offered a hand-hold. I screeched as my left hand slid, and my chin smashed into the roof. I heard nothing but the roar in my ears and realized that death might come in quads this time. Why kill me? I couldn't get enough purchase to swing my leg up, and I didn't dare move my hands.

But the fabric of the cape was just inches away. Rip-stop nylon, solidly anchored on the crane. My hands were wet, slipping. I launched myself up onto the roof, snatching at the fabric. I got two handfulls, then slid back down, pulling the cape taut. I looked up to see a man in a Tobin Charles suit, with long black hair and white face, pull the fabric up. "Hold on!" Thom shouted. By the time I was even with the roof, an assistant, an RV driver, and a red-faced Thompson offered me hands, strength, and leverage.

Once I was down, I kissed the concrete of Seattle.

"You can't leave Seattle without eating at the 13 Coins. It's a Seattle tradition. And it's on the way to the airport."

"Watch me," I said. My bags were packed. My taxi was due to arrive.

Thom and Esmerelda had peeled me off the roof of the EMP, then she had taken George and Irma to the airport. I barely remembered saying goodbye. Possibly because I'd been hunched over a martini, trying not to shake.

"Really," Darcy said. "It's the wrap party. We've been through so much. Don't be precious."

"I'm scared!" I shouted. "I'm not trying to get your attention or be a drama queen. I'm scared!"

"I know, honey," she said. "But Thom is going to sign vouchers, it's a public place. There'll be no ropes. It was an accident, a real live accident." She studied my stubborn expression. "We aren't meeting for a few hours. Don't you want to shop a little more, get something pretty for tonight? Hell, we'll be able to afford Balenciaga!"

I looked at her.

"Not my taste either, but I couldn't think of anyone else

off the top of my head. Lack of nicotine is contributing to brain death."

"How long has it been?"

"Almost four days. Seeing a murder. Made me think. I have three kids." She shrugged. "I got over the worst of the withdrawal, I think. I'll give it a shot and see if I can be clean. It would save on the dental bills."

I chuckled.

"C'mon, don't make me be nice to you! You need color therapy! It's your *dosha*. Friends don't make friends shop solo."

I squeezed her hand. "Will you do my makeup?"

"I promise. I'll make Freddie do your hair. He's been dying to since the lodge."

I couldn't believe how much I was going to miss these people. "Shopping it is."

She stood up and shouted at the door. "You owe me five hundred bucks, buddy."

"It's only because you promised her *my* coiffurage," Freddie said.

"So is your boyfriend still playing around here?" she asked me. "The nameless phantom lover?"

"You have a boyfriend?" Freddie said through the door.

I rolled my eyes. "Get out. Both of you. I'll be in the lobby in ten minutes."

"That is my new favorite store," I said as we left Alhambra, loaded with colorful bags of colorful clothes.

Darcy looked at her watch. "We have time for a drive-by of The Bon," she said. "Then we have to hoof it to get to the restaurant in time." She picked it up. I was so focused on not tripping over my bags that I had to dodge a man walking straight into me. I sidestepped.

He did too.

And again.

He did too.

Alligator boots.

I looked up at him.

"Corpus Christi," he said.

"Uh . . . you," I said to my whiskey-voiced phantom. "Broad daylight and everything."

"I'll be inside," Darcy squeaked.

"Were you concerned I was a creature of the night?" His sunglasses were impenetrable, but I felt him looking at me. I didn't want to look away.

"Oh, I'm convinced of that," I said. "How else are you in a band?"

He laughed.

"What is your name, by the way?" I asked.

"How are you?" he asked. Deliberately ignored my question.

"Fair," I said.

He looked at my bags. "Only fair after all this retail therapy?" He looked back at me. "Do you need some other kind of therapy?"

My voice was chilly. "What did you have in mind?"

"Music," he said with a smile. "You're in town, and I'm playing. I'd love to see you in your new threads while you groove to my music."

"I'm leaving."

"Baby, you're always leaving. But here's the place," he said. "Turn around." He wrote the address in a matchbook, using my back as a table. "If you can. I'd love to see you come. Watch me."

His voice had to be illegal in at least twenty states. "I'll try."

"Later, baby." He walked away with a street savvy sway. He smelled like leather, Old Spice and smoke. The heels of his boots were polished.

Intoxicated in the middle of the afternoon—from a voice.

Chapter Nineteen

I was standing in La Perla underwear before the mirror. In heels, I could only see from my chest to my knees. They hung this thing for midgets. I turned sideways to see if any of the many lattes showed. The good thing about my job was that it was an all-day gym. Especially today, hanging . . . "Don't go there," I said out loud.

My cell phone rang. "Thank God you're coming home," Lindsay said. "I've worried about you."

"It's been crazy. Has anything been in the papers there?"

"Nothing. What flight are you on? Do you need a drive?"

"No, it's okay. I'm flying standby, and you know how that can be."

"Right. Well, when are you available for work again?"

That's Lindsay, always looking to the future.

I looked at the date on my watch. "I'm booking out for about two weeks."

"Taking that free holiday, then?"

"That's an idea," I said. "I haven't been to Mexico in a while."

"Well, be careful flying in. There's a wicked storm brewing. You might do better to wait until the morning, actually.

Listen to that—" She held the phone away and I heard muffled booms. "Hear that?"

"Artillery fire?"

"Thunder, darling. Terrifically loud, isn't it?"

I swore under my breath, but she didn't hear me. Loud and clear I heard more thunder on her end. "I gotta go," I said. "I need to call American. Again."

"Can't hear you, darling. Call me if you need anythin'. Ciao, now."

After hanging up, I looked at the matchbook with the phantom's handwriting. I looked at my fetish on the dresser. "Is this a sign?"

Those turquoise eyes told me nothing, but they matched my $45 panties.

I turned to my purchases. My bed looked like a National Geographic photo of an exotic market. Color, detailed embroidering and beading. I had on party makeup, new shoes and Freddie had parted my hair on the far side. "Sweeping," he'd said. "It's all about the sweep."

With my back to the mirror, I changed.

When I looked at my reflection, I blew Dieta a kiss. Color was her legacy. Happiness. Shiva. I picked up the fetish. "That's your name," I said, and placed Shiva in the tiny silk pouch I'd bought, then slung it across my shoulder.

We parked outside an ominously square office building and truly did step back in time. The entire restaurant was smoking, the booths were so deep and protected that I imagined pimps and coke dealers meeting here, and the music was Barry Manilow and Simon and Garfunkel interpretations for piano. The waiting time was usually an hour. Those waiting were sunk into black leather couches and reading old *USA Today*s. Garage sale decanters decorated the wall.

"Tell me there's a deeper meaning," Darcy said with vodka

breath, pointing to the assortment. "Are they collectibles or something, and I just don't know better?"

"Collectible or not, anything featuring the seven dwarfs is a little scary to me," I said.

"This is so not fair," Darcy said, sniffing the air. You could see the cloud of smoke.

The waitress led us to a super-private booth. Walls on each side made it more like a train cabin than a restaurant. The only view we had was of the bar, lined with giant egg chairs that *were* the 60s, in front of the exhibition cooking fires. "They should have filmed Austin Powers here," Freddie said.

Before the food came, Thom showed us some of the film.

"Damn, we're good!" Darcy cried.

Dieta would be so very, very proud. I had to believe that from somewhere, somehow she saw this.

The smells were divine and the menu was impressive. Thirteen coins were imbedded in the table, beneath the glass top. We snacked on bread and antipasti.

The atmosphere was poignant, we realized this was *it*. The limo outside was full of our luggage, this was our last Seattle experience together before saying goodbye. Except for me— my stuff was at the hotel, since nothing was flying to Dallas tonight.

Wine flowed, the portions were enormous, and it was unspeakably comfortable. We were survivors. We knew each other. And we liked each other. The only stilted part of the evening was Thom Goodfeather's presence.

He'd saved my butt, but I still didn't like him. I'd thanked him profusely. I wanted my check. I was out of here. He kept trying to catch my eye. I kept avoiding him.

"So, the story is," Darcy slurred. "Tobin was trying to get rid of Kim. Right?"

I glanced around. We might as well be in a crypt in this booth. Kenneth agreed with her, so did Freddie.

"Kim was trying to get rid of Tobin?"

Stephen and Nasmo nodded.

Thom Goodfeather looked uncomfortable. That would just make Darcy happier.

"Then Richard, God bless him, and Dieta, God rest her soul, got caught in the crossfire." She sounded glum and ordered another drink.

"Kim got her just desserts," Stephen said.

"The only thing I don't understand," I said, setting down my spiked coffee, "the only part of this that isn't sewn up, ha ha, is the suit—"

"Oh," Kenneth groaned. "That's worse than mine!"

My phone rang. The phantom's number! I smiled at them and turned to face the bar, my back to the table.

"It's her boyfriend," I heard Darcy say.

"She has a boyfriend?" Nasmo and Stephen asked in unison.

I answered the phone.

"Be quiet." It was the phantom; his voice was electrifying in its command. "Don't repeat anything I say. Listen. Don't talk to Thom about the gray suit. Do you understand me?"

The egg chair across the room from me turned. My phantom sat there, speaking into a platinum Nokia, the whites of his eyes and the gleam of silver all I could see of him. "Be cool. Get on your plane. Go home."

I swallowed. What was going on? I nodded.

"You're beautiful." He turned his chair back to the bar. My ears rang with dial tone.

I turned back to the table. Thom looked at his watch. "We have some flights to catch."

Everyone embraced outside. "Call me when you're in New York," Darcy said. "You can stay with me and the kids, or—"

"Stay with me," Freddie said. "I'll invite a bunch of lesbian friends over and watch them drool over your legs. Promise me you'll wear this skirt, it's what, two inches long?"

I swatted him. "Y'all are the best," I said, striving to seem normal. "Dallas is your home anytime you're there."

Kenneth gave me a bear hug, Nasmo kissed my cheek, and Stephen blushed and said he thought Dallas was a great name for a woman. Wes bent me backward with a big, fat kiss.

"This is the effect of color?" I said.

Darcy kissed me again. "Miss you." She grabbed Freddie's arm. "Why did you pretend to be Tobin's lover?"

Esmerelda pulled up in the limo.

I nodded; I'd wanted to know too.

Freddie shrugged as Kenneth and the guys got in. "Simple deal. I was his alibi for not killing Kim; without me he was number one suspect. I save his distasteful bacon, he wouldn't sue any of us. And there should be a little bonus with all your checks." He winked. "Those luscious robes from the Salish."

Kenneth and the guys got back out—a lost ticket or something.

A second limo pulled up behind. "I need you to take a short ride with me, Dallas," Thom said quietly. Everyone was grouped together by the first limo, getting inside. Thom pressed the small of my back. "We need to talk, Dallas. There's not a lot of time."

He shoved me into the second limo and closed the door behind us.

The first limo was pulling away; no one saw me leave with him.

The door locks clicked.

Who had Kim been talking to?

Thom Goodfeather.

Who had money?

Thom Goodfeather.

Who had probably known about the new Porsche and the old Porsche?

Thom Goodfeather.

Who was Filipino?
Thom Goodfeather.
Who played two ends against the middle?
Thom Goodfeather.
Who was sunk?

Be cool, I told myself. *It will be okay.*
"I needed to talk to you in private," he said. "It's such a tragedy."

We headed away from the airport.

"Kim," he said, "well, Kim had started some cycles in life that were going to collide with her one day or another. Dieta, however, was fresh, a new soul."

"She was," I said. If he was going to confess that he was Iago in this whole mess, then he wasn't going to let me go. Could I open the door and roll out of the car? Were those child locks I heard? Do they have child locks on a limo?

"You figured everything out," he said. "Didn't you?"

"Just what the police figured out," I said. My phone rang, then died mid-ring. *Please be someone following me, worried about me.* "What does that matter?" I said, trying to speak around the piece of heart lodged in my throat.

"It doesn't matter at all now."

Be cool, Dallas. Did he have a gun? I couldn't see him in the dark of the limo to check for signs of a firearm. Where were we going?

"Was there something you were going to say about the suit?"

"Uh, it's beautiful."

"That puzzled you?"

How could I answer his questions and not talk about it? "How could it . . . be so beautiful. Astounded me. Still does." Ohmigod. My hand clenched around my fetish. I needed strength like a bear right now.

"That's exactly what I wanted to talk to you about."

I'd talked about the suit. This was it.

He turned to me. "It was gratifying to watch you handle the fabrics, the care you took with each piece throughout the shoot. You respected those garments. It's for that reason I need you."

Confused pause. "Excuse me?" I said.

"I have to publish the promo piece, ship merchandise, deal with the merchandisers, the marketing people. Someone from Hollywood wants the Tobin Charles suit for the next award ceremony." He sighed deeply. "I don't have Kim. I wanted to hire Dieta, but . . . she's gone. I need your skills. You can help me, Dallas. I'll pay you handsomely. But I need you, this company needs you. It's an immediate need."

The limo stopped and he opened the door. "I have to catch a flight. The driver will take you wherever you want to go. Be well, and don't spend all that money in one place." He handed me an envelope. "We'll talk soon."

My hand clamped around the paper. "Bye," I squeaked.

He slammed the door and ran toward a helicopter through the rain.

"Get me out of here," I told the driver.

"Where, ma'am?"

"Airport!" When I could dial, I called the hotel. The lights glittered outside as we headed to the airport. The hotel said they'd be delighted to FedEx my luggage to Dallas. I was glad I'd flirted with the extremely handsome desk clerk.

Flights weren't going to Dallas; I knew that. I didn't care; I just wanted out of Seattle. How had the phantom known—anything? Had Thom's job offer been legit? I dialed Kreg's number.

"Which terminal, ma'am?" the driver asked.

"American."

" 'Lo," Kreg answered.

"I know you're drinking, and you're probably in the mountains, but I'm coming to Portland. Don't ask any questions. I'll call you when I get there."

Go home.

How had the Phantom known anything? Who was he? What was the suit?

I clenched my handbag; I'd thought this was over.

Chapter Twenty

Dallas. Ten P.M. The airport glowed with the sheen of lights on rain-slick streets. I was so happy to be home, I could cry. Lindsay was on her way, but she'd gotten stuck in traffic. I don't think anyone had followed me from Portland to L.A. to Phoenix—the flights had either been nearly empty or filled with easy-to-recognize people.

Kreg had been confused when I'd called back to cancel his meeting me, but he could wait until he got home for an explanation.

Home, I was home. Ten o'clock and I was sweating—definitely home. I breathed in the mingled smells of the Metroplex. None of them were good for me.

A Mercedes slid up to the curb. I took a step back. The window hummed down. "Need a lift?"

She looked familiar, but without her shorts or tattoos, it was hard to be sure. "Esmerelda?"

The door opened, and still I stood there.

"It's okay," she said, stepping out of the car, flashing a badge at me. "I'm a federal agent."

"Someone's picking me up."

"She'll be late." She said it with confidence.

I got in the car.

"How was your flight?" she asked, twisted around in the front seat. I didn't see the driver. Would it be Wes?

"Fine," I said. "Saw Mount Saint Helen's from the sky."

"That's an awesome view," she said. "It's even better if you are heading south. You fly over Rainier, Saint Helen's and Shasta. You get to see a volcano in all its stages."

I nodded. I didn't ask where we were going. I obviously wasn't aware of what was going on in my own life.

"Have you eaten?" she asked.

I nodded.

"Coffee?"

"No," I said, a little sharply. "I'm a little coffeed out."

"Anything?"

She wasn't going to go away. "Fine," I said. "Iced tea."

Esmerelda repeated my order to the driver, and a few minutes filled with inconsequential chatter later, we pulled in to a JoJo's. The lighting was surreal. But then this whole thing was. She made small talk while I sucked down iced tea with lemon and sugar. The driver waited outside. Esmerelda ordered some bacon and eggs, then scooted into the booth so she was sitting beside me.

Lindsay would wait, I guess. Or worry. It had only taken me twenty-four hours to get home. What was another hour?

The waitress set the plate down, refilled our drinks and left.

I finished my second glass. "What. Is. Going. On."

"You're confused?"

"Who are you?"

"I told you, a federal agent."

I turned to face her. "Why?"

"It was a choice I made in high school," she said, then wiped the grin off her face. "I see. Okay, Ms. O'Connor, would you like me to tell you what has been going on these past few weeks?"

"Yes," I said. "Since I was there, it would be nice to have reference points to fix my erroneous reality."

"You don't have to get testy."

"Is this some bizarre TV show?" I said. "I mean, screw the person's mind over then see if they can unscramble it?"

"Calm down," she said, sounding very official.

"Why were you there?"

"Tobin Charles Designs is suspected to be a key player in a money laundering scheme that weaves its way around the world."

"Yeah, right," I said. "This is bullshit."

"No, Dallas, it's not. Thom Goodfeather is our key suspect. He's up to his eyeballs in Mob money," she said.

Which one? "Anything else?"

"He's a tool. We need to get to whoever is behind Goodfeather."

"A Dallas person?"

She nodded.

"Can I go now?"

She threw some money on the table.

"You pay up there," I said, pointing to the cashier's booth. Esmerelda delivered me to the airport curb and I turned to her before stepping out of the car. "Did you really live in Yakima during the eruption?"

"I did. I'm a born and bred desert Washingtonian, but with my job and my husband's career I don't get to spend much time there. You'll be okay," she said. "This isn't about you."

"I'm *so* grateful to hear that," I said, then got out.

My house was in the same state of chaos I'd left it in, with the addition of UPS boxes and FedEx slips piled on the porch. The things I'd shipped back from Seattle. My renter wasn't here, and my mail had overflowed onto the swing. All in all, the place screamed "Rob me!"

The air was stale and I turned on the AC and opened the windows. My answering machine light was out, no messages either. The Caller ID box was blank. Power outage or something more . . . sinister?

I swore at the whole mess and went upstairs. At least I'd made my bed. I'd just stripped down when I heard a tap on my back porch door. I tied on the Salish Lodge robe and went downstairs.

There was a card tucked into the frame with a beautiful scrawl of black ink. "Baby. Come. See me play. Terilli's. Now."

I heard the music from outside and took my valet parking ticket with a blissed smile. I could postpone the worry until after the set.

Then I was going to interrogate the "Phantom."

He didn't have a band, he played alone, his hands moving with such grace and sensuality I felt dizzy for a minute. I stood by the bar, until I was forced to order a drink and speak over the beautiful music.

Oh, how I could go to sleep listening to this every night.

Now, I was scared. I didn't even know his name.

Did it matter?

His long-lashed black eyes opened and looked straight at me. He glanced at the back of the bar, the hidden seats. I got a table back there and waited.

"I'm going to take a break," he said to the audience. "Y'all enjoy this wonderful cuisine. I'll be back in a while." Women were fanning themselves.

I smiled as he walked toward me, in black jeans, white shirt, silver and black belt. He'd been playing hard, the tendrils around his forehead were sweaty. "Hey, baby," he said, sitting across from me. "Being home agrees with you. You look beautiful."

"Who are you? What are you? Why are you here? How did you get here? How did you know about the gray—"

The dreamy expression in his eyes vanished. "Don't talk about it. Don't ever say it, baby." He was that razor sharp man on the phone at 13 Coins. Like this, he was a little scary.

"Esmerelda is a good guy, Dallas. She's just doing her job."

"She was a plant from the start? That means she knew what was going on with Richard and Dieta's deaths. Which means she probably could have prevented at least Dieta's."

"You sure think a lot when you are flying all over the country, don't you?"

"My guess is y'all—and I assume you are one of them too?" He didn't bat an inky eyelash, just stared at me. "Y'all were watching Thom, or Tobin. You . . . you could have done something." I searched his gaze. "How could you let Dieta die?"

His voice was so soft, I could barely hear it. "Listen. Listen good. Tobin and Kim were having it out between themselves. You figured out the poison, we didn't know that."

"So Kim really did pay a hitman to take out Tobin and got Richard and Dieta instead?" I couldn't help it; I still couldn't believe it. "You never got a chance to talk to Dieta," I said as I watched tears fall on the table. "She was a wonderful person. So full of life." I looked at him. "Tell me, is that why Richard and Dieta died? Kim did it? Tell me the truth. I'll believe you."

He just held my gaze, then stretched his hands out, palms up. "Don't tear yourself up about things you can't control, baby." His palm wasn't soft—he was a man who used his hands. They were callused and very warm. He had three silver rings, but my eyesight was too blurred to see the designs.

"Esmerelda was there to keep track of Tobin. She got you permits for all your shots, made sure you had hotels and rooms that were clean, made sure we could keep an eye on you—"

Hence her perfect timing to rescue Tobin from the Brazilian.

"She kept y'all from having to deal with the cops."

I knew he wasn't a real cop—You wouldn't catch that happening to me again. "No wonder the investigation was so lousy. You didn't want any publicity or much scrutiny."

"No, baby. We were trying to work quietly."

"That's why Dieta's body was cut up and sent home before any of us got to see her again?"

He hurt for me; I felt it in his hands, I saw it in his eyes.

"Did you get whatever you wanted?" I asked. It must be something in or with the suit. Why else would it have gone AWOL, then turned up, re-stitched? Why else would I be forbidden to speak about it?

He nodded. "It was a good operation."

"Was it worth the cost?" I was crying again.

"Dallas, baby, you have to let this go. It's goin' to eat you alive if you don't."

"Then I guess I'm going to be eaten alive. I don't know how else to feel. I did the best I could with the shoot. But I can't hold it in any longer. A person as good as Dieta shouldn't die. Especially not like that, for no reason." I sniffed. "Inside, this is a turning point for me. I don't know how to hold on to hope anymore."

"And now, our accomplished Spanish guitarist is back," the announcer said.

The phantom stood up and leaned into my face. "Don't you dare leave. If this place burns to the ground, you wait for me to come get you." His eyes were fierce.

I nodded; my fingertips tingled.

Another forty-five minutes of music, soft and sexy, fast and erotic, heart-rending, fun, then a few notes I knew by heart, but had never heard on a guitar. "Ave Maria."

"I'm hungry," he said. "Is there anyplace that serves sushi this late?" It was after 2 A.M. I doubted it.

He closed the door of my Mustang gently. I loved this man.

We settled for Whataburger. "Drive me to water," he said. I took the scenic route to White Rock Lake. We got out and sat close together, his arm over my shoulder. He nuzzled my neck, his voice a whisper. "I'm going to talk to you, but it will look like I'm stealing a few kisses," he said. "I'm trusting you beyond everything I know, Dallas O'Connor."

My heart was doing a marathon.

"We busted the killer Kim had hired three hours after the Porsche accident. He told us about her. Richard was already dead, but we could use the information."

It was hard to think as he nibbled the side of my throat and ears. I groaned.

"Yeah, baby," he said. "You're doing good. Dieta was working with us." I probably would have reacted, but his hold on me was tight. "She'd known Tobin, she was going to get us the information we needed."

"The information inside the gray—"

"Yes. Your expert eye discovered some of that, I hear." He bit me on the neck, just a little. "We tried to return the item to the location of the accident, but a certain suspicious stylist was prowling around. We had to find another way."

He was kissing my forehead, my temple; I was trying to listen but getting distracted. "We pulled Dieta, Dallas. She's not dead."

You bastard, I thought.

He pinned me to the damp earth and held me there until the desire to get up and drive off had abated somewhat. My body felt like a board.

Fake cops, fake RV drivers, fake arrests, now a fake death? Fool me once, shame on you; fool me twice, shame on me. "That's cruel," I finally said through gritted teeth.

He braced himself over me; we were nose to nose, hidden

from the world by a fringe of black curls. "I've never lied to you. I've never let any harm come to you. You told me you would trust me if I told you. I'm telling you."

The voice of the man who helped me out of the water.

The man who arranged to comfort me at the Salish when he knew Dieta had been "hit." Played guitar until dawn. For me.

"You aren't supposed to be here, are you?" I said.

"I'm jeopardizing everything," he said. "Dieta is fine. She had figured out the way the company was conducting its business."

Money laundering through the suits. The inside of the suits. I didn't know what money laundering entailed, and I wasn't going to ask. *Dieta wasn't dead.*

"We thought she was getting too close. We didn't want her harmed, so we faked the accident while we looked at the . . . item."

I never saw her in the hospital. Esmerelda had been at the scene of the accident first. The decisions about everything were so fast, so final. They even gave me a bloodstained button and I bought the whole thing. It had all been a cover story.

Dieta was alive. I hugged him with all the joy I felt.

"You can't let anyone know you know, baby. Your grief is essential. Don't fail me there. People may be watching you, their side, our side. They can't ever guess." The razor sharpness was back, but he'd made himself vulnerable. He trusted me.

I felt his body full length on mine.

My colorful, bliss-hunting friend was alive.

I couldn't be happier. "Are you going to tell me your name?"

"Kiss me," he said. "I have to get to the airport."

Epilogue

Three days later I had Thom Goodfeather's check in the bank (plus a thousand dollar bonus), bright pink flip-flops on my feet, call forwarding on my main line. Goodfeather wanted to talk to me about the job. I didn't want to talk to him, not even to tell him I didn't want to talk to him. I was doing dishes looking out the window and watching the squirrels fight on the clothesline. My cell phone rang and I picked it up with wet hands. I knew that number.

"Wave to me," his sexy voice said.

As I lifted my gaze, a cherry red car with tinted windows cruised by. The passenger side window rolled down. Dieta smiled at me, then the window rolled up. "Later, baby."

The haunting music from Twin Peaks *plays in my head; a CD on endless repeat. Above the music, as though spoken by an ethereal voice, I hear:*
    Who killed Laura P—Kim Charles?
    Who *did* kill Kim Charles?